MURDER IN
HOLLYWOOD

Millicent
Binks
x

BOOKS BY MILLICENT BINKS

The Opal Laplume Mystery Series

A Most Parisian Murder

MURDER IN HOLLYWOOD

Millicent Binks

bookouture

Published by Bookouture in 2025

An imprint of Storyfire Ltd.
Carmelite House
50 Victoria Embankment
London EC4Y 0DZ

www.bookouture.com

The authorised representative in the EEA is Hachette Ireland
8 Castlecourt Centre
Dublin 15 D15 XTP3
Ireland
(email: info@hbgi.ie)

ISBN: 978-1-83618-916-9
eBook ISBN: 978-1-83618-915-2

For my sister Angeline – a beautiful actress who channels the golden age of Hollywood with effortless charm. Your portrayal of Marlene Dietrich in Piaf was unforgettable, one of the many roles where you've so vividly brought the era back to life. With love, your sister.

Virtue has its own reward, but no sale at the box office.

Mae West

ONE

PLATINUM SIGNET PRODUCTIONS, HOLLYWOOD

July 1934

The Honourable Opal Laplume's gloved fist hovered under the engraved plaque reading 'Millinery and Accessories Department'. *No, not quite ready to knock.* She smoothed her lavender-pleated dress and plucked a curlicue of her black poodle's fur off the sleeve.

The plaque, polished to a gleaming finish, offered a handy reflection of her blue eyes so she could check her mascara hadn't run in the heat. She tweaked her fedora jauntily over her dark curls. *Angles give attitudes!* The hat itself was *simply ripping*, a yellow confection that matched her silk blouse and gloves, with a fan of quills she'd stitched to the right side.

Finally, she rapped on the door. It swung open with alarming speed, revealing a firework of red ringlets.

'And who might you be?'

'The Honourable Opal Laplume. I'm here to see Mr Adrian Greenburg. I'm the new milliner.'

'Oh...' The girl's hair seemed to spark with nervous energy. 'I'd better speak to him.'

She made to shut the door, but Opal interjected, 'I sincerely apologise. I know I'm three days late...'

'And I'm your replacement. I'm sorry, ma'am.' The door clicked shut, a millimetre from Opal's pointed nose.

Opal gasped and dropped her hatbox. Rejection lapped at her feet. Not an unfamiliar sensation, sadly. School memories resurfaced; girls huddling in bathroom cliques, sneering, 'Go away, Carnival Float!' the name they called her for her habit of adorning her hair with garden refuse, feathers and blossoms. She had arrived in Hollywood alone, with high hopes of making a friend. Alas, this was not a good start.

Determined, she knocked again. *Blithering silence!* Huffing, she burst into the room. Three seamstresses stared. There was a man sitting at a desk whose hair shone like black-liquid silk, with a side-parting as sharp and straight as if cut by fabric scissors. *Adrian!*

'Please accept my sincerest apologies, Mr Adrian Greenburg. I did send a telegram, but my journey was an ordeal! The London train was delayed by a cow blockade, my ship tossed in a dreadful storm, and I missed the 20th Century Limited due to a Yankee fanatic's wife getting caught with a Red Sox supporter in coach B. I assure you, my tardiness is entirely uncharacteristic.'

The room blinked at her as if watching an English doll in an ostentatious hat come to life.

'Charming accent, Miss Laplume,' said Adrian. 'Shame that we no longer need you. Bonfire here has taken the position.'

The redhead, aptly nicknamed 'Bonfire' looked down awkwardly.

'This can't be true,' Opal protested, hands knotted in front of her. 'I've travelled for two weeks. Surely film sets always run behind?'

'I never run behind,' Adrian declared, though Bonfire sniggered. He ignored her. 'But your previous employer in

Paris did sing your praises. Perhaps another department has room.'

He scribbled a note:

I have a surplus of staff. Can you use this seamstress? Adrian

With an artistic flourish he waggled it in the air at her. 'Try a few doors down in the fitting rooms.'

Relieved she still had a chance in Tinseltown, Opal smiled faintly. 'Working as a dresser isn't my specialty, hats are. But it will be good experience.'

'That's the attitude. If you get to dress Jane Margeaux, that'll be an experience and a half.'

'Oh... who is that?'

'You really are from another planet! *Jane Margeaux.* Not only is she the next big ticket in Hollywood, she's an heiress to the York Tobacco fortune. It's so substantial it could provide enough cigarettes to fog up the moon. Although the director, George DeLuca, has an ego that eclipses even hers – he's the one to watch out for.'

Adrian returned to examining an oversized rhinestone belt buckle, as if contemplating whether it was beautiful or not. 'Jane designed this for *A Capitol Wife*. Her opening scene. I think it's gaudy. Actresses shouldn't push to design their own costumes.'

'Oh, I didn't know they *did*,' Opal said, glancing at her own modest horn belt buckle.

'Jane Margeaux gets what she wants. Premiere's soon. We'll see how it looks on screen.' He eyed Opal's hat. 'Smart. French flowers?'

'Yes, it's one of my own.' Opal flushed pink. 'I handmade these flowers with some spherical heating tools I bought in Paris.' She offered a Laplume Millinery business card with her little finger akimbo. 'My shop's particulars.'

Determined, Opal exited, resolving to worm her way back into millinery. Framed portraits of Platinum Signet Productions heroines – Garbo, Shearer, Crawford – lined the hallway, lifting her spirits. She mentally designed headwear for each gown before knocking on another door.

'Forgive me for interrupting,' Opal said in her politest voice. 'I'm seeking a position of any kind. Can I be of any assistance?'

'Yes. We need these yeti costumes covered in mud. Thirty of them.'

Opal hesitated. The department labelled 'Costume Break-down' was stocked with bricks, rocks, tubs of stains, anything to make costumes look worn. It was a dashed shame that Opal had left her black poodle in Studio Services, as making things mucky was the perfect job for him.

'Oh. I, um, may not have the proper credentials,' Opal said politely.

'It's just rubbing dirt into fur. We've got overalls.'

'I'll try next door first. Perhaps something more fitting to my... expertise.'

She knocked on 'Background Artist Fitting Suite'. The harried woman inside rejected her immediately out of the side of her mouth with pins sticking out. Opal didn't mind, it looked positively like a junk shop.

Next was 'Lead Cast Fitting Suite'. A pinched-faced woman in a maid's pinafore answered.

'Good afternoon. Opal Laplume. Sent by Adrian. Need any help with fittings?'

'As a matter of fact, yes.' She scrutinised Opal with flared nostrils, then extended a hand. 'Virginia, Jane Margeaux's assistant. Are you good with small buttons?'

'Oh, yes,' Opal affirmed, keenly.

'We've got two hundred to fasten onto Jane Margeaux and Betty Caruso. Here's a button hook.'

TWO

DRESSING ROOM DISCORD

Opal stepped into a bright room lined with mirrors and chinoiserie screens. Jane Margeaux stood before a mirror, script in hand. Her face was encircled by a peroxide blonde cloud. So light and fluffy was her hair that the bulbs around the mirror behind her shone through it like sunrays. Betty Caruso stood next to her in the same dress with her arms folded like tight twine. She was a dirtier blonde with more angular features that had a very pleasing symmetry. Both actresses wore identical mint-green satin gowns, unfastened at the back.

'Oh, these dresses are *simply ripping!*' Opal gushed. 'The beaded appliqués! The butterfly sleeves! Will you have headwear?'

'Just a diamond clasp,' Virginia said flatly. 'Do Betty's buttons while I do Jane's.'

'Is it a double act?' Opal asked, inspecting her button hook.

'A ballroom number about rivalling sisters,' Betty replied, her emerald eyes boring into Jane.

Opal knelt to button Betty's train, irony prickling her. A lady's maid would dress Opal when she was small. Opal's father, who was a baron, Lord Edmund Laplume, owned

Copperfields Hall in Suffolk and she had lived there until she was eight. Then, due to dwindling funds, they had to sell the estate to a mustard factory. She moved with her mother, Lady Phyllis Laplume, to London to live above their own hat shop, Laplume Millinery. Her mother still had a lady's maid called Effie who she was terribly hard on. But Opal had decided she didn't need the fuss.

Jane shifted, her script hovering above Opal's head, revealing pencilled doodles at the start of each line: an elephant, a spoon, a bird.

'What are those little drawings?' Opal enquired.

Jane smiled. 'My, haven't you got a bonnie accent! Are ya English?'

'Indeed I am.'

'I need to perfect my mid-Atlantic accent. Maybe you can help?'

'Mid-Atlantic?' Opal was utterly bamboozled.

'Hollywoodland prefers a more neutral, sophisticated sound. A mixture of American and British.' Jane sighed. 'And the drawings? Acrostic mnemonics to remember lines. An "e" word gets an elephant, "s" a spoon. I make a story from them.'

Betty smirked. 'If Jane spent more time learning her lines than drinking vodka, she might actually manage a coherent sentence.'

Jane's red nails nearly punctured the script. 'You've got more foundation than this town's buildings. Did you apply that to your face with a trowel?'

'Oh, calm down, Jane. It was play-acting. I didn't realise you'd take it so seriously.' Betty rolled her eyes.

'I didn't,' retorted Jane. 'Your performance was so wooden I half expected termites to start a union.'

Opal thought desperately of something to change the subject. 'Ladies, would you be so kind as to help me. Is there a nice hotel around here that would not be averse to dogs?'

'None. Unless you're an A-lister,' Betty said curtly and inspected her manicure.

'Try Palatial Pines,' Jane offered. 'They allow mutts. I know a spotlight operator who keeps a Dalmatian there.'

'Oh, Thank you. I'll see if they still have space.'

'Hollywood's full of canine auditions,' Jane mused. 'What kind of pooch is it?'

'Black miniature poodle, continental cut. Pom-pom tail, naturally,' Opal said fondly. 'I rescued the poor dear from a pile of coal sacks out the back of a kitchen in Piccadilly. He had a little piece of ripped burlap sack on his head in the shape of a bicorn hat. Naturally, I christened him Napoleon and made him a little bicorn to wear!'

'Well, isn't that somethin'.' Jane smiled. 'Where's the critter now?'

'I left him with a friendly chap over at Studio Services. Along with my trunk.'

'I'm sorry to interrupt your little courtship, but I have to brief Miss Laplume on the wardrobe plot.' Virginia handed Opal a thick wad of paper. 'The movie's called *Midnight at St Claire's*. You can read the synopsis on the front.'

MIDNIGHT AT ST CLAIRE'S

In New York City, 'St Claire's Emporium' is the pinnacle of luxury. Mavis, a homeless shop girl, toils by day among lavish clothes and perfumes. But by night, she finds refuge within the store's opulent halls, pretending it's her home.

One evening, thieves break in and she gets shot in the arm. The mobsters, feeling guilty, nurse her back to health. Mavis forms a bond with Jack, the gang leader.

When Mavis's secret life is uncovered, she confesses to Mr St Claire, the store's owner. Instead of punishment, he offers her a chance at redemption – a job as the emporium's night watchwoman and builds her a grand, master bedroom above it.

'I play Mavis – the lead, of course,' said Jane. 'There's one scene that's going to shoot my career to the stars, and, darling, I'll never come down.'

'You already achieved that when you played Lady Macbeth like a confused sous-chef,' sniggered Betty.

'Says the woman who played Ophelia like she was drowning in gin!' Jane said coolly and turned to address Opal. 'It's the stunt scene. Nobody's ever done a skit like this before. We've got a bird's-eye view camera, swooping down like a hawk, the sound of gunfire echoing through the heavens... All those *fancy footwork* bits, not to mention the Technicolor to capture my luscious-red dress. It's going to be the most *dazzling* thing on film.'

THREE

PALATIAL PINES

After salvaging her beloved pooch and trunk from Studio Services, Opal embarked on her search for accommodation. 'I say... Excuse me!' she said as she swung her trunk out of the way of an Egyptian Pyramid prop that wheeled past. Napoleon yapped at the stuffed camel perched beside it, offended by its glassy, unblinking stare.

Opal could only compare the bustle of Platinum Signet Productions studios to Harrods sale in London, and even that paled in comparison. Men in shirtsleeves and trilbies dashed about, scripts clutched in their hands as if they were life preservers. The echo of hammering mingled with the barked orders of directors and the occasional wail of a brass instrument. Opal gasped as she realised the man who had sidestepped her was John Gilbert, the silent film star.

His chiselled jaw turned to the woman beside him. 'Anna, I feel as unwelcome on set as a cigar in church.'

The woman, who had dazzling almond eyes and a black bob pierced with an oriental pearl comb, replied, 'Talking pictures aren't the enemy. They're just... different. Like trading a fountain pen for a typewriter. A bit noisier, but the words still shine if you use them right.'

That must be Anna May Wong! Opal longed to call out to the actors... but John Gilbert's forlorn expression discouraged her.

Everyone she tried to ask directions from was utterly preoccupied. She tried, in her most ladylike tones, to enquire about her destination, 'Palatial Pines?', but was met with either a hurried nod or a vague wave in an indeterminate direction.

At last, a teenage boy with very large ears and a flat cap paused to actually listen. He removed his hat in clumsy politeness.

'That's one hell of an accent coaching you've had!' he squeaked.

'Oh, no,' Opal said. 'I'm an English native.'

'I saw you leave from Jane Margeaux's costume suite. Are you acting with Jane?'

'*Me*, an actress? I'm flattered. But alas, no. I'm from the costume department.'

'Burton Ford... script clerk,' said the young man and held out his hand.

'Opal Laplume and Napoleon... Napoleon, no! That's not a real goose.'

Burton leaned in. 'I've been trying to get Jane Margeaux to read my script. Directors like George DeLuca won't even glance at an unknown writer's work. But if Jane liked it, maybe she'd pass it on.'

'Fortune favours the brave. I can certainly try,' Opal said and took the crumpled manuscript. 'Now, would you be so kind as to direct me to the Palatial Pines hotel? And furthermore, help with my trunk?'

'You're in luck, mam, as I lodge there too.' As Burton led the way through the maze of the studio lot, Napoleon trotted alongside, pausing to sniff a fake sausage stall, his nose twitching in confusion at the scent of plasticine and not pork.

They passed through the pedestrian gates under grand roman pillars, which marked the PLATINUM SIGNET PRODUC-TION STUDIOS territory. The road transitioned from a wide, paved boulevard to a more modest dirt track. The occasional palm tree cast a few welcoming patches of shade in the hot sun. Opal fanned herself with her fedora, lamenting her lost hand fan. Her mother-of-pearl hand fan had snapped in the gale on the way over the Atlantic.

The sounds of the studio became a distant whirr, replaced by the chirping of birds. Opal wondered what breeds lived in the trees. Her father, Lord Laplume, was an ornithologist and had a nickname for Opal – 'Bins'. This was short for 'binoculars' as she would be able to see very accurately from far distances and helped her father when she was little. Burton pointed to a particularly dilapidated wooden hotel made up of chalets, its sign barely visible behind the overgrowth of ivy. PALATIAL PINES.

'I suspect the name was chosen for alliteration rather than accuracy,' Opal said, sighing. 'It's not exactly a palace.'

'Looks like it was built by a set crew, doesn't it?' Burton laughed. 'Probably was.'

'My mother would have an apoplexy,' Opal said, eyeing the chipped steps and the sagging porch. 'I do hope the mattresses aren't lumpy!'

'I stay in the gents' quarters on the top level.' He plonked the trunk down. 'Well... good luck. I gotta get to a meeting... I mean a date.' He pulled his jacket closed and Opal saw the flash of something red in his inside pocket.

'Well, thank you, Burton. Jolly decent of you. Until we meet again.'

There was a single room available in the ladies' quarters and Opal paid a man in a burlap apron eleven dollars for the week.

Her room smelled of pinewood and carbolic soap due to the pungent bar sitting on the sink. Napoleon, being a dog, and not able to decipher between luxury and shabbiness, leapt happily up onto the cotton sheets and cosied his bottom for forty winks. After unpacking, Opal decided to explore her new surroundings. The chalets had five levels, and she ascended to the topmost one on the external, zigzagging staircase.

The topmost balcony offered a panoramic view of Hollywoodland. Its iconic sign was perched in the distance. The sky began to blush pink as the eighth hour approached. Though a beautiful view, Opal couldn't help feeling awash with a barren feeling. Hollywood, she mused, was built on a desert, but oddly enough it never quite got rid of the desolation. The streets may be lined with palms and the buildings all gilt and glass, but there was something in the air... hot, dry, and hollow... that whispered of things lost, rather than things found... like a postcard of paradise that's been left too long in the sun, edges curling inward.

Opal, being a hat aficionado, loved sketching fashion and headwear. But this poignant view she simply could not resist capturing. She riffled in her handbag for her sketchbook and a pencil. *Botheration.* She would need to resort to using the lipstick crayon she had. She began to make sweeping strokes of the horizon and smudged blots for the reddening clouds. The activity reminded her of a very special man she sketched with in Paris...

A commotion below distracted her. At an eatery called the Golden Hour Luncheonette, men in security uniforms loitered while a girl in a boater wound the handle of a tombola barrel. Opal visually zoomed in on one of the men. There was something achingly familiar about his stance... Then, as he turned slightly, she saw his dimpled chin and the way it would turn into an apostrophe as he smiled. He also wore a very familiar paisley cravat.

Good heavens above! Opal thought, clutching the wooden railing for support. *It can't be... but it is! Augusto!* Napoleon also seemed to spot the man, his favourite Paris babysitter! He yapped, sticking his snout through the railings.

This was the man who she had harboured an ill-concealed 'pash' for during the past spring in Paris. She'd spent the entire time wondering whether he was interested in her or not. She had gotten the inkling on their last goodbye that he *may* have a soft spot for her.

Could it be possible he had followed her to Hollywood? No, don't be so vain, Opal. It was a silly dalliance anyways.

She held her breath as, with a casual elegance, he turned and began to walk away up the boulevard.

'Augusto!' Her voice was drowned by a flurry of cars journeying downtown. Opal dashed downstairs. Napoleon galloped in tow. She burst out of Palatial Pines towards the Luncheonette. *Drats! He must have turned off into a side street.*

The girl in the boater called her over. 'Roll up, roll up, be in with a chance to win a seat at Jane Margeaux's new movie premiere!'

'What a marvellous publicity stunt,' Opal said, to try and charm the girl into giving her information. 'Do you know where the gentleman in the cravat went?'

'I don't. But I do know he'll be sitting in seat D2 at the premiere. He won a ticket. Lucky dame whoever gets to sit next to him.' She winked and nodded at the tombola for Opal to try.

'Oh, very well. When in Rome and all that.' Opal dropped a five cents piece in the girl's palm and dove her hand into the red lacquered barrel.

The ticket was quite impertinently inked with, '*No Seat, No Show.*'

Blithering fig! However could she track him down in this hive of a town?

FOUR

AN AROMA OF ACCUSATION

An exotic pomander of pink orchids stood on the dresser with a notelet, *Eternally Yours, Carey.* Jane Margeaux was seated in front like a white sunflower, basking in the light of the bulbs around the mirror. Adrian Greenburg was standing to one side, fussing over one of her dresses.

Opal sheepishly held out Burton's crumpled script. 'Forgive me if this is impertinent, but a sweet script clerk, Burton Ford, asked me to pass this on to you.'

Jane sighed. 'That boy is obsessed. I humour him because he's writing strong lead roles specifically for me. But he doesn't listen to my feedback. Just leave it on the dresser, will you.'

'I peeked at it, it's about a female propaganda artist. A jolly interesting idea,' Opal said.

Opal held out a jewellery case for Virginia to retrieve a string of pearls, but noticed they weren't shining as they should. 'Wait. I need to polish them first. May I?' She whipped off Adrian's neck scarf, rubbed the pearls, then presented them.

Jane was impressed by their renewed lustre. Virginia fastened them around the star's neck. Tiny droplets of iridescence raining down from the cloud of her hair.

Opal then hung Jane's opera gloves over her forearms like a waiter and curtsied. 'Don't forget talcum powder, ma'am. It will help them slip on easier.'

Jane arched a thin brow. 'Where did you learn these airs and graces?'

'My mother's lady's maid, Effie.'

'A lady's maid?'

'Mother is Lady Phyllis Laplume, daughter of Viscount Oulton. My father is Lord Laplume, a baron. I'm an honourable. I was dressed as a child but I always found it bothersome.'

Jane leaned in. 'Well, well, well... an honourable. That is something. You can gain riches, you can gain fame, but you can never gain that. You either are or you ain't.'

'Not everyone values it. My aunt rejected the life entirely,' Opal said.

'I think I could learn a lot from your accent and your decorum. Let's be friends,' Jane said, as if there wasn't any option not to be.

There was a triple knock at the door.

'Cover up.' Adrian slung Jane a tasselled shawl. 'It's the Tiger and the Penguin.'

Opal helped drape it over her shoulders. 'Who is that?'

'Emmett Zimberg, studio head, and George DeLuca, director,' Adrian murmured, smoothing his jacket before opening the door.

Zimberg walked in first with the gravitas of his big cat nickname. He wore a well-tailored pinstripe suit and light circumvented off his gold spectacles. The second, shorter man waddled with his arms pinned to his sides in navy tweed, his neck nearly non-existent.

Zimberg spoke. 'The scriptwriters have rewritten a pivotal scene. It's essential you understand it.'

'Yes, yes, Virginia's told me.' Jane waved him off. 'Meet the

Honourable Opal Laplume.'

Opal exchanged pleasantries with the studio gladiators. But they had glazed eyes, and minds absent. They asked her no questions.

DeLuca sniffed. 'Jane, have you been drinking? There's a strong smell of whisky.'

The air turned static and Opal scrunched her toes. Zimberg wrinkled his nose and made his glasses hop upwards. Adrian cleared his throat as if acid had dripped down it. Jane pressed a hand to her chest.

'Heaven's no,' Jane said. 'I don't even drink whisky! I drink vodka but only at the club.'

'It might be from the rubbing alcohol we used to clean a stain on Jane's slip,' Opal fabricated in Jane's defence.

'That's it!' Jane snapped her fingers.

DeLuca grunted. 'Fine. Just give me a sharp take. This could be an Oscar picture.'

When the bigwigs left, Jane flung her shawl on the floor. 'For crying out loud! Adrian, do I smell of booze?'

Adrian leaned into her candyfloss hair, his nostrils flaring a bit like sails of a ship catching the wind.

'No, mam. That is God's truth. You don't.'

'Wait a minute,' Opal said, eyeing the shawl on the carpet. 'Is it the shawl that smells?'

'Yes... yes, it is!' said Jane, snatching and sniffing the bunched silk. 'Some two-bit grifter doused my shawl in moonshine!'

'Calm down, Jane. Was there a spillage at a wrap party?' Adrian said in a parental manner.

'No spillage. And this door is always locked. Some dirty rat is trying to screw with my reputation. That scarecrow Betty Caruso, I bet!'

'Miss Betty Caruso hasn't been in here, Jane, and the door is always locked, as you said.'

'Where was my shawl hanging?' Jane demanded.

'On the door hook. Take it easy. You're on set soon,' Adrian soothed.

Opal took the shawl and hung it back on the door hook. It was a spherical gold knob. She narrowed her eyes as she studied it hanging there. *The person who doused it in whisky could have easily, with a comb, pulled her shawl out from under the door, applied the liquor and pushed it back over the gap in the top of the door. It would land on the spherical hook as it fell down inside*, Opal mused.

Opal demonstrated this for Jane and Adrian and smiled a triumphal banner of red lips and pearly teeth. Adrian just stood and clapped, lost for words.

'Aren't you the shrewd one?' Jane said, her brows disappearing up under her frothy hair. 'I owe you two favours. For that and for saving my skin earlier with that rubbing alcohol comment!'

After Opal's dressing duties were over, she noticed a cap from a miniature liquor bottle on the carpet in the hall. The lid said, 'Silver Spur whisky'. She hummed to herself in intrigue and pocketed it.

A man leaning in the corridor witnessed her doing this. He had a camera hanging around his neck. He had very tanned skin and a beauty spot above his right eyebrow that jumped up when Opal locked eyes with him.

'Don't mind me, lady. It's a little hobby of mine to take impromptu snaps of Hollywood life.'

'Goodness, what a maverick,' said Opal, a little shirtily. Surely this wasn't good manners.

'Domingo Lara, I'm a film editor here at Platinum Signet.' He removed his trilby.

'Opal Laplume... charmed,' she said and carried on down the corridor until he disappeared.

She noticed an office door was ajar. She slipped in and saw

a desk laden with piles of invitations all hand tied with a gold cord. She delicately inspected one. They seemed to say much the same thing – it was an invitation to Jane's premiere of *A Capitol Wife* at Grauman's Chinese Theatre. Apart from one invitation which stood up next to the typewriter. Opal was taken aback at how strange the language was. It read;

Dear Mr Huxley,

Special friend. Come, join us on a journey through magic, your seat will be A6. Every detail was meticulously crafted. Nestled amidst the glitz and glamor of Hollywood, the premiere of A Capitol Wife *awaits your presence...*

She stopped reading as the words seemed off. 'Special friend.' And unnatural sentence structures. And why a unique invitation written especially for Mr Huxley? *Who was* this Mr Huxley?

There was a headmistress-like throat-clearing noise. Virginia was in the doorway holding a jug of water. It was crammed with slices of lemon and Virginia's lips were pursed as if she had bitten one. She took Opal by the arm and marched her back into Jane's dressing room.

'I caught Opal nosing at the premiere invites,' Virginia reported, thudding the jug down.

'I was admiring the pretty stationery, please forgive me.' Opal scrunched her toes.

'Well, thank you for reminding me, Virginia...' said Jane, pulling a comb through her locks. 'Can you fetch a blank one, I need to invite the Honourable Opal Laplume, of course.'

Virginia's pointy chin jutted upwards as she left the room to obey.

'Mrs Margeaux, I would be delighted. Thank you,' Opal said, positively fizzing like champagne.

'As I said, I owe you one.'

'Might I request to sit in seat D1?' asked Opal a little shyly. 'It's just, I know a chap who won a ticket for D2 in a tombola.'

'A lady cannot go without a chaperone.' Jane winked. '*D2*, eh? Let's hope he's not too *dee*-stracted by *you* to watch my film.'

FIVE

GRAUMAN'S CHINESE THEATRE

No matter how beautiful the chinoiserie embroidery on the cinema curtains was, it could not pull Opal out of her blue mood. She looked at the empty D2 seat next to her. Why had Augusto not shown up? Most people would give their eye teeth to be present. Did he perhaps spot her and decide he did not want to sit next to her?

To distract herself, Opal scanned the audience, hoping to spot a famous face. There seemed to be an art to the Hollywood smile, a particular gloss to the enthusiastic wave. It seemed to cover a multitude of sins... chiefly the screaming loneliness underneath.

Opal's eyes landed on an especially hefty diamond necklace, above it the renowned doe eyes of *Joan Crawford!* Gosh, was it really Clark Gable, leaning back with languid grace? He shot Opal a rakish smile. Flustered, she whipped her head back round, anxious not to look like she was staring. She decided to just read the programme on her lap.

A Capitol Wife unveils the hidden life of Senator James Thompson's wife, Elizabeth. Behind the facade of a dutiful spouse lies Elizabeth's clandestine career as a playwright, her provocative works challenging societal norms. When her secret identity is threatened, she must defend her art, risking her marriage and reputation.

'Excuse me, ma'am.' An usher tapped her shoulder. 'Empty seats look bad. Is your guest running late? I have seat fillers ready.'

'It doesn't look like my guest is coming. You can fill it.' She sighed.

'Excuse me, is this seat D2?' a familiar Latin voice spoke behind the usher.

Oh fig! Was it? Could it be... Augusto?

The usher stepped aside to reveal the man in question. He was even more dashing than she remembered. He was clad in white tie, his hair slicked back with enough brilliantine to grease a small engine. His dark brows seemed to express a languid amusement, as if chuffed that Opal had orchestrated this little rendezvous. The soft slope of his nose led to the dominant feature of his countenance... a chin marked by a deep, dark dimple, the kind that gave his impeccable visage a rakish, devil-may-care air.

'Opal Laplume. What a pleasant surprise...'

She parted her lips to reply, but the spectators hushed as the curtains stirred. Augusto sat, gave her knee a gentle pat, and smiled. She melted into her velvet seat, bursting to speak but forced into silence.

The title, *A Capitol Wife*, flashed in blazing monochrome.

But the first scene stood out as a little *off* to Opal. It was a close-up of Jane Margeaux on a chaise longue. She was wearing the twinkling belt that Adrian had been complaining about on Opal's first day. It was very large on her tiny waist, and you could clearly see the ten-by-ten rhinestones. Jane's character

'Elizabeth' is being berated by her senator husband about something to do with 'public moral decency'.

There was a further close-up of the belt and Jane's half-moon manicure, tapping various diamantés on the buckle. Like some sort of impatient fidget while she was being scolded. She then placed her hand under the belt and then out again. She then fiddled with the large jewel on her finger. It lasted about half a minute, causing bottoms to wriggle impatiently.

The rest of the film was ripping, and Opal eagerly joined the standing ovation. Jane Margeaux and her co-star bowed beneath the screen. Jane waved with the reverence of a prima ballerina, her enormous orchid corsage cascading from shoulder to hip.

Opal rose on her tiptoes, scanning seat A6... the seat number assigned in Jane's queerly worded invitation. A bald man stood before it, his starched collar slightly askew. Mr Huxley? Opal made a note to observe him at the drinks reception.

'Finally, we can speak,' Augusto said, offering his elbow as they made their way up the aisle.

'Indeed.' Opal smiled, analysing his motives. He'd known she was coming to Hollywood... *had he followed her?* Instead, she asked, 'What brings you to the land of talkies?'

'I know you might think I'm following you,' – he gulped, adjusting his collar – 'but it was... how do you say in English... when something is good accident?'

'Serendipity?'

'Ah... *casualidad*, we say.'

'Bumping heads at a star-studded premiere, five thousand miles away... sounds very "casual" indeed!' She let out a nervous laugh that could probably be heard in Pasadena.

'Emmett Zimberg was looking to add to his security corps. They've been having trouble with spies.'

'Good grief. Spies?'

'Studio spies. Cox & Lumière Pictures, Platinum Signet Productions... they're all spying to get ahead.'

'Should I trust you, then?' Opal squeezed his elbow playfully.

Their tête-à-tête was interrupted by a ruckus. Behind a pillar, director George DeLuca had film editor Domingo Lara by the scruff of the neck. DeLuca, furious, was pink-faced, veins spreading over his bald head like blue forked rivers.

'I told you to CUT IT OUT!' he barked.

'Did George mean "cut it out" in the figurative or literal way?' Opal mused. 'You know, the way Americans ask people to cease unsavoury behaviour? Or did he mean literally "cut it out" as an editor would snip out a part of the film?'

Augusto gently steered Opal away from the unscripted drama. 'Whatever it is, I hope George DeLuca is in a better mood on set tomorrow. I have a security posting there.'

'On *Midnight at St Claire's*?' Opal asked. 'So will I! In costume, no less.'

'I shall drop by and have my collar starched to a state of military precision then.' He grinned.

In the foyer, a knife clinked a glass. Carey Margeaux, standing on a chair, his fat, oblong cufflinks glinting as he ran a hand over his blond sheen. 'In honour of my wife's sterling performance, I'm treating the company to Cristal... a vintage so rare it deserves its own applause!'

Jane clapped along with the crowd, orchids trembling on her shoulder. But as Carey stepped down, Opal lip-read her muttered words: '*We should NOT be paying for the champagne. Platinum Signet Productions should.*'

Carey turned dismissively to take a frothing flute from a swirling tray. Opal watched the tray make its way through the crowd. She noticed a thick hand with a dirty fingernail pluck a glass stem. Most ungenteel to be unmanicured before a white tie event! She followed the arm up to the head of a bald man, and as he turned away Opal noticed his crumpled collar. *It was the man from seat A6.* Mr Huxley! The recipient of Jane's mysterious invitation.

'Let's get closer to the trays of fizz,' Opal said, and snaked her way through the sea of sequins and chiffon.

She tapped Huxley's shoulder. 'Excuse me, do let me fix your collar for you. I work in costume and I just can't help it, I'm afraid.'

'Oh dear, what am I looking like? Thank you, my dear.' He bowed his head as she folded the collar neatly.

'I'm always on duty! Though I long to work in the millinery department. The post was taken when I arrived, but what I've got is far better than nothing.'

'Mr Huxley, producer, Cox & Lumière Pictures, glad to meet you.' He lifted his glass, revealing the grubby nail again.

'The Honourable Opal Laplume,' she said. 'What is Cox & Lumière Pictures?'

'A rival to Platinum Signet Productions. We might have a millinery placement for a new period drama set in Victorian Britain. Bonnets and whatnot. You'd be perfect.'

'Sounds positively charming. Is it a book adaptation?'

'Top secret. But come to the Cocoanut Grove on a Saturday. That's my hangout. We'll chat more then.'

Augusto pulled Opal behind a giant vase. 'I must leave. I have to be up at the crack of a sparrow's rear end.'

'Oh, Augusto! Already? You gulped your champers so swiftly!'

'I will see you on set.' He then did something that he never had done in Paris.

His mouth moved towards Opal like she was entering a tunnel. His brown eyes were on her lips. Opal could feel herself blush with so much pigment it would be enough to paint the entire Hollywoodland sunset. *Oh fig. What do I do? Pretend you don't notice, that's what you do.*

Opal barriered her lips with her flute and pointed at someone's hat. 'What a crest on that turban! I wonder if it's burnt peacock barbs. Singed and dyed. Or it could perhaps be egret?'

'I don't speak your millinery language, I'm afraid,' Augusto said and gave her hand a light squeeze. 'Goodnight.'

As he walked away, Opal detected a hint of disappointment in his sloping shoulders. Opal longed to be able to reciprocate his advances. But she felt like a fine violin yearning to join a street band... melodious, but hopelessly misplaced. Mother would simply not allow it.

She sighed deeply and sauntered over to the mirror above the mantel to adjust the tassels hanging from her capulet. But her eyes slid slowly to the left as she overheard a morsel of gossip.

'The word on the street is that Carey married Jane because his old flame was far too poor for his tastes! I've almost got the scoop on who the waif was... if you can get some photographs...'

The woman saying this was rather striking. She was skinny and a dash past the half century, shrouded in midnight purple and wore a Cossack hat tumbling with faux grapes. She had tiny pupils like drops of newspaper ink. Domingo the film editor was listening with his head on the side.

'I've got something else on the *reds*, Peridot,' said Domingo and whispered in Peridot's ear.

'*Jane and Emmett Zimberg?*' Peridot said as if these were the most unexpected names to hear.

Opal continued to tweak her hat and thought, *What is 'the reds' exactly? A red uniform? A surname? Or is it that Bolshevik ideology everyone seems to be in a flutter about? 'Red' for the fierce ones, 'pink' if you're more on the sympathetic side, isn't that how it goes?* She picked her glass up off the mantel, frowning deeply. *But wealthy Jane Margeaux and Emmett Zimberg... communists? Surely not!*

'Ahhh!' Domingo said, noticing Opal. 'The Honourable

Opal Laplume, Jane's assistant! Meet Peridot Ellington, Holly-wood's gossip queen, she's editor of all the big rags.'

'Honourable eh?' said Peridot with the overripe tone of a bad actress. She put out a hand. 'Jane has blue blood waiting on her now? Isn't that somethin'.'

'I'm helping Jane with her mid-Atlantic accent,' Opal said, and took Peridot's typewriter-induced swollen knuckles. 'I'm also in the millinery and costume department.'

'That's one of your own, isn't it.' Peridot's eyes dilated as she noticed Opal's capulet.

'Yes. From the Laplume Millinery Shop in Marylebone, London,' Opal said a little smugly.

Peridot Ellington's pupils pulsed at the opportunity to leverage this information. 'Take my card. If you can dig up any dirt on Jane Margeaux, I'll have a double-page spread in *Photoplay* magazine waiting for you and your hat business.'

SIX

STRAWBERRY JAM ON A PLATE

'Listen up, folks,' Jane Margeaux addressed the studio underlings, looking at each and every pair of eyes to make sure they were listening. 'Brace yourselves. This gunshot scene, yes, this very one, will surely jettison me into the history books. I can practically hear the Oscar committee filling their ink cartridges as we speak! Now, we simply must get everything exact, because, as I always say, "If you're going to shoot, shoot for the stars..." Preferably with impeccable timing and a bit of finesse! So, let's make this scene the talk of Tinseltown, shall we?'

The studio cheered in agreement and loosened up their shoulders before they posed with their prop or angled their equipment. The clapperboard slapped down. Action began in choreographed perfection. The mobster stunt artist aimed his gun at Jane, who dramatically swept her arms above her head like a ballerina getting ready to leap backwards and be caught.

BANG!!!!!!!!!!!!!!!!!!!!!!!!

The gunshot was so powerful Opal could feel air pressure whip the floor beneath her feet. The muscles around her eyes spasmed shut. She clasped a coat hanger to her chest. Her hearing swam as if a pair of conches were pressed over her ears.

After a couple of heartbeats, she could just make out a peppering of applause.

She peeled her eyes open slowly as the clapping got louder. She looked over the vast expanse of the Platinum Signet Productions sound stage. Beneath a bleaching spotlight lay the actress in her red-beaded gown. She was splayed like a flick of strawberry jam on a plate.

What a commendable display of acting! thought Opal. The starlet's fall had been executed with such convincing drama that the crew continued to clap in zealous appreciation for her artifice. The director delayed his command for the applause before calling out, 'Cut!' through his tinny megaphone.

But the actress did not rise. She didn't flick her eyelids open or swish her head to the side and smile. It became a heartbeat too long. A chill crept into Opal's bones. *Something's not right.* Opal's eyes, trained to notice the slightest imperfection, locked onto the torso of the starlet's dress. Among the sequined artistry in postbox red, a stain in a darker shade of red began seeping through the fabric, like magma. The red beads seemed to writhe, the blood oozing through them with a terrible, deliberate purpose. The room seemed to hold its breath.

A single drop of blood formed at the corner of the starlet's mouth. It quivered, poised like a redcurrant at the peak of ripeness, before it began its descent, tracing a path down her white cheek.

The moment was shattered with a sudden scream from a female member of crew, like the guttural cry of a prisoner facing the gallows. It set off a rush of movement like an electric model railway. Three figures descended upon the lifeless woman. The director, George DeLuca, among them, his earlier smugness replaced by a frantic terror. Opal dropped her coat hanger with a clatter and rushed forward. The arm of a sound engineer blocked her path. 'Wait,' he said sternly.

George took the actress's pulse with trembling fingers.

Necks all over the studio craned forward, desperate for a signal. George removed his fingers again, dragging them limply backwards across the floor. The manner in which he did so could only mean one thing. Jane was dead. The tip of his little finger touched something on the floor... he slowly lifted it into the light. It was a rounded lead slug with a smooth brass jacket, about one inch long, smeared with blood. It was not a blank.

Opal looked over at the stuntman, who had taken off his cap. And slowly other flat caps and trilbies followed suit. The stuntman's facial features contorted in confusion as he stared at the revolver in his hand like it was a poisonous tarantula. His voice, trembling with disbelief, rose above the ruckus. 'But I fired a blank. It was supposed to be a blank.'

The director whipped his head around and eyed him with flamethrower eyes. Blue veins spread across his bald head like a cracked egg.

'Arrest him! And where is the armourer? Arrest him as well! Lock them in the camera storage!' The commands flew fast and furious, in a desperate attempt to regain control of a situation spiralling into chaos. The stuntman was grabbed under the arms and taken away by security. He did not struggle as he was hauled off. He continued to mutter to himself, 'It was a blank, it was a blank.'

Jane's body was swiftly covered with a black tarpaulin that was usually used to block the Fresnel lights. Over her stood the Platinum Signet Productions boss, Emmett Zimberg, in a dark-navy suit. His eyes, usually twinkling behind gold-rimmed spectacles, were two black holes. The director's voice dropped to a harsh whisper as he conferred with the boss, a man whose usually fatherly face was now taut with the weight of the catastrophe. Opal strained to hear them over the ruckus.

'Nobody on the outside can know about this. Have the extras seen what happened? We can't let them out until we decide what to do.'

The boss gave a single, sharp nod. 'Lock the doors,' he commanded, his voice a low rumble.

'With all due respect, Mr Zimberg, most of the hundred crew and extras in here haven't eaten for nine hours,' a female member of the crew said hesitantly, a clipboard shaking in her hands. 'They're already starving.'

'Just lock the doors, damn you!' the boss shouted, raising his volume with each word, leaving no room for discussion.

The stagehands moved like hasty ants, the heavy doors of the sound stage clanging shut, the metallic sound echoing like the toll of a bell. Opal could sense a collective unease settle over the room as the air became cold.

As the last bolt slid into place, sealing them in, the lights above flickered once, twice, and then went out entirely. Darkness swallowed the studio.

SEVEN

THE GLOW OF A MATCH

Nobody could see the blood seeping through the tarpaulin that covered the body of Jane Margeaux. The sound stage was in pitch blackness. Opal had no idea who had cut the lights.

'Light a match!' a male voice yelled.

Little scratch sounds came from all over the studio. Up on the balcony, and in the rigging, at the back near the costume rails and up on the sound stage. Scratch, scratch, scratch.

Little orange pockets of light illuminated faces and the nearest glow to Opal revealed George DeLuca, Emmett Zimberg and Jane's blubbering assistant, Virginia. The big boss lit up a cigar that trembled in his hands as if he was sitting on a train. Opal stayed about two metres distant so that they wouldn't necessarily know she was listening.

'Will somebody get the damn fuse box!' George DeLuca yelled so loud it echoed.

A bunch of lit matches scurried around the back of the studio. George glanced at his boss's cigar and followed suit, lighting up a cigarette. His own match died and now they were a large and small firefly.

'Virginia, I need you to pull yourself together,' said Emmett

Zimberg, his gold-rimmed glasses aglow. 'Take these matches and keys and go into the editing suite. I need you to slip out the fire exit, go to my office and fetch one almighty reel of Platinum Signet Productions letterhead paper and as many pens as you can find. And try to grab us some sandwiches.'

'But—'

'No buts. Go!'

'I will have to alert the medic.'

'She's dead. No medic—yet. Security is in the camera storage with the assailants. I will brief them and we will alert the police when we have come up with a statement.'

'Whatever you say, Mr Zimberg.'

Her footsteps hammered away with the jingle of keys.

'We're not letting anyone out until they've signed a confidentiality agreement.'

'But there's a hundred and fifty people locked in here. That could take hours, and everyone is hungry.'

'Do you realise what could happen to me if this got out? The future of Platinum Signet Productions? DO YOU?' Emmett Zimberg's cigar clouded his face in thick, orange smog and his glasses looked like the chambers of a double-barrelled shotgun.

Opal decided to follow the sound of Virginia's footsteps. Perhaps the woman could do with help bringing the paper? She didn't know what else to do. She bumped shoulders with a few bodies in the dark and stammered apologies. The faint glow of Virginia's match led her behind a long row of tall studio lights. Opal noticed her feet patter in water as she walked over some sort of spillage.

Virginia's match illuminated a sign that read EDITING SUITE. Virginia fumbled with the keys and muttered to herself, 'It's already open?' as she pushed it ajar.

'Virginia!' Opal hissed. 'Virginia, do you need any help?'

'No,' she hissed back. 'That wasn't the instruction. Step back!'

Virginia pulled the door shut behind her.

Opal waited for a beat. What should she do? The extras were locked inside the holding area of the studio to the left. They were probably out of their minds with worry. And in the dark. She could hear faint shouting and the ruckus of a hundred people threatening.

She heard men's voices coming from down a corridor to her right. She felt with her hands along the wall and came to a door. She took her cloche off so that she could press her ear against it.

It sounded like Augusto's voice.

'You are saying someone must have tampered with the gun?'

Opal realised she must be listening though the door to the camera storage room where security had taken the stuntman and the armoury props man.

'Yes. A live bullet must have been loaded into this gun chamber. Look! All the rest are blanks.'

'Perhaps there will be fingerprints on the bullet.'

'Would fingerprints be detectable after it's gone through the body?'

'I don't know.'

'In any case, whoever put it in could have been wearing gloves.'

Suddenly the lights pulsed, fizzed and then burst into full, white light with a flurry of 'pings'.

EIGHT

THE CONFIDENTIALITY AGREEMENT

Opal squinted and stepped back from the door. She shouldn't be seen here. She dashed back up the corridor.

There was a bashing on the door to the room where the extras were being held. The lady with the clipboard seemed to be trying to calm down the person hammering behind it. They could be heard through the wooden door.

'There's fifty-two extras in here who are ever so hot in their toy soldier costumes. One older lady in particular is very faint. She won't take the amphetamines. We have children in here too. Let the children out – please let them out!'

Opal knew how to get out. The fire exit in the editing suite. She thought perhaps Virginia hadn't locked it behind her. Perhaps she could slip out and find a few morsels of food for them. The thought of it made her stomach swell. God knew she was hungry. The filming today had been so behind, compared to the other days, that they had not let anyone go to the canteen. She headed back towards the editing suite. Everyone was talking in clusters and nobody had noticed her.

The editing suite, a rather cramped affair, was furnished

with an array of metal cabinets and sturdy wooden tables, upon which rested the tools of the editor's trade. Spools of film, some neatly rolled and others hopelessly tangled, were scattered about like the entrails of a mechanical beast. The air smelled of celluloid and dust that tickled her nostrils.

Opal meandered around the tables on her tiptoes, heading for the fire exit at the back. She heard a faint clicking noise. Was it some sort of machine?

'Bah!'

'Ahh!' Opal shrieked and then clasped her hands over her mouth.

Crouched in the corner of the editing suite was the film editor, Domingo Lara, his camera in his hands. The clicking noise must have been him playing with the lens. His eyes were pink, as if he'd been staring at something for a long time, and the beauty spot above his brow trembled at her as if he'd been caught with a knife.

'Domingo. I, um... Please don't tell anyone, but I am on the way out to find some food.'

'Oh yes, that's alright. Let's just not tell anyone we've seen each other. I was, um... I just had to get away as I was in shock.'

'Quite. Quite. Of course, let's just carry on.'

Opal let herself out of the sturdy metal door and closed it behind her.

It was late and the Platinum Signet Productions allotment was pretty quiet. She headed towards the canteen in the humid air. Dusk had fallen and she shivered from multiple ailments: hunger, shock and anxiety.

Across the way was an open hatch to another sound stage in which another production was lying dormant. As she passed, something colourful caught her eye. It was a prop market with piles of powdered spices and a heap of yellow melons. Behind them she could see a couple of baskets of apples. Prop apples?

Opal stepped over some wooden crates and scooped one up. She sniffed it. Papier mâché? Or real? Some of the props would be real, surely, as they were so cheap. It was heavy like a real apple. Waxy and sweet-smelling. She rubbed it on her dress sleeve and tried to sink her teeth in. They sank and apple juice seeped into her mouth as she crunched.

Perfect. This would keep them going.

The baskets were exceedingly heavy but she managed to carry them, despite sore shoulder muscles, back to the fire exit.

'I have apples,' she announced, brandishing them.

'You've been outside?' The lady with the clipboard looked at her with wide eyes.

'Oh yes, I was told to,' Opal lied.

'By who?'

'Oh, I don't know their name.'

'What an excellent idea!' boomed a voice from behind. It was Emmett Zimberg, hands on his hips. 'What was your name again, young lady?'

'Opal Laplume.'

'You didn't see or speak to anyone, did you?'

'No, sir.'

'Alright... hand these out to those in need.'

It was two more hours before Emmett Zimberg managed to get everything under control. A long, chunky queue of crew and extras had formed before the vast exit doors of the sound stage, which were still locked.

George DeLuca stood on a chair with his megaphone. His face was white and his head seemed to have shrunk even further down inside his collar. Brandished before him was a sheet of paper.

'Some of you are witnesses to what happened this evening and some of you are not. There will have been a lot of rumours going round, I am sure. The sound of the stunt gun gave Jane Margeaux a fatal heart attack. This is what happened, and this is what the public will be informed.'

There was a rush of whispers. Opal put her hand over her mouth. *Why would they lie so horribly? Would poor Jane never get any justice?*

'We will let you out one by one,' George continued. 'You must sign before leaving. I will read what it says so that you don't have to read it individually:

"This document serves as a confidentiality agreement between Platinum Signet Productions Inc and the undersigned.

One: You are prohibited from disclosing any information related to the incident involving Jane Margeaux on the set of Midnight at St Claire's, *whether verbally, in writing, or through any other means, to any individual or entity.*

Two: In response to enquiries from law enforcement, media representatives, or third parties, you are to state, "I know nothing".

Three: A breach of this agreement will result in immediate termination of your employment, permanent blacklisting from future opportunities within the industry, and legal proceedings, including claims for damages incurred by the studio.

By signing, you affirm that you have read, understood, and agreed to these terms."

'Now, sign and move along.'

Opal scribbled her name underneath dozens of others with a weak hand that the bite of apple had been able to energise.

'I want to see you in my office at noon tomorrow,' Emmett Zimberg whispered to Opal as she passed him.

Opal nodded. *Oh goodness. What on earth had she done?* She dashed out into the allotment and towards the canteen with everyone else.

NINE

EMMETT ZIMBERG'S OFFICE

Betty Caruso's smile unfurled like a particularly self-satisfied orchid, the sort that had spent a good deal of effort quietly strangling a neighbouring bloom and was now basking in the glory of having the sunlight all to itself. Her skin shone peach, her usually dull-blonde curls had tinges of gold. Her heels echoed like happy castanets down the Platinum Signet Productions corridor.

Opal was walking towards Betty on her way to Emmett Zimberg's office. Opal tried to nod in acknowledgement, but Betty stared right past her as if she was on some imaginary red carpet and Opal wasn't there. *Had Mr Zimberg, perhaps, given Betty some good news?*

Sitting on a waiting chair in front of the looming office door was Augusto. Opal gasped and gripped her handbag handle with both hands. He was as pale as an egg. She'd never seen him this drained of colour. His brow was sweating and he was pulling his collar away from his throat as if it were a noose.

'Augusto? Augusto? Are you alright?'

'I'm finding it hard to breathe. Is it hot in here?'

'No. It's not hot in here... Would you like some water?'

'No. No, thank you.'

'Can you tell me what the matter is?'

'I... I've failed again.'

'Failed? Failed in what?'

'I... can't... speak.' He kept pulling at his collar, even though it was already undone.

A secretary opened the door and beckoned Augusto in. She noticed his strange pallor and the way he was gasping for breath.

'What's wrong with him?'

'He said he's finding it hard to speak,' Opal said, and placed a hand on his arm. 'Perhaps I should come in with him?'

The secretary checked if it was alright for Opal to join their meeting. It was, so with a hand on the man's back, Opal gently led him into the office.

Emmett Zimberg was sitting in a massive, high-backed leather chair, upholstered in rich, dark burgundy with brass studs along the edges. His wooden desk was dark, nearly black, and polished to such a sheen you could practically see your future in it. The wall behind him was covered in gridded maps of the Californian terrain. Perhaps he envisaged taking it all over with his studios one day. And tigers, of course. Platinum Signet Productions' famous feline was everywhere: carved into the bookends, gleaming atop the marble mantelpiece, even leering from the corner in the form of a bronzed statue that looked as though it might spring to life at any moment, should someone make a misstep.

Mr Zimberg's temperament was different this afternoon. He usually assumed the manner of a preening tiger, lazily observing his territory. Now, he channelled the spirit of another type of big cat: a black panther whose territory was threatened. And on either side of him he had a fellow panther.

'Good afternoon, Opal Laplume, Augusto Sevilla. Please

meet my lawyer, Mr Witlock, and my private detective, Mr Kensington.'

'What the devil's the matter?' said Mr Kensington when he stood to shake Augusto's hand.

Augusto tugged his collar down and opened his mouth a couple of times in an attempt to speak.

'He's not at his best. I think he is upset about yesterday,' Opal said, and helped Augusto into a chair. She then sank into the chair next to it and interlocked her hands upon her knees.

'Well, we all are,' Mr Zimberg said solemnly, leaning back into the shady depths of his chair. 'I've asked you both, and a dozen or so others, into my office as you were witnesses to what happened. A lot of the extras and crew were in the next room with their vision obscured, but you both saw what happened to Jane and had minor roles in what unfolded. As you know, the public will be told that Betty Jane Margeaux died of a heart attack from the sound of the stunt gun going off. The Los Angeles Police Department are going along with this story. But I, myself, need to know what *really* happened. I have hired Mr Kensington here to help us get to the bottom of it.'

Gosh, even the Los Angeles Police Department eat out of Mr Zimberg's hand, thought Opal. *I know that theatre is played out on the streets of Hollywood as well as on-screen, but I didn't know it would go so far as to spin fairy tales about murder!*

Mr Zimberg continued in a grandfatherly tone. 'So, if there's anything you can tell us that we may have missed yesterday – *anything* at all – then you must tell us. It won't leave this room. You will be protected.'

Opal looked down at the gloves in her lap, then glanced sideways at Augusto. He did not look like someone who had nothing to say. A bead of sweat fell down his temple and his Adam's apple bobbed in a huge gulp.

'Sir?' asked the detective, leaning forward in his chair, eyes glued on Augusto.

Mr Zimberg touched his fingertips together, his elbows on the desk, his arms making a pyramid shape. The lawyer's gold pen was poised above his notepad, quivering in anticipation. Augusto swallowed again and reached into his inside breast pocket. He very slowly pulled out... a pistol.

TEN

THE PERFECT SCAPEGOAT

Opal felt the air solidify. The men behind the desk did not move. Only their eyelids drew back in reaction to the unexpected object. The slow way in which Augusto pulled it out from his jacket, keeping his finger well away from the trigger, and laid it sideways on the desk, gave no threat of assault.

'I discovered this morning...' Augusto said in an ominous tone, not taking his eyes off the pistol, 'that one of the bullets in my gun was missing. I think the murderer stole the live bullet from my gun and put it in the stuntman's weapon.'

'May I?' asked the detective. He pulled a handkerchief from his pocket, flapped it open and picked up the piece. 'Smith and Wesson Model 10?'

'Yes. With .38 special rounds,' Augusto said.

The detective broke open the chamber. Five shiny bullets were visible and one empty hole.

'The brand of these rounds matches the one found by Jane's body. Remington UMC.'

Opal gasped and covered her mouth. Augusto's head fell forward and he shut his eyes tightly.

The detective continued, 'The blanks that had been loaded

into the stuntman's gun were .38 special rounds also, but the brand was Harbourline munitions.'

'Is Augusto correct then?' Emmett Zimberg asked, strumming his fingers. 'Whoever set this up took a live bullet from Augusto's gun and put it in the stuntman's?'

'It *is* possible,' the detective said. 'When did you last notice you had all six bullets in your gun, Augusto?'

'At breakfast at the Luncheonette. I checked it. I had all six.'

'When could the assailant have stolen the bullet from your gun, Augusto?' Opal asked, gripping her chair arms.

'There was an incident, shortly before the shooting. The drinking-water barrel was knocked over,' Augusto said. 'I was sitting at my post, with coffee, gazette and pistol on the table. I realise now I should have kept it strapped on my person. Perhaps the sight of it inspired someone to distract me in order to take the bullet. Anyway, I heard a crash and a gush of water. I left the table and rushed over to lift the barrel back up. I had no idea who had pushed it over... I didn't see. And when I came back – it must have been only thirty-odd seconds later – my gun didn't look like it had been touched.'

'We'll test it for prints,' said the detective.

'Were there prints on the bullet that killed Jane?' asked Opal.

'No. The heat of the bullet leaving the chamber destroys any of that kind of evidence.'

'This all reeks of spontaneity,' Opal said. 'If the murder was planned ahead, the murderer would have come to the studio with a live bullet ready. All set to put in the stunt gun.'

'Indeed. A spontaneous act.' Mr Zimberg nodded.

'So, the conjecture is that the person who pushed the barrel over is the person who stole the live round,' Opal said.

'If Augusto is found to be telling the truth, yes,' Mr Kensington said, wrapping the pistol in his handkerchief.

Augusto looked up sharply. Opal's mouth fell open.

'Excuse me, Mr Kensington, but why would Mr Sevilla come in here with this evidence if he wanted to get away with something? Can't you see he's trying to help you find the culprit?'

'Does Mr Sevilla not have a voice box?' asked Mr Kensington, clicking open the locks on his briefcase and placing the pistol inside.

'The lady is correct. I am here to help you find Jane Margeaux's murderer,' Augusto said, and fidgeted with his collar nervously again.

'Have you anything you might like to tell us, Opal Laplume?' Mr Zimberg said, lightening the tone in the room. 'You became friendly with Jane Margeaux quite quickly. Did you notice any malignant behaviour in those who surrounded her?'

Opal scrunched up her toes. She tilted her head to the left and looked into the dark nucleus of Mr Zimberg's glasses. She had noticed many a malignant behaviour. The jealousy of Betty, who stood to inherit Jane's acting roles; the greediness of Carey, who would inherit Jane's money and mansion; the corruption of Peridot Ellington, who could gain great power through gossip. But she did not know yet what she should disclose. She did not know what web she could get herself tangled in if she were to play by Mr Zimberg's rules.

'I have been very focused on the costumes. I want to get into the millinery side, you see. I'm very driven in that regard and have had no time to gossip or notice things.'

'Well, if you do, young lady, you know where to find me,' Mr Zimberg said after a pause. 'You'll be helping Adrian resize Jane's costumes to fit Betty. She will be taking over the leading role in *Midnight at St Claire's*.'

'You're still going ahead with the film?' Opal said, utterly shocked.

'My dear, a fortune has been poured into this. We only shot

a few scenes with Jane. It sounds barbarous but it's unavoidable. I will let you go and check in with Adrian now.'

'Alright. Good afternoon, Mr Zimberg, Mr Witlock, Mr Kensington.'

'If you can wait behind, Mr Sevilla,' the lawyer said.

Augusto nodded, still looking at his lap. Opal felt nauseous as she left the office and held on to her cloche in order to keep her balance. *Would they try to blame Augusto?* In this world of lies they could surely do whatever they wanted. They had to blame someone and a foreigner that nobody knew would make the perfect scapegoat.

Something told her that what Augusto had meant by 'failed again' was that he'd failed to protect his principal, Jane. The same way he had failed in Paris when his principal, her cousin Clementina, was killed on his watch... Poor Augusto...

Before Opal shut the door behind her, Mr Zimberg called out a warning: 'Opal – one learns to walk with caution in Hollywood, lest a sudden shift in the scenery leaves one standing in the middle of nowhere.'

ELEVEN

ALL HAIL BETTY CARUSO

Opal dashed about, trying to keep her cloche on with one hand and keep hold of the dog leash in the other. Napoleon's nose was high in the air, in detection mode, hoping to sniff out his pal Augusto. They had been thick as thieves in Paris, marching up and down the Rue de Rivoli together, and Napoleon knew even the sound of Augusto's walk.

Opal was checking each and every security post in the Platinum Signet Productions allotment, desperate to find out what had happened to him. Outside Sound Stage 4 she spotted the teenage writer who had carried her trunk to Palatial Pines on her first day.

'Burton, Burton, can you help me?'

He removed his flat cap with fumbling fingers as she approached him. He had all manner of scripts and scrolls under his arm.

'Good morning, Miss Laplume. And Mr poodle... Napoleon, was it not? How may I be of assistance?'

'I've been desperately trying to find out what has happened to Augusto Sevilla. Do you know him? He's a member of the Platinum Signet Productions security corps.'

'Yes, I know him. The artistic fellow. He sketched me once, though he gave me extra-large ears. I think he's been replaced. At least there's a new man at his usual posting. The new guy is packing heat.'

'What do you mean, *packing heat*?' Opal asked.

'Gun in hand, not in his holster,' Burton replied, creating pistol fingers and holding them across his chest.

'I guess Mr Zimberg is asking them to be extra vigilant,' Opal said.

'If I see Augusto, I will be sure to let you know.'

'If you do, please tell him I'm based at Palatial Pines and to let me know that he is alright. I have been considering enquiring at the Platinum Signet Productions office to ask Mr Zimberg, but I'm a little scared of what the answer would be.'

'What are you scared of, mam?' asked Burton, his young face tilted on its side in concern.

'I think he may have been fired... or worse... arrested.' Opal sighed. Napoleon whined and pawed up her legs.

'Why?' Burton said, and his ears seemed to fly back.

'I'm not at liberty to say, I'm afraid.'

'Will you be coming to the miniature golf tomorrow, mam?' Burton said in an effort to lift the conversation.

'The *what?*' Opal screwed up her nose as if irked by such a nonsensical question when her nerves were on edge due to far more serious matters.

'It's a miniature golf course, mam. A lot of the Platinum Signet Productions gang are going. We've got a week off because of what happened to poor Jane. It's to take our minds off things and to honour her – she loved miniature golf, you see.'

'Well, it's alright for you. In the costume department it's "all hail Betty Caruso" as we are having to work around the clock to make sure the costumes are re-tailored for Betty,' she said, gently tugging at Napoleon's lead to make her departure.

But she noticed the look of disappointment on the boy's

face and added, 'Miniature golf, you say? I guess I should pay my respects, as it's to remember Jane.'

'Yes, it's the fad she was obsessed with. I'll be in my plus fours. I love the golfing get-up.'

'Well, I could do with cheering up. I may join you. But I shall have to bring Napoleon and I can't promise he won't be a rascal around the balls.'

Napoleon cocked his head on one side as if to reproach the word *rascal*. He was far more used to being described as babykins, biscuit-nose or Lord Floof.

'Seven o'clock, mam. There's a miniature Buckingham Palace and the ball swirls around the turrets to make the king pop out.' He smiled and smacked his flat cap back onto his crown.

'*Simply ripping!*' Opal said to humour him and then tottered off. From his pinked cheeks she had the suspicion he was developing a pash for her.

TWELVE

THE BEAUTY MICROMETER

Opal arrived at the dressing room that used to be Jane's. Bonfire, the redhead who had taken Opal's millinery job, was there. She was swapping the metal plaque that said 'Jane Margeaux' with one inscribed 'Betty Caruso'.

Opal clutched her beads. *Was this not a little insensitive, seeing as Jane had not even been dead a week? Couldn't they at least wait until after her funeral!* But she kept her mouth closed.

Bonfire glanced at Opal through the brassy spirals of her hair and seemed to read what she was thinking. 'Adrian thought it would be easier for everyone if Betty took over this dressing room rather than transporting all the costumes to another one,' she said, and a tear mingled among her freckles.

'I see,' replied Opal, and she sniffed hard. She could feel her bottom eyelids prick with the temptation to cry.

Jane Margeaux, though quite mad and ruthless in her ambition, was a kind woman who'd had her whole life ahead of her. It was adding insult to injury that someone she despised so much was benefiting from her death.

Opal entered the dressing room and what she saw was so shocking that she gasped. Napoleon hopped from foot to foot, not knowing quite how to react, so thought he'd cover most bases and growl. They were confronted with Betty wearing a terrifying contraption on her head.

The huge gizmo looked like a cross between a medieval knight's helmet and a futuristic gadget with dials and wires sprouting out. Virginia was twisting the knobs on it for her with a stoic expression. It seemed she had reluctantly taken on the job of assisting Betty now Jane was gone.

'Don't pop your clogs, it's the latest thing. A beauty micrometer by Max Factor,' Betty said with the little movement her mouth would allow in its clamp.

'What does it do? Does it hurt?' Opal asked, still frozen.

'No! It measures your face with precision and then calculates the optimal makeup techniques to hide any flaws. You wouldn't understand. And what's that *mutt* doing in here?'

'I do apologise. Jane used to allow Napoleon in here. Please let him stay, he will be a good boy! I haven't got anyone to babysit him today. Augusto, the security guard, was helping me on occasion, but I just don't know where he is.'

'Augusto Sevilla, the dishy security guard?' Betty asked.

'Yes.'

'Oh, he's been given the boot. Negligence of duty or some such. I think Mr Kensington the detective is keeping an eye on him. I must say he seemed a shady fella.'

'He was not shady, he was delightful – and he wouldn't hurt a fly!' Opal's mouth moved before she could calm herself. She felt her body shudder with unease. *Poor Augusto, what would become of him if he was accused?*

'Opal! Betty! Just relax. Napoleon can stay in the corner. I need Opal to get to work,' Adrian cut in from behind the costume rail.

He seemed to be the only person Betty would listen to. She wriggled her jaw closed inside the clamp. Napoleon, as if to prove what a creature of fine breeding and decorum he was, gently curled up on a pouffe in the corner with his paws neatly together.

'Can you get that thing off Betty now? We need to resize the headpieces on her as she has a larger crown than Jane did,' Adrian said, gritting the pins in his teeth a little hard.

'Well, it looks like your facial features are 97.895 per cent perfect. You need deeper contour on your cheekbones,' Virginia said, inspecting the dials.

'I remember Jane was 99 per cent perfect,' Adrian sniggered.

'Oh, I don't believe in this claptrap anyhow!' Betty seethed. 'Get the confounded thing off me.'

Virginia and Bonfire untwisted the knobs and heaved the thing off Betty's head. Neither of them cared whether they were hurting her or not.

'Ouch,' Betty yelled.

Opal looked at the booklet for the machine, which bore the slogan, 'Bring back the bloom of youth'. She scoffed disapprovingly.

'These beauty firms do love a dig... "Bring back the bloom of youth" indeed!' said Opal. 'If a husband tried that line on his wife, he'd be jolly well turfed! Yet beauty firms may peddle such cheek with impunity. My mother looks splendid, and young girls should hear language like *glow* and *radiance*, not this piffle about outrunning time. Give it a century, and they'll have seen sense.'

'I'm not so sure. Fear always peels pennies from the palm,' Adrian said as he rolled his shirtsleeves up behind Betty.

He began fluffing out Betty's hair before placing a pleated turban on her head. He wriggled it, but it wouldn't slide down into place. Instead it sat high like a gnome's hat. Betty glared at herself in the mirror, arms folded, completely devoid of amusement. Everyone else's lips were curled in a tickled fashion and even Napoleon puffed his nostrils.

'A little tweak is in order, don't you think?' Betty said.

'Bonfire, I'll leave the resizing to you. The tape measure says Betty's head is an inch bigger,' Adrian said.

Bonfire nodded and removed the turban. She was torturing her lower lip and Opal could see through her curls that her eyes looked panicked. *Did she not know how to resize a fixed turban? It would be tricky with the intricate pleats.*

'Opal, I need you to prepare the foundation garments,' Adrian said curtly.

Opal took a deep breath and stepped behind the costume rail to where the undergarments were kept. How was she going to be able to get through the day without worrying about Augusto? He was innocent but a perfect scapegoat. He would be in danger if the real killer wasn't found.

With jerking movements, she began to match the appropriate stays and slips with each dress. She lifted a lace slip off a side table and noticed Betty's crocodile handbag lying underneath, its clasp open to reveal a diary nestled inside. She was completely hidden from the others by the rail. *Should she take a peek at the diary?*

Opal gently plucked the leather book out of the bag and riffled inside to find the past month's escapades. There were many 'weigh-in' appointments, tennis, dinners with 'Georgie' – George DeLuca, Opal assumed. It all looked rather innocuous, until Opal's eyes zoomed in on something that made her blink rapidly, then stare in disbelief...

THIRTEEN

PINS, PLOTS, PERFIDY

In brazen blue ink, Betty had scrawled an appointment: *Voice Coach – learn Jane's songs in* Midnight at St Claire's. *Bring life to them.*

Opal tilted her head to the left in thought and read the entry over and over. The date of the session was the week before Jane died. *Why on earth would Betty need to learn Jane's songs... Unless...?*

'Opal, I need you to stitch a new collar to this tea dress. The accessories department has the correct thread – go meet Bonfire there so she can give it to you.'

Opal hastily slipped the diary back into the croc bag and replied, 'Certainly, sir.'

She made her way to the accessories department, the garment slung over her arm. She heard some warbling and the odd expletive. When she entered, she noticed Bonfire hunched over a table with a pair of small scissors and the turban in front of her.

'I say... Is everything alright?' Opal asked.

'No! I can't do this. I can resize hats for smaller heads, by padding them out. I can block hats from scratch. But I can't make them bigger. That's just something I've never had to do. And something as intricate as this...?'

'Oh fig,' Opal said sympathetically. 'That is a ghastly debacle with bells on. Have you told Adrian? I'm sure he'd understand.'

'No. I lied to him when I started, saying I could do it all.'

'Well, you're in luck. I know how to resize that. One inch, was it? But it will take me a good four hours, so we'd have to swap jobs – he's asked me to affix this collar.' She held up the garment and collar.

'Oh, Opal, would you? That would be so kind.'

'Of course. I'm a milliner. It's what I do.'

'Could we keep it a secret? I couldn't bear Adrian knowing I was a liar.'

'Well, if we must.' Opal sighed. 'I think there's been enough drama, don't you? Don't worry, we will work together.'

'Thank you, Opal. You're a kind lady. I was a little scared of you at first. It's those piercing eyes of yours, staring thoughtfully at things, noticing everything – I never know what you're think-ing. I wondered if you were judging the state of my hair at first. I mean, I know it looks like I've combed it with an egg-beater.'

'Nonsense, your ringlets are *simply ripping*. I do apologise. I have a tendency to get in my own head. And yes, I do notice everything. In Paris I solved two murders and a diamond heist, in fact.'

'Golly.'

Opal then paused in threading a needle and tilted her head to the left. She eyed Bonfire intently. 'I'd be very interested, Bonfire, in knowing what you think happened to Jane.'

'I was back here when it happened, so I was oblivious to Jane being killed until I was told. The lights were affected too but, thanks to my cigarette lighter, I was able to find some candles and went on sewing like I was in a Victorian sweatshop. My eyes still hurt from that. But' – she looked around before

continuing, even though there was nobody else in the room –
'Virginia told me Jane didn't die from a heart attack like the
public statement said. She was *shot*. The stuntman or armourer
used a live bullet. What did you see? I know we signed the
confidentially agreement, but we can talk, you and me,
can't we?'

'Yes.' Opal sighed sadly. 'Our dear Jane was shot. The
stuntman and armourer are adamant they had no idea about the
live bullet. Mr Zimberg is carrying out internal investigations
and there have been some developments. I think they may be
targeting or even framing the wrong man – my dear friend
Augusto.'

'How terrible! If anyone wanted to kill Jane Margeaux, it
was definitely Betty. Or at least it would have been Betty who
orchestrated it.'

'You think so?' Opal said, twiddling a thimble between her
thumb and forefinger.

'It's as plain as day. Betty's always hated Jane – she was so
jealous of her. And George wanted Betty to play the lead in
Midnight at St Claire's all along! She has benefited immensely
from Jane's death. Mr Zimberg is so doe-eyed over Betty he
would never suspect her. Or at any rate, he can't risk her being
charged for murder because he needs her in this film.'

'Where exactly was she when it happened?' Opal asked,
pulling her sketchbook from her handbag.

'Backstage, in one of the dressing rooms, practising her
lines,' Bonfire answered, peering over at Opal's red artworks.

'I'm going to sketch a floorplan of the sound stage and
connecting corridors and rooms. Then we can mark where
everyone was at the time Jane was shot.'

'Why are you using a lipstick?'

'Oh, I never have a pencil when I need one. I don't like this
colour on my lips, so I use it as a crayon. I like to sketch hats

with it... So, you were here' – Opal daubed a splodge to represent Bonfire – 'and Betty was...?'

'There. In this same corridor, a few doors down.' Bonfire pointed on the page and Opal marked a dot for Betty.

'Did you physically see her?' Opal asked.

'Yes, I did. I had to fetch her some candles.'

'I guess she could have swapped the bullet earlier.'

'That's possible.'

'I'm going to patch up the mechanics of the whole day and make a timeline and figure out exactly where everyone was and who saw what,' said Opal, closing her book and snapping the lipstick lid back into place.

'Good luck with that, Miss Laplume. Nobody tells the truth around here,' Bonfire said, fluffing up her curls.

'That certainly seems to be the case. It's as if everyone is their own scriptwriter.'

'Are you going to the miniature golf event that's being held in Jane's memory?' Bonfire asked, scrabbling in a box of pins.

'I most certainly shall... *if* we finish this.'

'That security guard, Augusto, you were speaking of earlier... I think he might be going,' Bonfire said, fluttering her eyelids at Opal as if she knew he was a beguiling subject.

'Do you? How?' Opal said, failing to hide the shrill excitement in her tone.

'I'm stepping out with one of the fellas in the Penciltown Sketch Club. He's mentioned that Augusto is a member and I know the club are going.'

Opal could feel her cheeks go pink and fingers jitter as she attempted to thread a needle. *Quick, divert your thoughts elsewhere... There'll be plenty of people to interrogate at the golfing affair.*

FOURTEEN

COLONEL THWACK'S TACTICAL GREENS

Napoleon's pom-pom tail was wagging excitedly at the distant sight of flying golf balls over the hedgerows. What were these white, airborne dumplings ready to be snapped in his jaws? In the horseshoe driveway, they approached a row of gleaming Cadillacs, Buicks and Packards, their polished chrome winking like conspirators in the lamplight. Opal's favourite was the custom Duesenberg. It was resplendent in a shade of Pacific turquoise and flowed with a grace of a swan gliding across a pond. Its polished mahogany dashboard was adorned with platinum-rimmed dials and a clock. On its right-hand door was the word 'Margeaux' in silver italics. *Must belong to poor Jane's widower, Cavin Margeaux.*

The people who spilled from these mechanical chariots were dressed to the nines, or at least, to the plus fours. Men swanned about in their golfing attire, knickerbockers billowing, their argyle socks tucked into mirror-shined brogues. The ladies sported outfits that were equally spiffing. One lady, Opal noted admiringly, probably an actress, sported a large golf-club brooch stabbed into her cloche.

Opal passed under a colourfully painted arch of letters

which read Colonel Thwack's Tactical Greens. From every direction came the sound of wooden clubs *thwacking* golf balls. The fluttering laughter of the ladies followed by a terse silence from their male companions as yet another ball was lost in the wild grasses.

The course was utterly whimsical. It stretched out like a landscape that might result if Salvador Dalí had taken up horticulture. There was a giant papier mâché Sphinx glaring at players negotiating the labyrinth of hedges at its feet. A little further down, a replica of the Eiffel Tower loomed, its spindly legs forming a gauntlet for shots between them.

Napoleon's eyes almost popped out with so much stimulation! Whichever ball should he focus on? He became paralysed by the excitement and only his eyeballs and ears twitched. It was almost as riveting as Wimbledon! Though he seemed not to be able to fathom why the humans insisted on whacking the balls instead of chasing them properly and giving them a good shake.

There was a beach-hut-looking thing where you lined up to hire your clubs. As the crowd parted, Opal spotted a few members of her Platinum Signet Productions gang. Burton, Domingo, George, Bonfire and Carey stood about chuffing smoke and comparing clubs. Opal was taken aback to see Carey. Would he not be mourning his wife? It was an event to remember her, but Opal assumed he'd be too cut up to attend so soon after his bereavement.

Though he did seem forlorn. He was not clad in his usual loud and lurid jewellery. His face had lost its cocky handsomeness, and the corners of his mouth drooped. He may also just have been keeping 'down' appearances as this was a very public event. He was a failed actor, if Opal remembered correctly, so it would not have been hard for him to *act* upset.

Opal thought it pertinent to approach Carey before anyone else. She tentatively floated over and said, 'Mr Margeaux, I do hope you'll forgive my forwardness. I am the Honourable Opal Laplume. I simply could not let the evening pass without offering my deepest condolences. Your late wife Jane was very kind to me. But I must say what a jolly fine way of celebrating her life: organising this little golfing excursion in honour of her, at a place she loved.'

'Thank you, Miss Laplume.' His eyes came to life when he saw her and he removed his trilby and held it to his chest. 'She was always smiling and laughing here. It's the only place I really saw her happy, to be honest.'

'Well, I hope visiting here will bring some comfort to you,' said Opal. Then, hoping to offer a brighter subject of conversation, she picked up Napoleon. 'This is little Napoleon, I hope he will be more of a retriever of the ball than a rascal with the ball.'

'Nice to meet you, little man,' Carey said, taking his pom-pom paw. 'Napoleon will be excellent at miniature golf, he's always had a thing for small territories.'

'Indeed, let's hope he doesn't go into exile if he loses!' said Opal, pleasantly surprised that Carey was able to joke.

But his face fell when he dropped Napoleon's paw, seeming to remember his predicament. 'I really need to take my mind off the looming funeral,' he said sadly.

'Oh,' said Opal, placing Napoleon back on the ground and resuming a comforting tone of voice. 'It'll be alright, sir. When is it taking place?'

'In a few days. A private, family affair. That's why I organised this. Something less maudlin, where everyone who knew her could come and celebrate her life. She was cracking at this game.'

'She handled that putter like Dillinger handled a Tommy gun!' interrupted Domingo. 'I'm going to miss playing our Jane. We played a least once a month for the past three years.'

'Oh, I'd not realised what good chums you'd been with

Jane,' said Opal, gently tugging Napoleon away from a stray ball.

'Domingo and Jane were the best of chums. In a sort of brother and sister way,' Carey said.

'We were,' Domingo said and threw his cigarette stub on the grass limply.

'Opal Laplume!' beamed Burton, nuzzling in and removing his flat cap. 'Shall we play together?'

'No, I insist on playing you, Burton. Man to man,' Domingo said, and lifted his golf club between the two of them as a barrier.

Burton looked a little perplexed at why Domingo so badly wanted to play him. 'Oh, alright then, if you really want to be beaten! I guess I'll play you next round, Opal?'

'That's a good idea because I wanted to play Opal,' Carey said and looked at her. 'I need a little talk with you, and this could be a good time.'

'Oh, yes, yes, if you need to speak,' Opal said, but a little nervously. *What could Carey want to say to her?*

'Excuse me,' said George DeLuca, brushing Carey aside with his golf club. 'Bonfire and I are going to have a go as we are novices.'

Carey waited until they had passed then, placing his club under his arm in a militaristic manner, he ushered Opal forward. 'I've got our clubs and balls... After you.'

Opal hugged her shoulders and followed on, Napoleon in tow. She was secretly hoping she would have clapped eyes on Augusto and partnered with him for a round of golf, but she could not see him amongst the clumps of punters.

'The obstacles seem expressly designed to baffle, bewilder and enrage,' chortled Carey as they watched George DeLuca ahead of them on the first tee. It was a miniature windmill, its blades whirring with a manic glee as they prepared to swat away DeLuca's golf ball like tiny, spinning cricket bats. George squished his head into his neck and hit the ball with the determination of a man about to go over the top at the Battle of the Somme. He watched in disbelief as the ball was flicked aside, landing in the adjacent pond with a spiteful plop.

Opal clasped her hands over her mouth to chortle. Napoleon took advantage of the fact she'd dropped the lead and darted into the pond after the ball. Moments later he emerged, a sodden lamb, his proud canines clamping the golf ball. The end of his tail was no longer a pom-pom but a dripping, black flag.

'I suppose the dog has to be useful for something!' George said, hands on his hips. 'You wouldn't catch me wading into that quagmire!'

'Napoleon can be your retriever for the evening, George. I'm sure you're going to need him,' Opal called.

'Thank you, Miss Laplume,' George said with his cigar between his teeth as he gave it another bash.

'It's a shame Betty isn't here to witness her darling George's skills,' Carey said quietly to Opal.

'Oh yes. I assume Betty, Adrian, and Virginia for that matter, are far too busy prepping the costumes?' Opal said.

'They're manic, yes. Betty I should expect would be devouring the script as fast as she can.'

'Funny you should say that,' said Opal, before she could stop herself. 'She'd been practising Jane's songs before Jane had even died. I can't fathom why, can you?'

FIFTEEN

LOVE OVER LUCRE

Carey coughed on his cigar and removed it from his mouth. He frowned down at Opal, then looked up at the sky. 'Dammit. That Betty Caruso was totally bent on poaching Jane's roles. She was probably doing it to prove to Mr Zimberg she would yowl the songs out better.'

Opal blinked at him doubtfully and opened her mouth to speak, but he continued.

'Of course, I know Jane's death wasn't a heart attack,' he said, tossing his chin over his shoulder. 'Everyone knows the official heart attack tale isn't true. But I can't help thinking it was an inside job.'

'Mr Margeaux, I don't mean to be rude but someone could hear us. Are you sure we shouldn't speak in private?'

'This is as private as it gets. If we just keep our voices down and we're seen talking in public, it looks normal. The moment we get a table somewhere or you're seen coming up my driveway, that's when it looks suspicious.'

'I concur...' said Opal. 'Do go on...'

'I assume you've met the snake in a silk dress that is Peridot Ellington?'

'I have indeed,' said Opal, her eyes darting about the bushes in case of prying ears.

'I don't trust that woman. She's an executioner who uses blood for fountain-pen ink. If I'm going to accuse anyone in this town of Jane's murder it's her and her partner in crime, Emmett Zimberg. They work together very closely. I'm not quite sure who puppeteers who, but they are in this together.'

'I can envisage that,' Opal said, under her breath. 'From the brief moment I met her, Peridot Ellington did not seem a model of ethical integrity. She seems to have an inflated sense of power too.'

'But she *is* powerful. Can I ask what she spoke about?'

Opal scratched her forehead. Should she be opening up to Carey? Could she trust him? Not that she had any useful information; she hadn't been able to hear what Domingo had whispered into Peridot's ear about Jane and Emmett Zimberg.

'There was a spot of back and forth about suitable stories for articles. I do remember Peridot telling Domingo that you, Mr Margeaux, had ditched your last lover because she was too pauperish to marry. She was mildly threatening to publish this information...'

'That abominable narrative has to stop. I was NOT with Jane for the York Tobacco money. I loved her with all my heart!' Carey said this loud enough for all those in the vicinity to hear and gripped his golf club in two hands as if it was a truncheon. He then lowered his voice again. 'I've got a thing or two to say about Peridot. I know she fabricated a lot of her *LA Times* column. If that got out, she would lose her book deal.'

'What did she fabricate?' Opal lifted her eyebrow and looked at him sideways.

'She claimed she was an orphan with a tragic past in order to gain readers' sympathy. It's far from the truth. But all I care about is Jane. The reason I believe Peridot and Emmett Zimberg wanted Jane dead was to stop her moving over to Cox

& Lumière Pictures. She wanted more serious roles, something that would show off the facets of her dramatic talent. Mr Zimberg would rather she was dead than let Cox & Lumière have her. And Peridot does Mr Zimberg's dirty work.'

'You think they orchestrated Jane's death by setting up or engaging the stuntman? If this was the case, then why has Mr Zimberg hired a detective and asked him to find out more about Augusto?'

'To make it *look like* they're investigating.' Carey looked Opal dead in the eyes and held her gaze.

'But why? When the public already think she died from a heart attack?'

'They may need to make it *look like* they're investigating internally because so many people on set saw her get shot. It's all a game of double bluff.'

'I'm terribly sorry, Carey, I'm giving myself a headache trying to decide what is theatre and what isn't. I just want to get my dear friend Augusto out of the firing line!'

'Well, Miss Laplume, all we can do is keep our wits about us. And pray to God Jane gets the true justice she deserves.'

The conversation fell dead after that and Opal tried to focus on the golf and not the awkward silence between them. Due to her excellent eyesight she was able to do very well on the first two obstacles. Carey was sloppy and distracted, nervously rolling his sleeves up and down before every hit. The third hole was a hill that had been decorated to resemble a large loaf of bread, and this caused no end of trouble. Opal squinted, furrowed her brow and swung, only to watch her ball bounce unpredictably off the surface, skittering away. Napoleon leapt out of a bush and chomped down on the ball. He sat proudly holding it up for Opal in his teeth, his soggy tail whipping the grass.

By the seventh hole, Opal had given up any hope of thrashing the course and had resigned herself to a sort of dazed amusement. She was more interested in looking out for Augusto to appear. While waiting for Carey to conquer the Buckingham Palace hole, she bent down to give Napoleon a little dry off with her neck scarf. All the bounding around still hadn't dried him off fully from his dip in the pond and he looked jolly well like a ragamuffin.

From her low vantage point, she could see underneath a little bridge. It framed a perfect view of Burton and Domingo. Their body language had the sort of simmering hostility more appropriate for a duel at dawn, not the ludicrous setting of a miniature golf course. *What the deuce was going on?*

SIXTEEN

A MOUTHFUL OF MISCHIEF

Opal squinted at them and kept completely still so she wouldn't be noticed. Domingo's feet were planted wide apart, and his hands were hung over the club behind his neck as if he was in the stocks. He was watching Burton with a menacing look, chin low.

Burton was trying to putt a ball into the mouth of a Bakelite frog. Burton was red-faced and his big ears seemed to jut back. He glared at the infuriating amphibian as if it had personally insulted his lineage. He thwacked the ball, it shot forth, circumnavigated the mouth of the frog and then careened off course.

'It was only ten feet, Burton, not the English Channel,' sniggered Domingo.

'Damn frog!' Burton shouted, really wound up.

For his next effort he gripped the putter with white knuckles, jaw shut so firmly it seemed it might crack. He gave a swift tap, and this time it went into the frog's mouth with a 'conk' sound. He froze, not quite believing what had happened, then with a satisfied nod, he adjusted his collar. Domingo nodded at the hole to signal that Burton should collect his ball.

But when Burton looked down inside the mouth of the frog, his ears shot bright red. He dropped his putter with a clatter and clasped his mouth with both hands. His eyes expanded to the size of golf balls. He couldn't have looked more shocked if there had been a severed head inside. With a fast motion he snatched inside the hole and pulled out a rectangular piece of paper. Was it a photograph? Or was there something written on it? Opal strained her neck forward but she couldn't make it out.

Domingo casually stepped forward and plucked the thing out of Burton's hand. Domingo didn't look at the paper, he simply put it into his inside breast pocket. That signalled to Opal that Domingo already knew what was on the paper and had planted it there for Burton to see.

Burton stood up and faced Domingo, eye to eye like a couple of stags. Domingo smiled menacingly and said something that Opal was too far away to hear. The freckle above Domingo's eyebrow rose up in a challenging manner when he stopped speaking.

Burton, being only a teenage boy, shrunk back. He lifted both of his arms with his palms facing upwards as if surrendering and said something back. Again, Opal was too far away to hear. He then looked around him to see who was watching. Opal ducked lower within the grass. Burton then picked up his putter and lifted it shoulder height as if to swing at Domingo. Domingo patted his breast pocket in a mocking manner. Obviously aware that what he had in his pocket was upsetting Burton.

Burton dropped the golf club, took three steps backwards, turned, and then bolted, dodging the obstacles on the way out of the park. Domingo, with the same indifferent smirk on his face, casually made his way out of the park too, club under his arm.

I say, what in the blazes was the meaning of that performance? thought Opal. *And what was so unsettling for Burton on that piece of paper?* She must tactfully grill them both about it.

It was all she could think about as she finished the course. That, and where the devil Augusto could be.

'Good show, everyone!' Opal said once she and Carey had caught up with the others in the cocktail area. 'Who won out of your lot?'

'I did, of course,' said Bonfire, and her freckles danced about her face as she laughed at George.

'The dame beat me fair and square. But I'm a film director, not a wrangler of rebellious golf balls,' George said and rearranged his tie.

'The ball did *not* want to listen to you,' Bonfire said.

'Perhaps you needed your megaphone, George,' Carey said in effort to join in.

George sniffed in Carey's direction in a dismissive reply, then turned his back and struck up a conversation with a nearby actress. Opal got the feeling George was not fond of Carey. *A little insensitive to shirk someone who has just lost his wife*, Opal mused.

'I've just spotted my beau. I'm going to go back to the start to play with him,' said Bonfire, fiddling with her beret.

'Allow me,' said Opal, and rearranged Bonfire's beret in a manner that was flattering with Bonfire's ringlets. 'Is it the gentleman from the Penciltown Sketch Club?'

'Yes, here he is... Bertram! Bertram, come and meet Opal Laplume.'

'Good evening, sir.' Opal extended a hand. 'I believe you know my dear friend, Mr Augusto Sevilla. I've been looking for him.'

'A slippery fish, that one. I know he's recently been "lying low" and spending time on Santa Monica Beach, in between looking for a new job. Platinum Signet Productions turfed him out and he wouldn't tell me why. He seems extremely upset about something.'

Opal bit her lip... she hoped Augusto was alright. Perhaps

Bonfire would cover for her if she took a longer lunch. She could even do a spot of stitching on the beach while she kept an eye out for him? That is, if he hadn't already fled California, or worse... been arrested by the police.

SEVENTEEN

SANTA MONICA BEACH

Opal and Napoleon had taken the one o'clock Red Car on the Pacific Electric railway line to Santa Monica Beach. The car itself, a splendid crimson conveyance with its polished wooden interiors and gleaming brass fittings, had carried them along smoothly with the occasional rhythmic bump. Napoleon's tongue hung out and lapped at the briny tang of sea air as they approached the pier.

As soon as they descended and Opal unclipped Napoleon's leash, he galloped across the boardwalk and onto the yellow plains, kicking up sand and barrel-rolling in it. He hadn't been on a beach since their last visit to Southwold in Suffolk and had now found a fragrant and long-expired fish on the sand. Opal had not felt obliged to play fetch with it, but he was obviously in search of something else smelly that she may like.

'Napoleon! Wait, boy! Oh, blithering fig!' Opal shouted as she tried to keep her hat on her head with one hand and remove her Mary Janes with the other. She hooked her shoes on a finger along with her sewing bag and trudged after her sandy sidekick.

If I'd known it would be so breezy, I would have gone for a bonnet, thought Opal. *Hailing from Suffolk, you'd have thought*

I'd have known what the seaside was like. A parasol wouldn't have gone a miss either, though the sun is pleasant on my bare arms. Now, we must find Augusto. Is he out at sea?

She looked out into the sparkling expanse of the ocean. There were a dozen or so bathers, but too far for her to make out, and the sunshine bouncing off the surface was distorting their faces. She approached an apricot-coloured parasol, resting on its side. It was enormous, the size of a small elephant. Opal careened around it to see if it could be concealing Augusto. It was not. Opal gasped and veered away as she realised it was Norma Shearer the beautiful brunette actress rubbing a lotion into her arms and saying, 'Freckles are as outdated as the Charleston,' to her valet, standing at attention with a tray of chilled daiquiris.

Opal may have to rely on her four-legged fellow to sniff Augusto out. 'Napoleon, darling, we're looking for Augusto. Find Augusto for me, that's a good boy!'

Napoleon's ears became animated as he heard his favourite marshal's name. He squirmed on his hind legs, then sprung forth with new vigour. His Paris partner in crime! They approached a myriad of sunbathers next to some rockery that had been used to anchor parasols and picnic hampers. The girls were all dreadfully pretty. Perhaps actresses or aspiring ones. Opal tilted her head to the left and admired the Californian beach-hat fashions. Pastel cartwheel creations were bedecked with oversized ribbon, others with delicate clusters of artificial flowers, and there were a few daring straw numbers with brims so vast they seemed to threaten a small eclipse. Silk scarves fluttered from under chins, catching the breeze with the carefree abandon of the women themselves.

Opal had the twitching temptation to make some fashion drawings of the bronzing posers. Her feet were getting rather hot anyway on this sand. She prepared a towel and perched her bottom on some rocks ten or so yards from the sunning belles.

She dragged her red lipstick crayon across the textured page of her sketchbook creating the horizon, then concentrated on the arching silhouettes of the hats. She got a little sentimental when she imagined how much Augusto would enjoy drawing this scene of Californian life.

Yap, Yap, Yappp! Yapapap.

'Will you cease that blasted yapping, Napoleon; the ladies are trying to relax,' Opal hissed.

But when she looked over at what he was yapping at... it was a tall Cossack hat with a cascade of silk fruit hanging from one side. This style was signature to only *one* woman, Opal knew...

Oh, holy fig on a hobby horse! Opal thought. *It's Peridot Ellington, the ruddy newshound! If Carey is right and she really was in on it with Emmett Zimberg to snuff out Jane, then would fraternising with her be pertinent? I'm glad I have the snippet of information about her fabricated orphan tales up my sleeve.*

Peridot Ellington was flapping her wrist to greet the bathers. They were obviously all vying for her attention, sitting up and offering her drinks from the cocktail flasks they'd premixed at home. When she noticed Napoleon, her round sunglasses followed him as he trotted over to Opal.

Opal quickly looked over at the horizon with her hand covering her face, pretending to gaze at the fishing vessels. But this was a pointless attempt at hiding. Napoleon was the only bicorn-sporting miniature black poodle in town and he was owned by Opal Laplume.

'I'd know an Opal Laplume hat when I saw one!' Peridot called over, waving royally.

'By Jove! Peridot Ellington, I could do a backflip of joy. It's made my day, seeing you!' Opal said, but wondered if she sounded perhaps too contrived. Acting was not her strong suit.

'My dear, we do have so much to catch up on.' Peridot

lowered her sunglasses and her expression changed to forlorn. 'The world doesn't seem the same without Jane!'

'Yes, awfully tragic.' Opal looked sadly down at her knees but tried to keep the conversation light. 'The sunshine is medicinal in keeping ones hopes up though.'

'I guess you've been busy resizing the costumes for *Betty Caruso*.' Peridot said Betty's name in the same tone one might describe ghastly soup.

'Yes, I've brought some stitching to do on the beach. There's no better lamp for sewing than the glorious orb above.'

'May I perch?' Peridot enquired, pointing a talon at the edge of Opal's towel.

'By all means. Delighted to oblige!' said Opal over-enthusiastically.

'Now I may not have come over in my best light when we last met at the premiere. I was very much on a hunt for article material, and it can come across as a little... pushy,' Peridot said in a softer voice than usual, then pulled her sunglasses down to the bridge of her nose to look Opal dead in the eye.

Opal gulped and leaned back on her hands to move away from the intensity of Peridot's face. 'I daresay. I thought you were perfectly charming.'

'Well,' – Peridot slid her sunglasses back up her nose – 'you don't need to go that far. But you English are always very polite. I am enamoured by how you speak.'

'Jane, the poor thing, wanted me to give her lessons in speaking,' Opal remembered. 'That strange mid-Atlantic accent she was trying to conquer.'

'I was very fond of Jane. I know you overheard me gossiping with Domingo about Carey only marrying Jane for her money, but I was never going to print that. I just needed leverage to ease information out of her.'

'What about? I heard Domingo mention the reds. Are Jane and Mr Zimberg communists?'

'*Jane and Mr Zimberg… red?*' Peridot's face contorted into a freaky circus expression. 'Don't make me laugh. That would make a *story* and a half. No. The very opposite of communists, in fact. Domingo told me they were setting up a secret meeting about how to stomp it out in Hollywood.'

'It's becoming a problem then?' asked Opal.

'Wealthy families like Jane's and Mr Zimberg's are fearing redistribution policies will strip them of their wealth and influence. The ideology is spreading slowly but surely.'

'Was Carey Margeaux involved in these anti-communist meetings?' asked Opal.

'I would think so. Poor lad. I thought they were a very fine match. He must be going out of his mind wondering who was behind the murder.'

'Some people seem to think Carey himself is behind the murder, taking a hands-on approach to the laws of inheritance,' Opal said, before she could get a grip on her mouth.

'Oh, so it *was* a murder then?' Peridot said in a low voice and pulled her sunglasses down once more to reveal her ink-drop pupils.

EIGHTEEN

SUNGLASSES, SHADE AND SLANDER

Oh, blithering fig! Opal looked out to sea to quickly think of what to say. *How could I have been so stupid! Of course, the official story is that Jane had a heart attack. And that's the story Peridot would have been told to run with.*

'Oh, yes, yes it was a heart attack, I just mean I feel sorry for him that there are some wretched rumours about it being a murder due to Carey's greed and inheritance,' Opal stammered.

The laughter that emerged from Peridot sounded like a pigeon on heat. 'I'm only double-bluffing you, dear.' Her laughter then stopped. 'I know she was shot. The stuntman, armourer and security guard are getting it in the neck at the moment.'

Opal sighed with relief to know she hadn't trifled with the confidentiality agreement but was also anxious to hear Peridot knew that a *security guard* was potentially to be punished.

'How do you know about all this? And, in particular, the security guard getting blamed?'

'I'm contractually sworn to report it as a heart attack, but Mr Zimberg and I are good friends, and he's told me the truth. I am doing some digging of my own for him. I'm not sure that his private detective, Kensington, knows this town well enough to truly get to the bottom of it. He's been trying to hurry it along by focusing on those three men. The stuntman, the armourer and the security guard.'

Peridot lifted her chin to bathe her face in the sun.

'I see. Well, I'm mostly concerned that the wrong person could get blamed for Jane's death. The poor security guard,' Opal pressed.

'But why are you so concerned about the security guard... Augusto, I believe his name is? Do you *know* him?' Peridot sat up in a manner that made Opal shrink down.

'No, no. I don't know him. I just think it sounds sad that a man who wasn't paying attention for a split second and had a bullet taken from his gun is now somehow a suspect,' Opal said. She wasn't going to give Peridot the morsel of information that she was soft on Augusto. God knows how she'd try to use it.

'The best thing we can do to help in this situation is to keep an eye on Betty Caruso. My money is on her. She's been after Jane's parts for years. Betty is the only other blonde bombshell at Platinum Signet Productions. Betty was second rate but had a much better singing voice than Jane ever did... so it stung. Her director lover, George DeLuca, benefits too from Jane being out of the picture because he *literally* wanted her out of the "*picture*". He adores Betty but he's too much of a numbskull to pull off an operation like this. He's too loyal to Emmett Zimberg and would *never* do this to Platinum Signet Productions.'

'But wouldn't Mr Zimberg let Betty off the hook even if she did orchestrate Jane's murder? Doesn't he *need* her now? He's apparently doe-eyed over her,' Opal said.

'He might be inclined to turn a blind eye, but the Los Angeles Police Department would not. Emmett Zimberg has paid them off to accept the heart attack story, but if there was enough evidence and outrage over Betty, then we could take her down. That's why I want you to keep an eye on her for me.'

Opal blinked rapidly, then stared at her toes scrunching the sand. She weighed up telling Peridot everything she thought was suspicious about Betty Caruso. She could say that Betty may have doused Jane's mantilla shawl with whisky to make her smell like she'd been boozing on the morning of a shoot. She could also tell Peridot that she'd seen Betty's diary entries about learning Jane's songs a week before the shooting. But she still didn't trust Peridot and she might also need the information as currency to exchange later.

'I can keep an eye, but I can't promise I'll be able to find anything useful, Peridot,' Opal said and shrugged.

Yap, Yap, Woooof. Napoleon was pawing at something in between the rocks.

'Napoleon. Napoleon. Come away! The ladies are trying to bask in seaside tranquillity. Stop being such a blighter!'

The dog's nose seemed to lock on to a scent connected with an unknown object in the rocks and followed it, snout to the ground, over a selection of footprints that lead up and over a sand dune. The dog disappeared over it. Little black lollipop tail last.

'Are these your drawings of the girls' hats?' Peridot leaned over to peek.

'Yes... I want to design more seasonal styles. Our shop in London doesn't usually stock beach styles as we are not close to the seaside. But I think we should start to.'

'Don't the gentry go to... what's it called? Brighton?'

'Yes. Or I prefer Whitstable, for the oysters. Or Southwold as a child in Suffolk.'

Peridot started to natter on about her upbringing as an orphan near a poor seaside town, Port Hueneme, Ventura County. And it all sounded very convincing. Opal did wonder how Carey knew it was lies.

Napoleon's head appeared again above the sand dune. His tongue was hanging out in an especially happy manner. Like he had just lapped up a whole caramel ice cream. His little front feet rose proudly like he was competing in dressage. From behind him came another head.

The dark hair, slicked back by the ocean's hand, clung to his head, giving him the look of a chap who'd emerged from some aquatic adventure. There was a dimple in his chin so deep you could lose a blackcurrant in it. His shoulders were something out of a Victorian strongman poster. He wore a striped speed shirt, tucked into high-waisted shorts. Opal blushed as his legs came up over the sand dune. Bronzed and muscular, with a light covering of dark hair. He stood at the top with one hand on his hip. His dark eyes surveyed the scene with an air of confidence, as if the entire beach were his personal fiefdom. The actresses' tittle-tattle faded off and they fanned themselves with slack jaws as they caught sight of him.

'Opal!' Augusto called down to her and descended the dune with wide strides.

'Augusto!' Opal said and scrambled up to standing.

'I thought you said you *didn't* know him?' asked Peridot, the sun glinting off her sunglasses.

Botheration. I've put my foot in it, Opal thought. *Well, now Gossip Queen Peridot knows Augusto and I are friends. I guess it was only going to be chatted about sooner or later.*

'Oh, only vaguely,' Opal replied.

'Doesn't look vague to me, the way he's striding over to you!' Peridot smirked.

'Hello, mam,' said Augusto to Peridot when he noticed her. 'We briefly met at the Platinum Signet Productions offices, didn't we?'

'We did and I was charmed. I had no idea you knew the Honourable Opal Laplume.'

'I do, very well. We met in Paris.'

'Opal said she knew you only briefly!' Peridot said, pulling her sunglasses down, thoroughly enjoying herself.

'Yes, yes, when I meant briefly, I meant that we've only known each other since the latter end of last year,' Opal said. 'Pleasant dip, Augusto?'

'Yes, exquisite temperature. How funny that you're in the same spot as I was earlier. I'd been drawing here. Look... Napoleon has dragged out my sketchbook and followed the footprints to me in the sea...'

'Clever boy. Timing could have been better, but clever sausage. I was drawing the ladies here too. And I thought immediately that it's the kind of scene you'd like to study.'

'They are very attractive girls, aren't they! Why don't I introduce you both?' Peridot said.

'That's ever so kind, Peridot, but I've only come here for a short lunch break and need to get this stitching done. I should grab a bite to eat and then find a quieter spot.'

'Why don't we get some salt water taffy, Opal?' Augusto suggested.

'What in the Dickens is salt water taffy?' Opal said.

'It's a sweet chewy treat, an American delicacy.'

'Well, when in Rome! And, Napoleon, you may have a hot dog.'

Napoleon's pom-pom tail windmilled so fast you'd think he might take off.

'Opal... remember what we spoke about before. You wouldn't want me to give away the magazine feature to some other milliner, now would you?' Peridot said, standing up to take her leave. 'I can see a double-page spread!'

NINETEEN

BOARDWALK MEETS RUNWAY

Opal, Napoleon and Augusto skuttled out of earshot of the Hollywood gabble-guts and were soon approaching the Santa Monica Pier. They ascended the seaweed steps onto the boardwalk. A dazzling Ferris wheel turned languidly against the blue sky; it creaked and groaned amongst the lapping sounds of the waves against the pier's legs and the laughter of children. The tantalising scent of sausages wafted across from hot-dog stands, whilst vendors peddled their gooey salt water taffy with merriment.

'The refreshment vendors' uniforms are terribly sweet. Look at the salt water taffy girl's boater. The lilac-and-pink striped ribbons to match her sunsuit!' said Opal. 'Let's sketch them.'

'Good idea. Why don't we perch on the edge of the boardwalk.'

'Boardwalk meets fashion runway!' Opal said, and looped the pup's lead around a bollard. 'Yes, Napoleon, I will get you a sausage if you behave.'

'Wow! So, Peridot Ellington is going to do a feature on you in a magazine!' Augusto said.

'At what price though? I don't like being at her beck and call. She's a manipulative woman. But don't get me wrong, I am tempted. She's like Eve from the Bible, but instead of an apple it's a colour magazine. Tell me, what's been going on with you? I was looking all over the allotment for you. Then at Colonel Thwack's, to no avail.'

'I'm sorry. They told me they were going to let me go and that I was not to leave Hollywood or they would find me. They suggested I go look for a job elsewhere. So, I've been trying the bars but with no luck. I was going to head back to the studio to ask after you, but I've got a horrible feeling I'm being watched by Emmett Zimberg's men. That Detective Kensington seems to want to frame me somehow.'

'I can't let this happen, Augusto. Let's go through the timings and mechanics of the incident.' Opal whipped out her sketchbook and opened it to the page where she'd drawn the diagram of the studio and dotted where Bonfire and Betty were when the shot went off. 'So... the significant events were... you noticed all six of your bullets were intact in your gun at breakfast at the Luncheonette around seven a.m. You were stationed by stage door one. Your gun was on the table... you heard the water drinking barrel get knocked over at around eight p.m. Did you see anyone around?'

'The barrel was concealed from my sight by a set wall. Milling about beyond it was a gaggle of extras in toy soldier costumes, but they were quite far away. All of the extras next door, all fifty-two of them, were dressed the same, weren't they. So, it makes it impossible to tell who was who.'

'Alright, so you left your station to pick the barrel up. When you returned, the gun looked untouched. Did they get any fingerprints back from your gun?'

'No, they didn't. Not sure they're interested in finding anyone else. They seem to be wanting an angle to pin me down.'

'I wonder why they're not interested in the stuntman or the armourer.'

'Too many people know them and know it's not in their character. I'm from out of town. A stranger. A foreigner. Far easier to rub me out.'

'I'm going to have to ask as many extras as possible tomorrow if they saw who pushed the water barrel over. I need to find someone who saw the barrel fall. And who turned the lights out. So far, I've not spoken to anyone who was actually on set. Bonfire and Betty were backstage. Peridot, Carey and Burton weren't there. Domingo was editing. Mr Zimberg, George and Virginia were on set and closest to what happened. I can't speak to Mr Zimberg, but I can at least try to squeeze something out of the other two.'

'You can, but be careful not to step on Detective Kensington's toes. He's not going to like it if you go snooping around.'

'I know that... But remember Detective Inspector Prosper Delacroix in Paris? His incompetence only lit a fire under me.'

'A fire? A flaming rocket!' Augusto laughed.

Opal took a deep breath of the sea air and mustered the courage to say, 'I'm staying at Palatial Pines if you need to find me. It's a blasted nuisance not being able to contact each other.'

'Wonderful, *señorita*.' Augusto's eyes sparkled brighter than the sea. 'I shall call on you once I've found a job in this town.'

The corners of Opal's lips pricked upwards, but her eyes didn't smile. It seemed she could never be truly certain when she would see this man again. Like chasing the retreating surf.

TWENTY

TOY SOLDIERS

Adrian had scheduled Opal to arrive at the costume department unspeakably early as they were behind. Five thirty in the morning! *The only things that are supposed to stir at this hour are bakers and lunatics*, Opal thought as she held out her arms and accepted a stack of warm, pressed costumes. The laundress closed the door behind her with a steamy waft of industrial soap and lavender.

'Let's get these to Betty's dressing room,' Virginia ordered, and marched in front with her own arms full of starched garments. 'I feel sorry for the laundresses in there. They must re-press all fifty-two of those toy soldier costumes for the extras from the scene. They were put away ever so scruffily and, being made of cotton, they look like the back of nothing.'

Along the corridor were long costume rails that had been lined up for the laundresses. The extras' 'toy soldier' costumes consisted of a midnight-blue coat, festooned with gold braid and brass buttons, white trousers and boots, a high-crested shako helmet, and clownishly painted mask. It was for a scene that had fifty extras step out of giant toy boxes onto a shop shelf and do a midnight dance routine.

'I say. That is a lot of pressing,' Opal agreed. 'But I guess having been locked in for so long after Jane died, the poor extras were sitting on the floor or even lying down, so it couldn't be helped.'

'Unprofessional, if you ask me.' Virginia sniffed. 'They could have taken turns sitting on the chairs that are back there. Because of the panic, there was nobody keeping them in check. It's not the first film set that's gone on late with no food. If you can't hack it, then don't be a background artist.'

'I think they were frightened and worn out,' Opal said, feeling sorry for the dears.

'Do you know, I saw one of them push the drinking-water barrel over.'

Opal stopped on the linoleum and her Mary Janes squeaked. She blinked several times and said, 'What?'

'An extra toppled the barrel to the floor and water started spurting out. The cheek of it! I was too far away to reprimand them. But the fool deliberately crashed it down and hid behind one of the screens. That security guard, Augusto, came to pick the barrel up, so I assumed he would sort it out.'

Opal marched a few paces ahead so that she could look Virginia dead in the eyes. 'Virginia, this is very important information. Did you notice anything else? Which direction did the toy soldier go afterwards?'

Virginia shrugged so that the costumes covered part of her face. 'They avoided Augusto by hiding behind the screen, but then they went to the back-right corner of the studio. It was dimly lit back there so I lost sight of them. But I assumed Augusto would catch them and tell them off. Why is it important?'

Opal knew the back-right corner of the studio was where Augusto's gun was lying on the desk, unattended.

'It is the moment Augusto left his gun out on the desk. The moment the murderer stole the live bullet from it. They must have gone and put it inside the stunt gun. What time did the barrel get knocked over?'

Virginia stopped and looked up at the ceiling. 'Gosh... did I really witness something important? I think it was about seven thirty p.m. I was helping untangle a loop of Jane's hair that had been caught in one of the beads on her dress when I saw the barrel topple.'

'Did anyone else see it happen?' Opal urged.

'Not that I know of. Mr Zimberg, George and the tech crew were all scowling at the scripts and arguing loudly at a part Mr Zimberg thought was trash and had complained about. Of course, all the other extras were behind stage door three wait-ing,' Virginia said, her pace slowed as she thought hard.

'Golly. Now, perhaps we can conject that one of the *extras* killed Jane? The one who pushed over the barrel,' Opal said, and quickened her pace down the corridor. She was finally on to something.

'It could have been anyone. All they had to do was go into the extras' area, take a costume and put it on,' Virginia said.

'Indeed.' Opal nodded in agreement. 'How many toy soldier costumes, exactly?'

Virginia pondered. 'I'm pretty sure it's fifty-two.'

Opal looked back at the rails lining the corridor and her eyelids fluttered in thought.

'We don't have time for you to count them all now, Opal.' Virginia sighed.

'I'll only be a jiffy. You walk ahead, I'll catch you up,' she insisted.

Opal, her eyes quivering as she scanned the hangers, mentally counted ten hangers on five rails and then one on the last rail.

'Virginia! Virginia, there's only fifty-one toy soldier costumes,' Opal panted as she caught up with her. 'One of them is missing! Can we possibly deduce that the person who took it is the *killer*?'

TWENTY-ONE

EAVESDROPPER EXTRAORDINAIRE

'Really? We'd better consult Adrian first, since we're manically busy at present, see if he'll let us do a search for rogue costumes. Then, if it really is missing, we can report it to Detective Kensington,' Virginia said.

'Do you think he really will get to the bottom of it, or has he been hired just to make it *look like* he's trying to solve the case?' Opal asked.

'I think Mr Zimberg wants to know the truth and has hired Kensington to do an honest job,' Virginia said, in the straightforward manner of a loyal employee who would never question their superiors.

'Who do you personally think was behind Jane's death?' Opal asked.

'I, like many others, think her weasel of a husband, Carey Margeaux, bumped her off. Wouldn't surprise me if it had been him dressed up in that toy soldier costume and mask. The person I saw was too far away for me to make out features, but judging by their height, I reckon it could have been him.'

'You have more of an idea of Carey and Jane's marital life

than anyone, seeing as you were practically living with them. Was it domestic bliss in the Margeaux household?'

'They were forever griping about money. He always came home with some catalogue or phone number of someone trying to sell him something. She'd beg him not to blow everything on a private plane. Or a chateau in France. He rarely listened to her, even though she was the one with the cash. Now he has it all and is free from her wrath.'

'Goodness. Sounds like he chased after money like a dog after sausages,' Opal commented.

'He did. Relentless, single-minded, and with a fair bit of drool involved,' Virginia added.

Opal continued to muse on it. *Now that I have reason to believe the person who took the bullet was disguised in toy soldier costume, alibis are much more important. I need to find out where Carey was that evening. Assuming the killer was the one to knock the barrel over.*

'Opal.' Virginia paused and looked back over her shoulder at her, her pointy chin pulled into her lace collar. 'Please keep this between the two of us. I don't want Carey coming after me next.'

'Of course,' Opal said, and blinked slowly as if her eyes were doing a kind of humble bow.

'Carey?' a shrill woman's voice came from the next doorway down. 'What are you talking about *Carey* for, ladies?'

Opal and Virginia jumped like a couple of pieces of toast popping out of a toaster, almost crumpling the garments in their arms. Virginia's eyes looked like she was being electrocuted, they showed so much terror. They both whipped around on their heels to see Betty, wrapped in a kimono, leaning against the door frame.

'Betty. Miss Caruso. I do apologise. I didn't know you'd be here so early. I assumed we were the only ones in the corridor.'

'I should be so lucky. Adrian's fitting me this morning. Voice coach mid-morning, then rehearsals, rehearsals, rehearsals.' Betty clicked her fingers as she repeated the words in mock exasperation. 'So, what's the word on the street? Or the studio allotment, I should say. What were you two dames talking about Carey Margeaux for?'

'It was nothing, Miss Caruso, we were discussing...' Opal said, looking into Virginia's blank face for inspiration and finding none. 'We... we... were discussing the match I played with him at miniature golf. He was as precise as a caffeinated squirrel! And Virginia was just saying she would not want him to come asking her for a game!' Opal stammered and cringed inwardly because it did not sound convincing.

'More like Virginia doesn't want Carey coming after her to *kill* her.' Betty brought her face close to Virginia and said conspiratorially, 'I know what you girls were discussing – and I must say... I *agree*.'

TWENTY-TWO

RED BUGLE BEADS

Betty placed her hand on the dressing-room door, red nails splayed like a poisonous spider, and pushed it open. The ladies followed her inside nervously.

'You... you agree with *what*, Miss Caruso?' Virginia asked.

'I *agree* that Carey did Jane in for a quick payday,' she said, hands on hips, kimono sleeves dangling off her elbows. She looked back and forth into Opal and Virginia's faces to get some reaction. 'I mean that's what *I* would have done if *I* were him.' Betty then sank onto her pouffe in front of the dresser.

Virginia drew a panicked breath through her nostrils. 'With all due respect, Miss Caruso, I was not talking about Mr Margeaux in that manner.'

'Oh, give me a break!' scoffed Betty as she grabbed a peach from the fruit bowl. 'He did me a favour... *and* the box office too, for that matter.' She then took a large, juicy bite.

Opal desperately wanted to quiz Betty further on why she thought the culprit might be Carey, but Virginia's face was white and she moved with stiff jerking motions as she hung up the laundered garments. They were almost two-dimensional in their pressed perfection. Opal knew Virginia was desperate to change the subject of conversation, but this was the perfect opportunity to find out Betty's alibi, or whatever she might concoct as an alibi. Betty was still one of the prime suspects in Opal's mind.

'The whole thing was so dreadfully upsetting. I wish I hadn't witnessed it all, Miss Caruso. Where were you when the shot was fired?'

'I was back here with Adrian. Bonfire helped me find some candles, which was heaven sent,' Betty said, inspecting the peach, deciding where to bite next.

That's precisely where Bonfire said Betty was, Opal thought. *So their stories did match.*

'Anyway... you were telling me about the golfing event the other night, Opal,' Virginia chimed in, and it was clear she wanted to steer the conversation away from the murder.

'Oh yes, yes. A terribly bamboozling course and everyone was taking it so darn seriously. Especially Domingo and Burton. They had a little brouhaha at the end of the night. I still haven't found out what that was about.'

'Burton Ford.' Betty yawned. 'I feel sorry for the sap. He was Jane's biggest fan and even wrote scripts with her in mind, but she spoke to him like he was an annoying mosquito buzzing around her. That reminds me, actually. On the evening Jane died I saw her speaking to him like trash. They were at the back of the sound stage between takes. She was sneezing and he handed her a hanky. But when he pulled it out of his jacket, something red fell on the floor and he scrambled to pick it up. She sort of looked at the floor, then back up at him and said, *"You won't last long around here"*, or something to that effect. He looked upset. She was so cruel. All he did was hand her a hanky and she didn't even say thank you.'

Opal froze while hooking a silk blouse onto the rail. She tilted her head and blinked fast in thought. 'What time was this, Betty?'

'Oh, I don't know, sevenish? I had to get back in here to prep at seven, so, yes, it would have been just before seven. And she was shot pretty soon after that. It would have been in the planning for months this murder, I reckon.'

'Excuse me, ladies, I'm getting quite emotional. I'm not sure I can discuss that damn night anymore,' Virginia said, and with a blubbering sound, she walked out of the room, shutting the door with slightly too much force.

Betty looked at Opal through the mirror and made a sad-clown face to mock Virginia. Opal looked at the carpet and scrunched up her toes nervously. A few moments later, Adrian entered and Bonfire's explosive hair bounced behind him. She was balancing a stack of hatboxes. Adrian began trying the newly resized millinery on Betty's head. Betty was savagely munching the peach and humming the movie's numbers like some obnoxious school bully.

Opal felt a stab of melancholy in her gut. *Jane Margeaux should be sitting there. The sooner I get to the bottom of what went on, the better for everyone.*

'A marvellous job you've done resizing the headbands and adding material where needed, Bonfire. You'd never know these weren't brand new,' Adrian complimented Bonfire, who was handing him the hats one by one.

Opal felt another pang of sadness in her stomach. If only she was being praised for the secret work she'd done on Bonfire's behalf. Bonfire bit her lip and looked over at Opal. Her ginger lashes quivered a *'thank you'*. Opal smiled back and thought, *I don't mind saving Bonfire's skin as she's a sweet girl. I will just have to find another way of showing off my skills to Adrian.*

'Opal, will you come with me to the accessories department a moment?' Adrian asked.

Opal followed him out.

'We need to find some red bugle beads...'

'Oh. Like the ones on the dress that Jane died in? We're not fixing that one for Betty, are we?'

'Good heavens no. That dress is cursed and destroyed and we'd never use it. One of the most beautiful dresses I've ever created, ironically. No, I'm not making another one of those. I would refuse, even if I was asked. I think Mr Zimberg wants that entire scene cut and changed to something else.'

'That sounds appropriate,' Opal commented. 'And Betty seems very happy to be taking the lead.'

'She does. But not as happy as George DeLuca. He is more passionate about this film now than ever. He is in love with Betty but he also believes it needed an exquisite singing voice as the songs are so strong. He thinks it'll be an Oscar-winning musical,' Adrian said, sauntering into the stockroom.

'Happy enough for it to be a motive for murder?' Opal said, hands against the door frame. She couldn't see his facial expression.

There was a pause. Then he pulled open a long drawer, writhing with bright beads. 'I saw nothing. I was in the dressing room with Betty when it happened. All I know is... George was happy about Jane exiting the movie. I know one of his secrets. He was considering a move to Cox & Lumière Pictures, and would have gone ahead with it if Betty hadn't stepped into this part. Platinum Signet Productions and Emmett Zimberg do not know this, of course.'

'How do you know that George was thinking of leaving?' Opal asked, intrigued.

'I visited the Cox & Lumière Pictures allotment to buy some costume stock from them. The costume storage is next door to a meeting room at the back of their offices. Unfortunately for them, there is a ventilation grate in the wall through which conversations can just about be heard. Muffled, but you can hear them. I heard George in there, negotiating a contract to leave Platinum Signet Productions midway through filming

Midnight at St Claire's. He was saying he *hated* working with Jane.' He spoke in a casual tone as if spreading light tittle-tattle.

Opal joined him at the drawer and touched a dish of blue sequins. 'Golly. Would he really orchestrate a murder just so he could direct the movie with Betty?'

'There's a lot of money and reputation at stake with how well a film does. Aren't those sequins pretty.' He changed the subject. 'Can you go through these drawers and find some red bugle beads.'

Opal obliged, opening and shutting the drawers filled with scintillating hues. *Slide, rattle, thunk, slide tinkle, thunk.* Opal decided to just break the silence and come out with it...

'Adrian, I need your help... It is likely that the person who stole the live bullet from the security guard's gun did so while it was left unattended on Augusto's desk. He let it out of his sight for a moment while he went to pick up the drinking-water barrel. Virginia witnessed someone in a toy soldier costume toppling the barrel on purpose. We don't know if it was an extra or if it was someone dressed as one. But I counted this morning and there is a toy soldier costume missing. The laundresses are pressing fifty-one and there used to be fifty-two. The mask and helmet are missing too. Do you know where it might be?'

'Aren't you the little fedora-wearing gumshoe,' he said, giving her a slightly amused side smirk. 'Well, you could look for it on stage three, where the extras were held that night. But the place has been entirely cleared, as far as I know. And if it was binned along with all the garbage, there's no hope of finding it. The bins have been taken away.'

Opal tilted her head to the left in thought as she sifted through brown packets of beads. *Whoever it was could well have blended in among the other costumed extras, but then would have faced the rather tricky problem of discarding the costume without being observed... otherwise, they risked being recognised. But where could they have ditched it?*

Opal spotted the red bugle bag stuck down the back of a drawer. Adrian complimented her eyesight, telling her she was like a hawk with a monocle, before sending her on her way. Opal headed straight for stage three. *There were many rooms down the technical corridor,* she recalled. *I wonder if the person got changed inside one of those rooms. I remember Domingo was hiding in one of them. Was he the killer? Or did he witness the killer getting changed?* She pondered how she could quiz him about it without giving away that she might be on to something...

It turned out that Adrian was right in assuming stage three had been cleared of everything. Empty dressing booths and stacks of wooden chairs were all that remained. The toy soldier costume, she had to conclude, was missing.

She mopped her brow with a glove. She was glad they gave the dogs ice cubes in the water bowls over in Studio Services. She was gasping in this heat. She pulled on her lace collar. It was the kind of heat that turns a collar into a noose. She went in search of the water barrel next door. The one that had been knocked over when Jane died.

The floorboards a few yards from the watering station were covered in a spaghetti of wires, some attached to lights above. Opal sipped the tepid water, her brow furrowed. Her gaze meandered along the chaotic tangle, following the cables until they reached the mains box on the back wall. It was a messy-looking contraption that would make an electrician break out in hives. She drained the last drop of water and her eyes widened and blinked in realisation. Opal was no electrical whiz... but... *Could the water spilled from the barrel have triggered the power cut? And was it by accident or was it a deliberate ploy by someone trying to keep everyone in the dark?*

TWENTY-THREE

BONFIRE'S NERVOUS EMBERS

Opal unlocked her Palatial Pines door to find her poodle sitting upright in the centre of the room. Napoleon's eyes sparkled like onyx and his tail bashed the floorboards with all the enthusiasm of a drummer boy in the Queen's Own Regiment. In his jaws was a torn piece of sketchbook paper.

'Blast it, Napoleon! Have you been at my sketchbook? No wait. I've had my sketchbook with me all day. What is *this* then?' She wrestled it out of his mouth and to her utter delight it was a note from Augusto. The hotelier must have slipped it under the door.

Dearest Opal,

I have been successful in finding myself a position as a barman at Café Montmartre on the Hollywood Boulevard, thanks to the little French I picked up in Paris. I will be here most nights but would be delighted if you could visit me this evening. I have a break at nine. We could do some fashion sketches.

Yours cordially,

Augusto

Opal was absolutely done in after a long slog on set, wilting like a geranium in the desert under those infernal studio lights, but the mere thought of seeing Mr Sevilla filled her with such a giddiness that her limbs tingled with renewed vim. She flung open her wardrobe to select the perfect hat for the occasion. Her hand alighted on the metallic embroidered cloche with ostrich spray. This was just the ticket.

She was just pulling it over her head at an angle when something made her freeze.

There was a terrifying scream!

Was it a woman's cry? Or was it some sort of animal outside, like one of those coyotes?

Napoleon had obviously heard it too. He was standing up on the mattress with his front paws on the brass bedstead, his soft triangles for ears perked up. His whole body jolted as the wail came again. He looked at Opal. Their eyes communicated the need to go and investigate, and they both hurtled towards the door.

Napoleon scrambled towards the noise. It was about six doors down from Opal's and Napoleon sat bashing his tail on the floorboards in front of it. He whined and then yapped as if to ask if the person was okay.

The door yanked open a smidge and a red ringlet popped out. *Bonfire!*

'It's happened again,' she sobbed, still hiding behind her door.

'Bonfire! What? What's happened again?' Opal asked frantically, pushing her way inside.

'I just got back from Platinum Signet Productions and I found mysterious money on my bedside table.' Bonfire sniffed and pointed at a bundle of banknotes splashed on the nightstand.

'Oh... How queer!' said Opal, walking over to examine them. Napoleon trotted over to the nightstand, stood up on his hind legs and sniffed. 'Well, one doesn't often get upset about receiving money. But entering your room to deposit the loot, and the significance of why it's there, is indeed frightening.'

'I don't know who put it there or why. Maybe someone is threatening me.' Bonfire shrugged.

'Take a deep breath. Let's keep our voices down. I'll close the door.' Opal did so as Bonfire wrung her hands.

'How much money exactly are we talking about?' Opal asked, riffling through the pile of green bills.

'Twelve dollars. Last time it was eight.'

'When was last time?'

'The night after the miniature golf. That was scary because I woke up and the money was on the nightstand. Like a revenant had come in while I was sleeping. My door and window were locked and it wasn't there the night before!'

Opal tapped her fingers on her mouth and blinked as she thought, then looked at Bonfire and said carefully, 'Don't take this the wrong way, dear, but you weren't on the sauce were you? And forgot you'd put it there?'

'I don't drink. You think I have time?' Bonfire snapped, but seemingly not at Opal, more at the situation.

'Then today it's just appeared on your nightstand while you've been at work?'

'Yes,' Bonfire said, and sank onto her mattress with a creak that described her mood very aptly.

'Right...' said Opal, perching next to her with a slightly more positive-sounding squeak. 'Well, let's think. Perhaps the maid left the money by accident. Took it out of her pinny when cleaning and forgot to put it back? She's the only one with a key to the room, isn't she?'

'I asked the maid when it happened the first time. She said

she'd no idea and then looked at me as if I'd had a gentleman caller and forgot about it. Mortifying.'

Opal tried to stop herself from blushing. 'I say. Well... we simply can't have folks coming to that conclusion! It's an unusual one. Because usually people are stolen from. Not given to. Unless you're being paid for something you don't know about.'

'That's what I was afraid of. Someone bribing me in some way,' Bonfire said and screwed her hands up into her hair.

'Have you got any secrets you're keeping for anyone?' Opal asked.

'No...' Bonfire said. Opal detected a flicker of thought in Bonfire's eyes as she said it, as if trying to flip through scandalous things people had told her. She then changed the subject. 'What's freaking me out is how anyone can get in here! I'm not sure I want to sleep here tonight.'

'I can't say I blame you. I'm off to Café Montmartre, but you can always stay in my room with me. We can top and tail. I've heard siblings sometimes do that. I never had a sibling, so it'll be a novelty for me!' Opal smiled reassuringly. 'If you don't mind doggy snores, that is.'

Napoleon stopped licking his pom-pom tail, eyed Opal and huffed.

'I'd be so grateful. I really am spooked,' said Bonfire.

'That's settled then. Here's my key. You need to rattle it to the left slightly as it's stiff.' Opal spun on her heel to leave but then stopped, looked back at her friend and said in a low tone, 'There's also a pair of scissors in my sewing basket... you know... in case the dollar demon comes back.'

TWENTY-FOUR
CAFÉ MONTMARTRE

It was as if the jazz singer was conducting the music with her hands. She coiled her wrists and undulated her fingers to the accents of the percussion and spiral of the brass. A blue light fell down onto her, making the jewel in her turban scintillate like shards of twilight. Opal was bewitched but couldn't help making one small aesthetic critique of the chanteuse, Lotus Hartley. Opal would have added a taller egret feather emerging from the jewel. The current one was a tad short.

The singer locked eyes with Opal as she sang the lyrics, 'I know who you are.'

Opal blinked rapidly and looked down at her lap, abashed. Then back up again. Yes, the singer was certainly looking at *her*.

'She knows you!' said Augusto from behind the bar in Opal's ear.

Opal swivelled round on her bar stool. 'I don't think she does. She was just picking someone out.'

'What can I get you, *chérie*?' he asked. The golden sconce on the wall cast a shadow over the side of his face and made his chin cleft appear even deeper.

'*Chérie*? You haven't called me that since Paris.'

'We're in a little piece of Paris, aren't we?'

'It does have a distinctly Gallic flair in here. It feels like we're only a croissant's throw away from the Eiffel Tower. You even sell Gauloises cigarettes.'

The scent of said cigarettes wafted under Opal's nose and brought her vividly back to the French capital.

'What libation shall it be? Absinthe? Belle époque style?'

'I'm not sure, Augusto, I think I might go teetotal this evening. I'm stitching up a split trouser crotch early. Betty's dance scene didn't go smoothly.'

'But I wanted to show off my cocktail skills. What about a French 75?'

'Oh alright... you've twisted my arm. But if it's acrid tasting I'm not sure I'll be able to finish it.'

'You'll love it. It's champagne and gin.'

Opal watched him tinker with bottles with her chin in her hands. She hadn't seen him in this kind of attire before. He was looking dashing with his hair parted severely to one side. He wore neatly pressed trousers, a waistcoat with a gold pinstripe and gold sleeve garters to hold his shirt cuffs out of liquids' way. He slid the flute along the marble counter for her. He glanced behind her and his countenance dropped suddenly as if he'd had ice water thrown in his face. He froze and gripped the gin bottle neck as if it was a pole to steady himself with. *What in the blazes was he looking at?*

Opal whipped around to witness three men entering the club. It was the purposeful stride of studio head Emmett Zimberg, followed by the willowy private detective Kensington and then at the rear was the penguinesque waddle of director George DeLuca.

'They're here to intimidate me. Or get more dirt on me,' Augusto said in such a low tone Opal could barely hear it amongst all the clinking of crystal in the bar.

'It's a popular club, Augusto, they could just be coming for a drink,' Opal said, placing a hand on his tense arm.

George DeLuca parted from his crew and approached the bar. 'Augusto! Good to see you. Can we have a bottle of champagne sent over. Oh, and some Silver Spur whiskey on the rocks for me. Do you have it? I think it might be discontinued. I've got one bottle left in my office but I can't find anything else like it.'

'Mr DeLuca.' Augusto nodded, his forehead moist. 'Certainly and, yes, I believe we have Silver Spur.'

'Bring it over personally, will you. Good lad,' George said, twiddling his fat fingers in a goodbye wave before joining the other two men at their table.

Something about what George said sent a spark through Opal's brain. *Silver Spur.* She tilted her head to the left and riffled in her handbag. Between thumb and forefinger, she pinched the whisky cap that she had found on the carpet after the hoo-ha when Jane's shawl had been doused in alcohol. She pursed her lips together and made a *hmmm* sound. Up until now, Opal had theorised Betty had been the culprit, but had George DeLuca doused Jane's shawl in an effort to make her look bad in front of Emmett Zimberg in the dressing room that day?

Augusto took a clunky square bottle of Silver Spur off the shelf. He also took Fernet and splashed it into a highball with cola and shot it back himself.

'It's alright, Augusto. I think they're only here for a meeting. When you go on your break, I'll tell you all the discoveries I've made so far and how we're going to try and get you in the clear,' Opal said in just a loud enough whisper for him to hear.

'I'll be back in ten minutes,' he said stoically and went to fetch a champagne bucket.

Opal took a sip of French 75 but jolted when she heard a lady at a table nearby.

'Will you cut that out, you lousy shutterbug!' she hissed, her mass of dark curls quivering in frustration. She held her Martini at a threatening angle as if to slew the contents at the person she was hissing at. Opal swore those arched brows were famed starlet Clara Bow's.

Opal looked sharply to her right in the direction which the star was complaining. There was a clunky camera held over the face of a man who had a dark beauty spot above his eyebrow. He slowly brought the gadget down to reveal his smirk. It was Domingo, of course.

'Sorry, Miss Bow,' Domingo smirked, clearly not sorry at all. 'I hope the lighting is bright enough to come out. The lamp above should help.'

He then twisted his lens and took a snapshot of Opal.

'I wasn't even ready. You got the side of my face! I will look a berk,' giggled Opal. 'Anyway, Domingo. Jolly good to see you.'

'I don't do staged or posed photographs. I think I might be the only one making anything real in this town,' he said, and cocked one thigh up onto a bar stool.

'I have to concede, that's most refreshing,' said Opal.

'I'll have a Sidecar!' he hollered at one of the barmen, then turned back. 'Opal Laplume. The last time I saw you was at Colonel Thwack's.'

'Yes. I just about survived without butchering anyone's ankles. Napoleon was in his element playing the retriever. I didn't get to say goodbye to you though, Domingo. You had jettisoned off.'

'Oh, I had to get back to the editing suite.'

'You seemed on the verge of fisticuffs with young Burton Ford.'

Domingo fidgeted on his stool, and rested his glass on the bar. 'You saw that?'

'I did. You appeared to be taunting him with a piece of paper.'

'Oh that. That was the scorecard for the game. He was very

upset that I beat him. And we'd put a bet on it. I didn't take anything from him though, he's only a kid.'

Opal tilted her head to the left and squinted at him. 'I thought the scorecard paper was green. The thing you had was white, or at least the back of it was white.'

Domingo looked over at the stage performance as considered his reply, then said coolly, 'We didn't use the official scorecards, it was a scrap from my pocketbook.'

Opal nodded and took another sip of her cocktail. She knew Domingo was lying. It certainly was not a tiff about miniature golf scores and getting a ball inside a Bakelite frog's mouth. Their body language had been positively primitive, suggesting something far more consequential and sinister.

'I hope you are friends again,' Opal said.

'Oh, we're fine. He's a young lad who's prone to bouts of anger that extinguish easily.'

'You seem to ruffle a few feathers around here. I remember seeing George DeLuca hold you against a pillar after the premiere of *A Capitol Wife* and say "I told you to cut it out." Was that literal, about the editing... or figurative about something else?'

'Gee. You're more on it than Detective Kensington. You keep your eyes peeled, don't you, Miss Laplume?'

'I do, I'm afraid. My father nicknamed me "Bins" – short for binoculars.'

'When George said, "I told you to cut it out," it was literal. I didn't cut a few things that he'd asked to be cut out of the film, that's all,' Domingo said, leaning an elbow on the counter. 'How's your Argentinian?'

'My Argentinian? You mean Augusto?'

'That's the one.'

'He's not South American, he's Iberian... a Spaniard,' said Opal. 'But you're not the first one to say so. A tango dancer in Paris said he's about as Argentinian as a gaucho's poncho. He drinks Fernet, a popular drink out there. But he fiercely insists he is Spanish.'

'Wonder what he's got to hide,' said Domingo, and his beauty spot shot upwards with his brow.

'He has *nothing* to hide,' Opal said firmly, but she could not be entirely sure. 'Everyone needs to leave him alone. We think that Emmett Zimberg and Detective Kensington may be trying to pin Jane's murder on him. I mean, they have to blame someone – Detective Kensington needs to cash his cheque. So why not the unknown foreigner... the alien. But I'm determined to get Augusto out from under their claws.'

'How do you plan on doing that?' said Domingo, with a faintly amused twitch of his lip.

'I have a few ideas. But it would be helpful if you could tell me anything you know. Anything you suspect.'

'I know nothing. I hope whoever orchestrated Jane's death will get their comeuppance... but I am not pointing any fingers,' he said smoothly.

'That's strange. Everyone else seems to want to point a finger,' Opal said, and then lowered her voice to almost a whisper. 'What were you doing in the editing suite the night when she was shot?'

'I had been editing until the power cut out. I was avoiding the commotion and taking a moment's rest.' He shrugged.

'Did you see Virginia rush through to the fire exit?'

'Yes. And then I saw you come in and that was it.'

Opal looked down into her glass and watched the tiny bubbles bursting. She was tempted to ask Domingo about whether he'd seen anyone getting changed into a toy soldier costume or where the missing soldier costume could be. But if he was the killer... she didn't want him to know she possessed that nugget of information.

'Delightful songbird, isn't she?' Domingo said as he swivelled on his stool to face the stage and pointed to the singer,

Lotus. 'I'd like to capture her portrait. She's got a gaze that could cut glass... piercing, unwavering...'

'I'd say her gaze was attempting to hypnotise me into handing over my drink!' Opal said, wriggling uneasily on her stool.

Lotus was staring intently at her, the jewel in her turban becoming a mesmerising third eye. *Does she really know who I am? Why is she still staring at me so incessantly?*

TWENTY-FIVE

A PORTRAIT OF LOTUS HARTLEY

'Opal, I'm going on my break in two minutes.' Augusto leaned in between them and said, 'I'll meet you outside at the back door? You can get to it around the side.' Then he disappeared into the steam of the kitchens.

'Jolly good. Excuse me, Domingo.'

Opal spotted Augusto outside the kitchen, down a narrow alleyway. She had to squeeze past men in various states of culinary undress, sleeves rolled up, aprons slung over shoulders, leaning against the brick walls. They were wolfing down ham baguettes and muttering bitterly to one another, saying things like, 'It's absurd that they need twelve variations of Martini' and one of them, spotting Opal, commented, 'Miss, I'd wager that hat of yours has seen finer places. Best not sully it down here.'

When she'd emerged from the web of virile limbs, she found Augusto sitting on a metal bin. His arms and feet were crossed and he was staring at the wall opposite with red-rimmed eyes. Made redder by the fact his eyes were so dark. The bent cigarette in his mouth exuded smoke that looked like steps ascending into the sky.

'I say!' Opal laughed. 'Mother wouldn't be best pleased

knowing I was hanging out around the bins at the back of a *roistering joint*.'

'Oh.' Augusto looked up and smiled. 'Yes, I am sorry about this. I just wanted to show you the view of the stage from here. It's a great angle of the singer.'

Opal looked through the open kitchen door which led to a corridor stacked with pots and crates of onions. At the very end was a perfect view of Lotus Hartley onstage. She was a vision saturated in blue light. The jewel in her turban was like a disco ball.

'It would make a great sketch, wouldn't it? Lotus, framed by the corridor of the Café Montmartre kitchens.'

'Oh, I simply must,' Opal agreed and unsnapped her handbag to pluck out her sketchbook.

Opal and Augusto scribbled in silence for a moment. She in lipstick, he in charcoal. Opal drew the turban with a much larger egret plume; as she thought it should be.

'Well, my drawing is almost as beautiful as the lady herself.'

'Oh, jolly good, let's have a ganders,' said Opal.

She blinked at his page and clutched her choker. In soft and unfurling scrawls, Augusto had drawn a woman with dark curls, bright eyes, a pyramidal nose, cherry-shaped mouth in an embroidered cloche with a frothy scribble of ostrich plumage. He had drawn Opal. She swallowed and looked up slowly from his Adam's apple, his cleft chin, and up into his warm eyes. Had he called her *beautiful*?

'Golly. I um... think it's a very good depiction of me. You've never drawn me before.'

'Oh, I have... from memory. I drew you soon after you left Paris, in case I never got to see you again.'

Opal shifted her weight from foot to foot and looked back down the corridor at Lotus Hartley. What in heavens name should she reply? She was utterly magnetised by him but that inner monologue in her mother's voice repelled her whenever she got too swept up.

'So... did you serve the big bullies?' She decided all she could manage was to change the topic.

'Yes,' said Augusto, lowering his sketchbook onto his lap. 'They asked me a few probing questions about my background. It seems they're digging. They want me to come in for questioning in Emmett Zimberg's office next week.'

'Well then. We've got a week to find the real culprit. Or at least offer them some compelling evidence to put you in the clear.'

'Yes, Opal Laplume on the case,' Augusto said flatly.

'Was that sarcasm, Mr Sevilla?' Opal clutched her choker again.

'No... it wasn't actually. Only weariness. What you did in Paris was amazing. I have a far better private detective in you than Emmett Zimberg has in Mr Kensington.'

'I'll tell you now what I've seen and heard.' Opal looked over at the bounders in the alleyway to make sure they weren't listening. 'Virginia saw one of the toy soldiers push over the water barrel. It could have been an extra. But I don't think it was... because they would have put the costume back the same as everyone else. But the costume is *missing*.'

'Okay that gets us a smidgeon closer.' Augusto lit up another cigarette and flicked the match at the wall opposite.

'Virginia said the toy soldier hid behind a screen as you picked up the barrel, and then he headed for the back of the room in the direction of the desk where your gun was. So, I think it was likely the toy soldier stole your bullet,' Opal said.

'The costume was fully covering the person, wasn't it? The face, hair, feet, including gloves?' Augusto said.

'Yes, unfortunately,' Opal said, sighing.

'They would have headed for the armoury box next.'

'Where was that situated?'

'Over on the far-right wall, close to the door that leads to the technical corridor.'

'I don't have a witness that saw anyone go inside that box. But Betty saw something else. She said she saw Burton offer Jane a hanky around seven o'clock. Then something red fell out of his pocket. He picked it up and she said something like, "*You won't last long*" to him.'

'Oh, that boy? He adored Jane, didn't he? Writing all those scripts for her. He couldn't be involved in any way.' Augusto shook his head.

'And another thing. George DeLuca: I found out tonight he drinks Silver Spur. There's a chance he doused Jane's shawl with it to make her smell like a day-drunk on set. This was well before the murder but it shows he wanted her off the movie.'

'George DeLuca. If it's anyone I would say it was him. I just don't like his demeanour,' Augusto said, narrowing his eyes to black almonds.

'There's also her widower, Carey Margeaux. He's been acting devastated but he's an actor. He could well be a suspect. And I saw Domingo hiding in the corner of the editing suite. I just know he knows something I don't.'

'Keep working on it, *chérie*. I know you can do it. I'm so thankful to have you on my side. I would help but I'm not allowed back on the Platinum Signet Productions allotment unless I'm called to Emmett Zimberg's office.'

'I'll be alright going solo... well, as a duo if Napoleon is with me.' Opal looked back towards the stage. 'Oh, Lotus has finished singing. I can finish these last bits of the picture without her being there.'

Just then, Lotus Hartley tottered into the kitchens and slid onto the counter. She pinched a profiterole off a plate. She stuffed it in her mouth and started yapping to the chefs with chocolate sauce on her lips. 'You don't get profiteroles like this in Australia, even at the Royal Albert Hotel. Maybe it's the cream.'

Lotus's hazel eyes caught sight of Opal and jumped down off the counter. Her interest was piqued by Opal's sketchbook, and she floated over, hips swaying in a figure of eight, and said, 'Hey, I don't suppose that's a scrawl of me?'

'Yes, yes, it is,' said Opal over the clatter of the kitchen pans. She held the sketchbook to her chest, abashed.

Lotus, in a playful manner, snatched the book out of Opal's hands. Her lips parted when she got a good look at the artwork. 'I love this, can I have it?'

'Well, it's just a little fashion sketch... not quite finished. You can when it is.'

'Looks finished to me.' Lotus smiled and ripped it out of the book. 'Anymore and you'll spoil it. Can you sign it?'

Opal produced a fountain pen, then paused with the nib hovering above the paper. 'Do you know my name?'

'No, mam.' She shook her head innocently, the egret in her turban quivering.

'When you sang the lyrics, "*I know who you are,*" you looked at me. It seemed deliberate... conscious.'

'Oh, that was just a bit of audience allure... Whenever I do that, the person comes up to me afterwards to ask how I know them. Every time! Sometimes I make up little tales to amuse myself.'

'I see. Theatrics. Well, you could have fooled me!' said Opal, scrawling her signature in the corner of the artwork; *The Honourable Opal Marion Laplume.*

'You see, I know you for real now... Opal Laplume. And who is this stud?' Lotus said, dragging her eyes up and down Augusto, causing Opal to feel a flurry of jealousy.

'Augusto Sevilla,' he said, quite deadpan.

'I'm back on in a moment,' she said, the egret spray on her turban flopping backwards in the direction of the stage. 'But you two should come to the Cocoanut Grove on Saturday. I'm always there Saturdays.'

Opal couldn't help but feel jinxed by that third eye in the chanteuse's turban. There was something siren-like about her... Opal was tempted to know more but sensed it may be wiser to steer clear. A bit like deciding whether to bathe in a beautiful warm lagoon without knowing how deep it was or what was lurking at the bottom of it.

TWENTY-SIX

'23 SKIDOO!'

'Good morning, Burton, may I sit with you? Don't mind Napoleon, he'll stay under the table,' Opal said when she'd spotted the boy in the Luncheonette.

'Why, of course,' Burton replied, the tips of his ears going pink in abashment at seeing her. Opal was cute, sure he was dippy for her. 'Sleep well?'

'I did actually, thank you, Burton. Much better now I'm not top and tailing with Bonfire. She had a bit of a fright the other day. Something odd had appeared on her bedside table, so I let her bunk in with me. It hasn't happened since so I've got my leg room back.'

Before Burton could ask what it was on Bonfire's bedside table, the waitress approached with pencil poised above her pad.

'Good morning,' Opal greeted her with famished urgency. 'I don't suppose you can rustle up kedgeree, can you? It's what I have at home, I've been missing it terribly.'

'Keder-whaaaat?' the waitress asked in a Southern drawl.

'Kedgeree. Do you have it? You know rice, smoked haddock, a hint of curry powder... eggs, of course.'

'No, we don't. Sorry, queenie.'

'Oh, I, umm. Is oatmeal... porridge?'

'Yes, mam.'

'I thought so. Porridge, if you please, and some English breakfast tea,' Opal said in her politest tones.

Napoleon whined under the table in such a dramatic fashion you'd think that the Treaty of Versailles had just outlawed sausages for dogs.

'Oh, and a sausage, please,' Opal added for the hungry beast.

'Corned beef hash and a glass of buttermilk.' Burton handed back the menu.

'Where's your friend? The one that's always taking unsolicited photographs of people?' the waitress asked, bobbing her curls with a palm as if she'd done her hair especially for said friend.

'Domingo? Tanned... has a beauty spot above his brow?' asked Burton, and the waitress nodded. 'I don't know where he is. I'm sorry.'

'He's usually here every morning at seven sharp and this is the third day he's not been here,' she said, slightly ruffled.

Opal scrunched up her toes and caught Burton's eye. His mouth stretched in concern, and he shrugged, his linen jacket bunching around his big ears.

'Perhaps he's very busy re-editing and skipping breakfast?' Opal said to the waitress and tried to make light of it.

'I guess.' The waitress sighed and went about her business.

'Was she sweet on him or something?' whispered Burton.

'I don't know, but this sounds truly worrying,' Opal said, leaning forward.

'In the light of what's been happening, it does. But you're probably right; he could be busy finishing up the re-edits for *A Capitol Wife*.'

'I'll go to the editing suite this afternoon and check on him. The poor chap might be overwhelmed.'

Burton looked down at the script on the table. The typed pages were covered in pencil marks and arrows.

'I wish Jane had seen this script. I think it may have been one she would have really liked.'

'What's it about?'

'It's set in London. Jane's part is a fearless investigative journalist who infiltrates high society to expose a powerful criminal syndicate. Then she does a 23 skidoo – a quick escape – to Australia.'

'I know London society better than the contents of my own handbag. Should you require a gentle nudge in the right direction, you've only to ask,' Opal offered. She pulled the script towards her, frowned and pointed at a word. 'Oh, we never say "gotten" in England, its "got".'

'Oh... I guess I'd *gotten* lazy with the dialect,' said Burton and giggled.

'And we certainly would never say 23 *Skidoo*. We would say "vamoose like a shot". And "the pickles elbow" I heard the other day, awful!' Opal winced. 'It's simply ripping, tip-top, top-notch, bally marvellous, spiffing, splendid, smashing... that's the sort of thing we say.'

Burton scribbled the alien language on the back of his script.

'It's great to know a native. Jane tried to study your accent, didn't she?'

'Yes. To sound more mid-Atlantic. Strange business, that accent. But she was very kind to me. A smashing woman. I hope we can uncover what *really* happened to her.'

'I don't know if we ever will. Platinum Signet Productions are the masters of cover-up.'

'What do you think happened?'

'Well, I was on set. I was assisting one of the script editors.

I'd just used the bathrooms down the technical corridor and was coming back in when the gunshot rang out. Then there was all that commotion and the blackout.'

'The conjecture is that someone knocked over the drinking-water barrel earlier in the day, and while Augusto was picking it up, they took the bullet out of his gun and put it in the stunt gun.'

'Well, I didn't see nothin'.'

'*Anything*, Burton. I didn't see *anything*. Anyway, we think it was either one of the extras, or someone in an extra's costume.'

'I said I didn't see nothin'– *anything*, I mean.'

'Alright. Betty said she saw you offer Jane a hanky when she was sneezing. Then when you pulled it out of your jacket something red fell on the floor. Jane seemed to tell you off. She said, "*You won't last long*", or something to that effect. Can you tell me about that?'

'Betty witnessed this? Well, yes, it was a packet of cigarettes. Marlboro Red, a red packet. Jane didn't like me smoking.'

'But Jane smoked herself... A lot.' Opal frowned. 'Rather hypocritical to chastise *you* over doing the same thing.'

'I know. But she didn't like it. She wished she didn't have the bother of it. She thought I was too young and it was a sign of moral decline. I'm only seventeen.'

'I guess being only seventeen has its perks. Like Domingo not holding you to the golfing bet.'

'What? What golfing bet?' Burton looked utterly bemused.

'I saw you both have a little disagreement at Colonel Thwack's and I asked him what it was. He said he was taunting you with the scores on a scrap of paper. He said you got upset because you'd made a bet. But he let you off the hook.'

'He said that?' said Burton, going slightly pink. Opal didn't know if that was due to the fact he was embarrassed he wasn't man enough to hold his bets or because what Domingo said was not true. After a moment of him looking out the window, he continued. 'Well, that *is* what happened, and we made friends again.'

'That's what he said. Your stories match,' Opal said, and smiled down at the bowl of porridge that had been placed before her.

Burton slathered mustard onto his beef hash in silence. Napoleon whined for his breakfast.

'Who will you want to play the lead in your new script?' said Opal, dropping the sausage under the table to resulting gobble noises.

'Anyone but Betty Caruso,' said Burton.

'Oh. Any reason?'

'I just don't think she's a good enough actress. Great singer. Not a good actress... far too dramatic. She doesn't seem to realise you don't need to play it so big in the talkies.'

'She plays it big in real life too!'

'Oh, and then some.' Burton nodded. 'Shall I give you a lift to Platinum Signet Productions when we're done? I've been driving George DeLuca's car, a brand-new Lincoln Model K. It's *top-notch*.' He tried to say the final expression in Opal's accent.

'What are you doing with Mr DeLuca's car?'

'He gives me a few bob to look after it and to drive him here and there sometimes.'

'In that case, a lift would be smashing,' Opal accepted.

As they made their way out to the waiting motor, she wondered for a moment whether Burton should have been more concerned over the whereabouts of Domingo. They were not each other's greatest fans, but even so, he had not been as curious as she would have expected. Then again, this was cold, lonely Hollywood, where the only ones interested in a studio employee going missing were the eager candidates waiting for a vacancy to open up.

TWENTY-SEVEN

WHITEMAIL?

Alighting at the Platinum Signet Productions parking precinct, Opal and Napoleon hopped out of the red Lincoln. As she closed the passenger door, Opal noticed a spattering of grey bird droppings with dark oval fragments within. A faint sense of missing her father crept in. Being the insufferable, bird-obsessed swot that he was, he used to play a guessing game with her when she was little to determine which bird species any droppings they came across belonged to. Mother, of course, would tell them off for indulging in such '*low pursuits*' and call them '*hopelessly uncouth*'. Now, finding herself in the wilds of California, she wouldn't have the foggiest notion what manner of bird had produced this particular mess.

She felt tears prick the back of her eyes and rubbed them. *Oh Papa, I wish I knew the truth about what happened out there in the Papuan forest.* But would the truth ever come out?

'Hey, what's the matter?' asked Burton, his big ears twitching back in concern.

'Oh, it's nothing. The heat.' Opal sniffed, then smoothed out her skirt. 'Have a good day, Burton Ford! Budding hitmaker!'

'Thank you, Miss Laplume. And to you. I'll come and consult you if I've gotten stuck.'

'*Got* stuck. *GOT* stuck,' Opal corrected him with a finger in the air and a mock schoolmarm's glare.

She then checked her watch. She was a little early. Perhaps she could take a peek in the editing suite to see if Domingo was in there...

She knocked at Domingo's workroom door.

'What now?' a gruff voice came from the other side of the door. It was far deeper than Domingo's.

'Oh... excuse me... I've come to see Domingo,' she said politely through the door.

'Domingo?' A man yanked open the door three inches and peered out with one pinkish eye that slid up and down Opal's body, then he said curtly, 'Domingo has taken French leave.'

'What does that mean?'

'Vanished. Disappeared. Gone pouf. No idea where he is. Kapeesh?' He tried to close the door again but Opal curled her fingers around the frame.

'Who are you?' she said.

'I'm his assistant. And I'm a very busy man. I've had to get the re-edit of *A Capitol Wife* finished without him.'

'I'm very worried. Is Domingo sick or injured, I wonder? Has anyone checked the hospitals?'

'Yes, and his lodgings at Palatial Pines. He's not there. Emmett Zimberg has Detective Kensington on the case. It beats me. It's very unusual to bail at this crucial point of the project. George and Mr Zimberg are so angry with him for not showing up. If he does show up, I don't think he'll ever work in this studio again.'

'Oh... why are they so angry?'

'Platinum Signet Productions will miss the release date of *A Capitol Wife* because of his absence. I mean, I've taken over and I'm going as fast as I can but...'

'May I come in, please?' Opal politely laced her hands in front of her.

'Why?'

'I want to see if he's left any clues as to his whereabouts.'

'I'm too busy, mam.'

'I won't disturb you.'

'Kindly remove your fingers. Goodbye, mam.'

He shut the door. But Opal was not to be swayed. She looked down at Napoleon, who panted with his tongue out, looking about as threatening as a stick of black candyfloss. She couldn't use her dog for any kind of leverage. She glanced up at the photographs of production scenes that lined the walls of the technical corridor and had a stab of inspiration. *Ah ha!*

Opal Laplume was not a liar and detested fibbers. But, in this case, she decided what she was going to do was more theatrical acting than downright deception... or blackmail. Blackmail for a good cause. Whitemail? *Oh, just get it over with woman, toot suite, before your moral conscience sets in.*

She knocked. Rat-a-tat-tat. He ignored.

'Sir... sir.' She pressed her nose against the door so that he could hear her. 'I've seen some pictures Domingo took of you. They are... morally questionable.'

'*What?* What do you mean?' He wrenched open the door and looked almost cross-eyed with outrage.

'Domingo showed me his collection of secret prints once. He had a rather unflattering picture of me. And I noticed one of you amongst them. I think he hid them in this room and that's what I'm looking for. If you let me in to have a quick look around, I won't tell anyone what I saw. And if we find the stash, we can destroy the unsavoury ones.'

'I've done nothing to warrant any kind of blackmail or anything sinful,' he said, but his hand clutched his neck and his eyes were flickering as if he was desperately trying to figure out whether he had.

'I mean, the photograph of you is more *humiliating* than *incriminating*. I think you may have been blotto when this picture was captured and wouldn't have any recollection.'

The man squinted and looked up at the ceiling. He seemed to have a drunken memory that horrified him and he hurriedly said, 'Oh alright, come in...'

'Much obliged.'

'Just don't disturb me. I have to deftly splice the scenes. They must flow like a well-practised waltz.'

The room was awash with the flickering glow of the projector. There were reels of film stacked like so many pancakes on the tables. The editor flitted about, wielding scissors amidst a storm of celluloid.

'What in the blazes are those?' asked Opal, peering at the devices.

'A moviola, a splicing block and a rewind bench,' he said, and wound two crank handles attached to spindles. He then threaded a strip of film through a curious contraption.

Opal manoeuvred herself delicately around the room and over to the filing cabinets where Domingo had been crouching the day Jane was shot.

She didn't find anything except a voice recording vinyl labelled, 'Betty Caruso Vocals, *Midnight at St Claire's*, recorded 07/01/34.' American dating made this the first of July. Opal decided to hold onto it.

She glanced up at what the editor was doing. Barely able to see the screen due to the smoke from his cigar, she wafted the smog away with an arm. It was that curious, drawn-out scene she remembered from the premiere.

'Will you be scrapping this?' Opal asked.

'George wanted this scene cut completely, but I have to make sure the continuity isn't affected.'

Opal watched him play it over a few times. She noticed something strange. Jane wasn't just randomly fidgeting with her belt buckle. She was purposefully pointing to diamantés on the buckle in a sequence. Opal got out her sketchbook and daubed the ten-by-ten dots of the buckle with her lipstick.

She watched carefully. Then with a pencil, marked the order in which Jane tapped. She tapped diamanté 3 and 4, then the top of the buckle. Then 1, 1, 8, to the right of the buckle. The last gestures were her putting her hand under the belt and then pinching the stone on her ring. Then the clip was over.

There simply had to be a reason why Domingo disobeyed George and left this clip in for the premiere. Were Jane and Domingo working on some secret code together?

'Thank you kindly, sir. I'll be off now!'

'Did you not find his photo stash?'

'No, no. I'm dreadfully sorry. It seems our indecorous proofs are still out there somewhere.'

'But wait, mam. Before you go. Can you please tell me what was *in* the photograph he took of me?'

Opal felt sorry for him. The poor man's nerves seemed so frayed you could have used them to string a banjo.

'Not to worry, it was only a picture of you in a very ugly hat. It looked like a... hedgehog in a tutu. I guess *ugly* is subjective though. Nothing to worry too much about.'

He looked over at his perfectly normal homburg hat hanging next to the fire exit and scratched his bald spot. Opal vamoosed like a shot. Napoleon trotted happily after her with a bounce in his step.

Opal's mind flooded with intrigue. Another queer element of the premiere of *A Capitol Wife* was that Mr Huxley had attended after receiving that strange invitation from Jane. Did he hold the key to the mystery of the belt buckle scene? Opal knew he frequented the Cocoanut Grove on Saturdays... if she wanted any answers, she'd have to trot off and extract them from him.

TWENTY-EIGHT
COCOANUT GROVE

One of Napoleon's greatest contributions to Opal's well-being was his ability to quash her loneliness. Or at least soften its edges in that loyal, tail-wagging sort of way only dogs can manage. But standing alone without him in this nightclub queue just brought back stinging memories from London. Back in the old city, she'd occasionally be summoned to some society affair, where she'd trot in solo, trade stiff pleasantries with an old classmate or two, and do her best to dodge Cecil Turks-Leyton, AKA 'Turkey', the suitor her mother had tried desperately to thrust upon her.

At least she'd had Jane when she first washed ashore in Hollywood, a friendship she currently missed. A true friend should stand by you in storm and sunshine, but in Hollywood, you'd be more likely to be dropped the moment a brighter sunbeam beckoned. If a chance at fame presented itself, even the most bosom of companions was liable to recall a pressing engagement elsewhere.

The only other potential comrade Opal could have invited would have been Burton, but any shared outing would fan the embers of his pash for her. Augusto, poor man, was on duty tonight.

When her freshly polished Mary Janes had tottered to the front of the line, she was confronted with a doorman collecting tickets.

'It's the Greater Los Angeles Orphans' Aid Society Dance tonight, mam. Do you have a ticket?' he asked, like a parrot that had squawked it hundreds of times.

'Good evening. No, sadly, I don't. May I purchase one?' she said politely, her purse abreast.

'It's sold out I'm afraid, mam.' He shook his head.

'Oh, what a conundrum... I'm supposed to be meeting someone. It's terribly important...' Opal lied, batting her lashes as hard as she could, then moved closer to his ear and breathed, 'What if I paid double? Triple?'

'Makes no difference to me, mam, it all goes to charity,' he said, and looked over her shoulder. 'Next!'

'But it's for the Helpful Doorman's charity,' Opal said slower and lower.

He ignored this and repeated, 'Next' to the person behind her. It was hard to tell whether the chap was a paragon of virtue or a few bricks short of a chimney.

With an indignant toss of her head, she marched off to formulate a plan. There had to be another way in. The kitchens, perhaps?

Sure enough, she spotted the culinary staff entrance tucked down a shadowy alleyway alongside the grand edifice. A few waiters in immaculate white ties were loitering, puffing away and grumbling with a passion. She caught snips of their disgruntled exchange.

'That Madame Coco Chanel's here tonight, if you please,' one of them muttered. 'Sent her drink back twice already. Too warm,' she said. 'As if we're expected to nip off to the Alps to chip off some ice caps!'

Ah ha! Opal thought. *Chanel. The demanding fashionista. I know how I can get in.* Dodging the cigarette smoke wafting her way, Opal squeezed towards the kitchen doorway.

A chef, built like a boulder and stationed by the door, gave her a look like she was a suspicious parcel. 'No ticket I see?' he said, crossing his arms. 'Sorry, my pretty, but I know every trick in the book.'

Opal didn't miss a beat. 'I'm here to deliver French cigarettes to Madame Chanel,' she announced as if she was performing a public service. 'The poor woman's run out and is rather in a state. She finds the local variety positively ghastly, I'm told.'

The chef furrowed his brow, considered the matter, and then shrugged, muttering something about rich folk and their whims. 'Well, we'd better see to it if it's for *her*. Maurice! Escort this lady to Madame Chanel.'

'Oh no, no, that's quite alright... I can find her,' Opal insisted.

'I will escort you. Follow me,' said the assigned waiter and she tottered behind him.

Emerging from the clattering and humid kitchen, she blinked in awe at the grand nightclub. The ceiling was as high as a cathedral. Chandeliers hung from it in resplendent clusters, casting dappled light over the scene like a diamond-leaf canopy. The décor was jungle-themed and boasted towering palms swaying lightly under the breeze of ceiling fans that wafted the swing music. She was hit with a fragrant barrage of perfumes, each one battling for supremacy. Chanel No. 5 jostled with exotic jasmine oils with a faint undercurrent of freshly polished floors.

The conversations going on had a peculiar shrillness, as though everyone was attempting to outdo the last person's enthusiasm. It was the sound of people afraid of being drowned out, of voices raised not in joy, but in a desperate bid for attention. It seemed even those who had found what they were looking for... money, status, a place at the grandest tables, walked around with a hunted look, as if they'd been let in on a terrible secret, that *'having made it'* was simply another phrase for *'having something to lose'*.

The hors d'oeuvres balanced precariously on a silver trays were little works of art. Ossetra caviar on doll-sized pancakes, smoked salmon stuffed with Roquefort, and sweet tartlets bejewelled with berries. Opal could not resist pausing to sample a prosciutto-wrapped melon boule and to pinch a couple of the mini beef Wellingtons, which she then wrapped in a hanky, stuffing them into her handbag for Napoleon later. The waiter escorting her gave a disapproving side-eye at her greedy fingers.

Opal could not see Chanel yet. The place was positively rammed with guests, and she had to manoeuvre carefully, lest her sleeve be impaled by an errant sapphire brooch or, worse, crushed underfoot by a Charlestoning stiletto. When the dancers spun apart, Opal could see Peridot Ellington by a palm trunk, chatting animatedly to Marlene Dietrich and Claudette Colbert. They stood out like orchids in a field of daisies, commanding the room with their luminous beauty. Opal felt nervous just looking at them.

'I assure you, I am quite able to locate Chanel without your assistance. I wouldn't dream of encroaching further upon your precious time,' shouted Opal above the raucous strains of music to the waiter.

'She's here at this table, mam,' he said, pointing with a white-gloved finger.

They approached a circular table laden with desserts and highballs and Madame Chanel was seated at the far end, whispering something into the ear of Mr Huxley. Her peach linen lapels zigzagged down her chest and long strings of pearls laid with grace upon them.

'Madame Chanel,' said the waiter, presenting Opal with the

swoop of his arm. 'This lady is here to deliver the French cigarettes you requested.'

Chanel's cloche swooped up in surprise. '*Magnifique!*' she said with a smirk, stubbing out her current cigarette in an anchovy biscuit. 'I was just thinking about this. How I miss my French tobacco. How did you know? Do you have Gigantes brand?'

'You did not request these cigarettes?' asked the waiter and slid Opal a side-eye, his nostrils flaring, smelling a fibber.

'No, I did not request them. But I would like them very much. Do you have Gigantes?' Chanel pressed, looking at Opal almost like a begging puppy.

Opal swallowed hard and pretended to search in her bag. She turned to the side so that they couldn't see the beef Wellingtons stuffed in it. 'Oh botheration! I must have dropped the Gigantes cigarettes. But Café Montmartre just down the street has them, I will go and fetch some now for you.'

The waiter clasped his fingers around Opal's forearm and said, 'You tried to get into the club by spinning this yarn at the kitchen door! I will now throw you out.'

TWENTY-NINE

CHARITY COMES WITH A SPOTLIGHT

Opal felt the capillaries in her cheeks flush with blood. *Blithering fig!* How exceedingly mortifying in front of Madame Chanel.

'Leave her alone.' Chanel pulled the waiter's arm off Opal's and tutted. 'I know you, girl, don't I?' She gave Opal a once-over with her cheek turned to the side. 'Where from?'

'Yes, indeed. We met in Paris at Misia Sert's salon, madame,' Opal said.

'That's it!' The fashionista beamed. 'You had the darling poodle Napoleon with the little bicorn hat.'

Mr Huxley, who had been deep in conversation with someone else, now looked up, got to his feet and took Opal's hand. 'Opal Laplume... you finally made it to Cocoanut Grove.'

The suspicious waiter wound his neck in and sidestepped away in the crowd.

Opal parted her lips to reply to the film producer, but had to clasp her hands to her ears.

SCCCRRREEAAAACHHHH.

The ghastly sound of microphone feedback was coming from the stage. The crowd on the dance floor stopped bobbing and parted. Opal rose up on tiptoes and saw Carey Margeaux in a white dinner suit flicking the microphone, his eyes crossing as he tried to fix the infernal noise.

'Oh, not this poor berk,' muttered Mr Huxley.

'He looks as oiled up as an Eton rowboat,' commented Opal on Carey's obviously drunken state. 'He's even got some buttons done up in the wrong holes and his cufflinks are odd!'

Carey was swaying slightly and hiccupped before saying, 'Ladies and gentlemen.' *Hiccup.* 'I have an announcement to make. I'd like to honour my late wife, Jane Margeaux, by presenting this cheque to the Westward Hope Orphanage in Port Hueneme, Ventura County.'

He held up a giant cheque for $50,000 on a whiteboard and the crowd clapped and whistled like the sound of a rainforest storm.

'That's some serious cabbage,' said Mr Huxley into Opal's ear. 'Seeing as that's half of what his mansion is reasonably worth. He must have cashed in all of Jane's stocks!'

Marlene Dietrich, over by the palm, said in an overly loud voice, 'My, I didn't realise charity came with a spotlight and a press release,' and nudged Peridot and Claudette.

Claudette giggled back. 'He's giving with one hand and taking credit with both.'

Peridot simply glared at the stage, arms folded, a mixture of fear and fury on her countenance. Could the mention of the orphanage be something that was ruffling her?

Opal's lashes batted as she thought hard. *Was Carey making a large altruistic gesture in public to quash his motive for having Jane bumped off for money? Or was it a genuine tribute to Jane?*

'It is not a good thing that we have so many kiddos in orphanages,' Carey said, completely ignoring the actresses' remarks. He lowered the cheque and looked out in their direction. 'Isn't that right, Peridot Ellington? Peridot! Will you please come onto the stage?'

Peridot, who'd been leaning against the palm, straightened up, the dark fruits on her hat quivering. Opal felt a tad queasy, and it wasn't the canapé she'd scoffed. She was remembering the miniature golf event when Carey told her Peridot had lied about her orphanage backstory to get reader sympathy... was he about to expose and humiliate her?

Peridot floated coolly with her chin held high all the way to the stage, ascended the steps and stood next to Carey with an artificial smile stretching her lips. Her ink drops for pupils showed her true emotion – seething rage. No wonder she was a failed thespian.

'How unexpected, Mr Margeaux,' she said, twisting the fingers of her gloves as if she wanted to do the same to his neck.

'Peridot Ellington, were you not an orphan at Westward Hope in the eighties and nineties?' Carey said, offering her the microphone, his eyes twinkling with angst.

She snatched it reluctantly and said, 'Indeed I was, and it is very generous of you to gift that cheque. I'm feeling rather bashful and overwhelmed, dear. Now may I go?'

'Not yet, Peridot...' Carey took a second microphone. 'Tonight, I have invited another orphan who *also* grew up in the *same* orphanage at the *same* time... Nellie Ainsworth. Nellie can you please join us up here. Where are you?'

Nellie appeared from the midst of the crowd. She stood out because of her nondescript frock of dreary grey, the sort more suitable for laundry days than soirées. A well-worn shawl draped over her shoulders, she navigated the glittering throng of Hollywood guests. She walked up onto the stage with a huge genuine smile. Clearly delighted to be invited by Carey to attend and speak.

'Do you recognise each other, ladies? I know it was forty or so years ago...'

'No, no, we don't.' Peridot glanced at the woman as if looking at an unclaimed sock on a railway platform. 'There were hundreds of us. I was very different back then, a little mousy thing and rarely spoke.'

'Good evening, everybody,' Nellie said in a sweet and excited voice, revealing her wonky teeth. 'No, I don't remember Peridot, to be completely honest, but I've forgotten a lot of my childhood.' She ended the sentence with a sad break in her voice. *The poor dear*, Opal thought.

'What a great shame that you don't recognise each other...' said Carey, shaking his head in mock regret. 'Peridot... I heard from Nellie there was a giant portrait on the stairwell that was of a particular person. And it's still there... can you tell us who was depicted in that portrait, Peridot?'

Peridot's blueish complexion made her blush show up in a purple tone, as she said, 'I too have blacked out a lot of my early years. I wouldn't remember.'

Mr Huxley leaned over and whispered in Opal's ear, 'If Carey doesn't shut up there'll be another dead body before the ink dries on that cheque.'

Opal made a mental note that clearly Mr Huxley thought it was within Peridot's remit to get Carey killed for this.

'Are you sure?' Carey went on in faux surprise. 'It was of the *founder of the orphanage*! The man who would oversee the yard work and floor scrubbing. A very harsh man that surely all the orphans remember? What was his name, Peridot?'

Peridot's voice cracked into a whip. 'As you said, he was a harsh man and I have blocked it out. If you'll excuse me, I don't feel comfortable discussing those years. They are over. Dead and gone. I'm sure Nellie here can help you.' She then rammed the microphone into Nellie's hands and strutted off the stage, the fruit on her head vanishing into the crowd.

The audience emitted a low rumble of gossiping chatter. *What a brouhaha!*

'Well, his name was Mr Thaddeus Finch. And that portrait is now to be removed and replaced with a portrait of Jane

Margeaux. Once we have renovated the building, that is!' Carey lifted his arms to encourage applause. Which he got. It was thundering in overcompensation for the awkwardness everyone felt.

'Thank you for your generosity, Mr Margeaux! It'll certainly transform the lives of all the children at Westward Hope,' Nellie said.

'Enjoy the rest of the night, folks, and don't forget to enter tonight's raffle!' Carey said with another hiccup and stumbled off stage right.

A band struck up a pompous swing number that was like slathering honey over the bitter atmosphere.

'That was excruciating,' said Mr Huxley. 'I can't stomach the tense air in the club now. I was meant to have a nightcap with Carey later as he wanted to discuss turning Jane's life into a film with Cox & Lumière Pictures. But a drink with Carey tonight, my dear Opal, is decidedly off. He is in no state. I'd better scarper before he spots me.'

'Gosh, a movie about Jane's life? Carey really seems to want to create a legacy for Jane, doesn't he?' Opal said.

'He's lost the plot,' said Mr Huxley, straightening his bow tie with a tug of disdain.

'Though he used to be an actor, so is it genuine?' said Opal.

'You're quite right, Opal, you can *never* trust an actor,' said Mr Huxley. 'But you can trust us boring old producers. Actually, I've been wanting to speak to you about millinery for the new period film we're producing. Why don't you come back for the nightcap? Chanel will be coming so I can discuss the costumes with her. There's a singer here that I want to sing in it, it can be a brainstorming session.'

'Well... I...' Opal stammered.

'Driver's just outside,' he pressed. 'I'll join you directly, just as soon as I retrieve the singer. I last saw her doing the Charleston. You go ahead...'

Opal, more than a little nonplussed by this unexpected invitation, adjusted her cloche with an eager smile. A golden opportunity, no less. Companionship with Chanel *and* a bit of investigatory digging on Mr Huxley. She wasn't about to pass it up. Though she had no idea who Mr Huxley's 'singer' was.

A few moments later, she found herself ensconced in the Rolls-Royce Phantom II beside Madame Chanel. The Parisian was chuffing on her American cigarettes with an air of distaste, but smiled when she looked over at Opal. The entire scene had the surreal quality of a dream.

'Oh, look – here comes Mr Huxley now with his chanteuse in tow... with a voice like that, you'd expect a lady. Such a shame she's devoid of manners,' said Chanel, arching an eyebrow.

Opal turned her head and her mouth fell open. Strutting next to Mr Huxley's brogues was a pair of satin mules, which led up to a gown in brilliant cerise, with a bodice of frothy tulle. At the pinnacle of this exquisite gown was the blonde head of... Lotus Hartley.

THIRTY

MR HUXLEY'S MANSION

The sun-kissed Lotus gave Opal a cheery little wave. She returned it, though her nerves from being strapped in a car next to Chanel made her hand wobble like a leaf in a gale.

'Opal, this is Lotus Hartley, Lotus, Opal Laplume,' said Mr Huxley and gestured for Lotus to get in beside Opal.

'Oh, we met down at the French joint. How are ya, sweetie?' Lotus said in her Australian lilt and slid in.

'Indeed, we did. Charmed to see you again,' Opal said, shrinking down into the leather.

Huxley settled in front, and, with a lurch, the car sped off. Lotus and Chanel were already acquainted it seemed, due to a mutual friendship with Mr Huxley, and they launched into lively chatter, leaving Opal in the middle feeling rather like the quivering filling in a very posh sandwich.

After making a pit stop for Madame Chanel's tobacco at Café Montmartre, they rode out of Tinseltown. Mr Huxley's mansion, perched upon a hillside, resembled a hunk of black Swiss cheese, with its dark arches and intricate-tiled terraces. Heavy wrought-iron gates swung open to reveal a winding pathway lined with palms, their silhouettes dancing like spectres in the moonlight.

Mr Huxley arranged for his butler to bring Martinis to the veranda so they could give their thoughts on his new pool in the moonlight. Opal asked directions to the powder room first... she needed to gather her thoughts and check her makeup before spending time in the presence of her idol Chanel.

'Past the study, third door on the left,' directed the very elderly butler.

Study, thought Opal with a blink of intrigue. *Is that where Mr Huxley may have kept his premiere invitations, I wonder? If I can find the one from* A Capitol Wife *I can give it a good scan.*

She floated through the dimly lit foyer that was adorned with low-slung divans covered in vibrant silks. Intricate mosaics adorned the walls, forming abstract patterns that lured the eye into a hypnotic dance. A grand staircase, with its dark mahogany banister and sumptuous carpets, curled upwards like a serpent.

Opal's footsteps on the tiles silenced as she halted at the study door. It was ajar and as she navigated her nose around the door frame, she caught sight of a desk. It was piled high with letters and paperwork, in a careless bachelor sort of mess.

On tiptoes she inched towards the desk.

Clack. Clack. Clack.

Oh, blithering fig! There were footsteps coming up the corridor. She must look for the invitation quickly as she may not get another chance. Her hands shuffled through the documents like a croupier in a high-stakes game.

The footsteps came closer. What should she do? Duck under the desk? She squatted, but realised this was pointless as her skirts were draped to the side of it. She dragged the skirt past the waste bin, which rustled. She blinked at it with a keen flutter of her lids. There was a gold cord hanging off one of the cards stuffed inside. Opal remembered that gold cords were wrapped around all the stationery for *A Capitol Wife*. She dipped her hand in, but paper crackled.

'What are you doing?' came the syrupy tones of Lotus Hartley.

Oh, Christ on a lindy-hopping kangaroo, it's the outbacker.

Opal poked her nose above the desk and rested it there. Lotus Hartley was leaning on the door frame with her arms folded and feet crossed, a look of mischievous capture in her smirk.

'I, um...' Opal blinked around the study, trying to find some explanation. 'I needed a tissue – I have a ghastly cough. I've just disposed of it in this bin.'

Opal pulled her hand out of the bin without the invitation. She had nowhere to hide it.

'You shouldn't be in here, ladies!' came a new female voice from the corridor. But this time it was a Southern-belle accent. A grey head with a maid's bonnet on popped her head in the doorway. 'Mr Huxley has left it in a real ramshackle mess. He shouldn't let his guests see it in this state.'

'I do apologise, I needed a tissue,' Opal stammered.

'Excuse me,' said the maid and took the waste bin that was next to Opal. 'I'm going to give this room a once-over.'

Opal's toes clenched in annoyance. All she needed to do was to get that blasted invitation.

'I was on my way to the powder room also. Let's go,' said Lotus. Opal felt enticed by the way she sang as she spoke, like a siren, and followed her to the powder room.

'Have you been in Hollywood long?' Opal said as a way to break the ice as they reapplied their lipsticks in the bathroom vanity.

'Only a month. I'm trying to break into the musicals or at least get in the chorus.'

'I suppose having a good singing voice now that the talkies

are in fashion is as invaluable as having a maid that knows where the marmalade is,' said Opal.

'Precisely. I don't have the best face. My schnozz is a tad large. But my voice – once I've learned a true American accent – will be my golden ticket,' replied Lotus, snooping at what makeup Opal had in her bag.

'Mr Huxley is a good one to have in your telephone book then,' said Opal, with a final blot of lippy in the centre of her lower lip.

'Yes. I couldn't believe my luck getting in with him,' said Lotus, pencilling a brow as thin as thread.

'Is there a film industry in Australia?' enquired Opal, whiffing the violet perfume she found on the vanity.

'Hardly. I mean they're still mainly silent films so don't need someone with a good voice. I was just bored of touring clubs, you know. I did a spot of entertaining in the roistering joints in Indonesia. I got bitten to shreds by sand flies and I swear one flew down my throat and did something to my vocal cords. It was like I'd invented a new way of jazz singing the way my voice warbled. I got over it though.'

'A case of jazz-fly laryngitis?' giggled Opal.

Lotus snorted back. 'The world wasn't ready for Lotus Hartley meets distressed bagpipes!'

'Well, you sang beautifully at Café Montmartre, if I do say so myself,' said Opal. 'Mr Huxley will be lucky to have you in one of his pictures.'

'Being one of Mr Huxley's favourites doesn't come without its burdens.' Lotus rolled her eyes.

'Oh?'

Lotus placed her hands on the washstand and leaned forward in the mirror as if to get closer to the reflection of Opal's face. She let out a big sigh and whispered, 'I will tell you, but please, I beg you, don't tell a soul!'

THIRTY-ONE

VIOLET PARFUM AND VENOM

The hairs on Opal's arms stood up in anticipation. 'I won't spill a syllable,' she said earnestly.

'You swear?'

'My lips are sealed tighter than Aunt Amelia's purse strings when the collection plate comes around,' Opal said in affirmation, widening her eyes.

'Alright,' Lotus said, fiddling with an eyelash in the mirror. 'He's started to call me... a silly name... when we're alone and cuddling.'

Opal darted her eyes about the powder room in bafflement, then fixed them on Lotus again. 'Might I, Lotus, with all due delicacy, enquire as to what this... silly name... was?'

'Miss Cuthbert,' Lotus said with a lisp, then expulsed a laugh into her cupped hand.

'Pardon me?' said Opal, flaring her nostrils in surprise.

'That's exactly what *I said* the first time and he looked startled as if he didn't realise he'd said it. Then he tried to play it down and said he'd like that to be my pet name when we're alone.'

'But... why *Miss Cuthbert?*' said Opal, trying to emulate the lisp.

'Well... I've gotten friendly with the housekeeper here and she's ancient and has been here since he was a boy. And it turns out that Miss Cuthbert was his childhood nanny that he was very *fond* of.'

Opal froze for a moment and tried to digest this ghastly information. Then in unison they both blew raspberries into their hands with laughter. Opal thought tears might spout.

'Lord, give you strength,' Opal said, once she could breathe and patted some of the violet parfum on her neck with a little smile. She was chuffed she had found a gal who could have a silly hoot. Most of the London set Opal knew back home were about as entertaining as a lecture on advanced sock darning.

They rejoined Mr Huxley and Chanel on the veranda. The circular pool had the reflection of the moon in it. Like a drop of cream on an azure saucer. Beyond, the fountain was shaped like a peacock, the water spraying up in an impressive fanned tail. Opal dipped and scooped her Martini from the little old butler's tray and perched on a striped lounger. While the others chattered gaily she watched the water lap against the tiled edges of the pool. She was desperately trying to think of a way to pinch that invitation later. Would it now be in the kitchen bins?

'Mademoiselle Laplume, I was just telling Mr Huxley how your black poodle on the grand piano was the muse at Misia's salon in Paris.' Chanel's smoke twirled in an S-shape into the night sky as she lounged like a caterpillar.

'Oh yes... One of Napoleon Laplume's finest moments,' agreed Opal. 'In fact, I still have the sketch I bought that night off the costume designer fellow who drew Napoleon.'

Opal pulled her sketchbook from her bag and flicked through the pages to find the insert. Something tickled her hand. *I say, what's that!*

Little black legs, eight of them, came creeping off the book and up along Opal's arm. The sensation was quite tickly.

'What a charming variety of spider,' Opal said, moving her nose close to it. 'It's a little black thing with a kind of red kiss mark!'

Mr Huxley spat the smallest amount of cocktail back into his glass and placed it down. 'Don't move!' he yelled.

Opal obeyed the command but only moved her eyeballs up to look at him.

'If it has a red kiss mark then that's a black widow!' He shouted so loud that birds behind them fled their tree.

'Lucky spider, it has *offed* its husband,' Chanel scoffed.

'Be careful!' Lotus said anxiously, putting her glass down and lifting her hands into a surrender position.

'Is it venomous?' Opal asked, quite calmly. 'I'm not new to exotic insects. I've been bitten before so don't worry.'

'Not like *this* you haven't. This beast is *deadly*. Stay still and I'll hit it,' Huxley said, taking off his house slipper and raising it above his head.

'You can't kill a creature just because it's dangerous!' Opal said, slowly moving her arm out of Mr Huxley's way. 'Otherwise, the entire human race would all be for the chop.'

'Now listen, Opal.' Mr Huxley crept closer. 'A black widow's bite is no picnic. You don't want to make an early exit from this mortal coil, do you?'

The moon reflected in his wide eyes, pleading for her to let him execute the thing.

'She sounds a nasty little blighter,' Opal replied. She was scared, but she also knew spiders would not bite unless they were threatened.

'I shall go and find a tree down the bottom of the garden and get it off my arm gently,' Opal said, standing up very slowly.

'Opal come back,' Mr Huxley said. 'Are all young women this headstrong nowadays?'

'You would be correct!' Opal called back over her shoulder as she navigated the pebble path and its low lamps.

When she found a suitable trunk, she rested her arm against it and blew softly to mimic a breeze. The little thing climbed onto the tree and scurried into the darkness, its back blowing a tiny red kiss to Opal before it disappeared.

When Opal got back, she sat on the tiles by the edge of the pool and dangled her hand in the cool water, while Mr Huxley sifted through some of Opal's hat designs.

'You like to use red paint?' said Mr Huxley.

'Oh, I got into a habit of colouring with lipstick. Can't use a paintbox on the go, can you!'

'How resourceful. Now, hat designs. Opal, can you do some research on hats of the early 1810s, please. It's top secret, but we're going to be filming a British novel from that era. We can't give any more away than that.'

'I say! I'd be utterly delighted!' said Opal, and almost spilled her drink as she beamed up at Mr Huxley.

'And... Chanel will be doing the costumes. You shall work together.' Mr Huxley tipped his glass towards the fashion diva on her lounger.

Opal gasped. What a dream come true! She sincerely hoped Mr Huxley wasn't spouting codswallop. These impresario types needed to be taken with a pinch of salt.

'I haven't decided yet, Mr Huxley. Don't get ahead of yourself. As for the 1810s, I'm not sure I enjoy that period of dress.' Chanel swirled her olive in her drink casually.

Mr Huxley ignored her dismissal and swooped his arm towards the singer. 'And... Lotus Hartley, I'm going to give a singing spot to you.'

'Are you really, Mr Huxley, or are you trying to charm a clueless Australian who's fresh off the boat?' Lotus winked cheekily.

Opal had to admire her gumption in retorting like that. Perhaps it was an Australian thing.

'I'm trying to do both, of course!' Mr Huxley flirted back, and ordered his butler to bring some cheese straws.

'I can do a cracking rendition of "Greensleeves", if that's what you're after.' Lotus giggled.

'Precisely. We also need a good scream during a gunfight scene,' said Mr Huxley. 'I expect your lungs could muster that. That is, if you're not too faint-hearted for violence.'

'As a matter of fact... I witnessed a real-life gunfight in Papua over a diamond. I didn't flinch, so I'm your girl,' Lotus replied, glancing over at Opal with a gleam in her eye.

Opal sunk her nose into her Martini. She must conceal the shocked expression on her face. *This is so utterly uncanny! Father was in a gunfight over a diamond in Papua. Lotus couldn't possibly be speaking about that very same incident, surely? Could that explain the strange, knowing eyeball she gave me?*

Opal swallowed a mouthful of Martini that was considerably more than ladylike, composed herself and looked up at Lotus, 'Oh really? That sounds like a terribly exciting plot.' she said, attempting a casual slant.

'It was. Indonesia, that was right adventure. Took the jazz band up there, we were quite the hit among the Dutch set. Wealthy sorts, all of them. Among their ranks was a lord, rich as Croesus and twice as crooked, He was there on some dodgy poaching escapade. Wicked as they come, and the next thing I knew things turned nasty over some diamond that was found. I'll spare you the details, but his son got murdered by another lord. I witnessed the whole thing. After that, well, let's just say things went cold between us.'

Opal's heart began thumping. She looked down at the pool edge, trying to hide her face with her hair. There was an insect drowning. She scooped it out with her palm, placed it on the dry tiles. She felt like she, too, was drowning.

The details that Lotus had reiterated were so similar to her father's story. Lord Peregrine was a poacher, just like in her tale. Convinced that her father, Lord Laplume, had been the one who'd shot his son, he had come after Opal in Paris as retaliation. But her father had *not* killed young Reggie Peregrine. Why was Lotus saying that he had indeed killed the boy and that she'd witnessed it? She must probe Lotus more at a later date... Opal knew Lotus would be singing at the Café Montmartre and where to find her.

'Holy cow. That sounds quite the plot,' Mr Huxley said, pinching his chin thoughtfully. 'Like an Oscar picture. We should get one of our writers on it.'

'I'd rather costume something like that,' said Chanel with a smoky croak, 'Indonesia, guns, lords... the kind of thing the duke and I like to watch.'

The conversation had now veered towards the subject of Chanel's illustrious beau, the Duke of Westminster, and how he'd insisted on making his own dinner, with calamitous consequences. Then Mr Huxley recalled the time Douglas Fairbanks tried to impress Mary Pickford with his *'pioneer cooking'* and set half of the Hollywood Roosevelt's lawn on fire roasting a marshmallow.

It all sounded like far away murmurs to Opal. She couldn't believe Lotus was going around saying she'd witnessed her father shooting a boy! She contrived laughter and held her tears back. She just had to get away to cry into her pillow. 'It has been an utterly delightful evening,' she said, when she managed to interrupt, 'but I must retire.'

'They work you like a sweatshop, I hear, on *Midnight at St Claire's*,' Mr Huxley said.

'They do indeed,' said Opal, standing up.

'You can take the driver. He'll be out front,' the gentleman offered.

Opal thanked him kindly, said goodnight to the ladies and made her way through the French doors. But then halted. Her father, the most important man in her life, had his reputation at stake, but so did the second most important man in her life, Augusto, and the cloud that was hanging over him was more pressing. She had to help.

If the invitation she was trying to find had been binned by the maid in the outside dustbins, she might have to go around the outside of the house to find them. She tiptoed back and veered right around the pots of geraniums, muttering to the others that she wanted to take the exterior route and to look at the beautiful brickwork of the house. *What a twitty thing to say*, she thought, *who's interested in brickwork for goodness' sake?*

Opal meandered through a fragrant herb and rose garden, the scent pulling her back to Regent's Park in London. She came across a shady alcove that reeked of dish soap... aha! Kitchens and bins! And there, to her relief, the desk's waste bin had been emptied atop one. Among the debris was a half-empty box of intriguing chocolates.

Might as well. Canapés had not been the most filling supper. She plucked a glossy sweet, unwrapped it, and popped it in her mouth. Praline melted luxuriously over her tongue.

'Ahem?' came a smoky French voice.

Oh, blithering fig. Chanel! She's going to think I'm a tramp eating from the bins!

Opal whipped her head around. Indeed... Coco Chanel stood there, smirking through a whirl of cigarette smoke.

'I followed you. Left that pair to it. The driver can drop you first.'

'Oh... oh yes.' Opal swallowed, turned back, and sheepishly placed the chocolates in the bin. But not before snatching the gold-corded invitation.

'Saving some for later?' Chanel teased. 'Bias-cut dresses may be stretchy, but they're unforgiving.'

'Waste not, want not,' Opal replied, dying inside. She'd just been cocoa-shamed by Coco Chanel. Talk about a bitter aftertaste.

In the car, she pushed aside humiliation. The sooner she could get back, the sooner she could study that invitation. There *had* to be something hidden in the text!

THIRTY-TWO

TAPPING INTO SECRETS

Opal tossed the beef Wellington parcels that she'd pinched for the dog onto the floorboards at Palatial Pines. Napoleon snapped them up with the zest of a crocodile.

'At least you haven't been judged by the Countess of Couture for being a gobble gannet!' Opal said, rolling her eyes at the creature. 'Golly, don't choke!'

She was lying on her bed on her front, mascara smudged, Mr Huxley's invitation laid under her cupped chin. She was going cross-eyed reading the words over and over, trying to make sense of it. She also had her sketchbook open with the numbers she'd gathered from Jane's cut scene. Did the two documents correlate in any way? She moved her nose so close to the paper the letters fuzzed in and out of focus.

'Opal! Opal!'

Cripes! A man was shouting for her outside.

Napoleon's ears pricked and he scrabbled towards the door, his tail wagging as it did when he recognised a voice. *Was it Augusto?*

Opal creaked open her door and sheepishly crept up to the edge of the balcony. Grasping the wooden balustrade with anxious fingers she looked over and down. The dashing Spaniard was standing there, looking up at her with twinkling, mahogany eyes. He took his trilby off and smiled delightedly like a squirrel that had seen a nut in a tree.

'Augusto!' Opal hissed, pulling her cardigan across her. 'What the devil are you doing here?'

'Can I come up?' Augusto hissed back, pressing the hat to his chest eagerly.

Opal's breath caught in her throat. She blinked in sheer astonishment. He *did* look rather devastatingly handsome, no question about it. But, really! The audacity! A man of his charm should know better than to offer such an unseemly proposition.

'Heaven's no!' Opal said and Napoleon barked with his nose through the banister, reprimanding him.

'Will you shut your traps, it's midnight!' someone shouted from a window aloft.

'I will come down. Give me five minutes,' Opal hissed at Augusto.

She slung her shawl over her shoulders, slipped the cryptic invitation into her sketchbook, put the leash on the pooch and met him down on the grass. Napoleon stood up like a tiny human with his paws in the air, his tail wagging so fast it became a blur. Augusto was evidently one of his favourite marshals.

'Hello, boy! Sorry, Opal. I hope I didn't wake you. I finished my shift and I just had to see you...' he said, his arms clamped to his sides as if to stop him from embracing her. 'I mean, to find out how you've been getting on with the case.'

Opal could smell the Fernet he liked to drink on his breath. She assumed this was what had given him the Dutch courage to come bounding over here like Romeo in a trilby.

'Oh no, I wasn't asleep, don't worry. I've been trying to crack this peculiar cipher.'

'Why don't we look at it together?' Augusto suggested.

'I could do with another pair of eyes. I'm going utterly squiffy looking at it.'

'Let's sit under the lamps at the Luncheonette sign.'

Augusto, ever the gentleman, laid his jacket under a pool of light from the neon signage and they sat on it like a picnic blanket. Opal enjoyed the warmth emanating off his chest as she leaned in to show him the puzzles.

'I need to compare these two documents,' she explained. 'The numbers from the cut scene mean something and the invitation is the instructions on how to understand it. The numbers I got from the scene are 3, 4, then a tap above the buckle. Then 1, 1, 8, and a tap left of the buckle. The wording on the invitation begins... *Dear Mr Huxley, Special friend. Come, join us on a journey through magic, your seat will be A6. Every detail was meticulously crafted. Nestled amidst the glitz and glamor of Hollywood, the premiere of* A Capitol Wife *awaits your presence. Embark with us as we unveil the cinematic marvel that is sure to captivate hearts. 1 night only, be among the first to witness the beauty of our latest creation...* It goes on and on like this!'

'It sounds like Walt Disney wrote it after one too many sherries,' commented Augusto, rubbing his dark-stubbled chin.

'It's claptrap! And all the other invitations were just to the point and brief. So, this has to be a code!' Opal said.

'Which scene was the one that was cut again?'

'It was the first scene... scene 1, remember the awkward belt buckle tapping scene?'

Opal blinked at the invitation rapidly. *Scene 1... scene 1... scene 1.*

'It seems like the vocabulary isn't important. The words were chosen for an alternate reason. Is it the *start* of each sentence? Jane used to use the acrostic method to learn her scripts! Perhaps, that's how she got a coded message to Mr Huxley?'

Opal highlighted the first letter of each sentence with her lipstick.

Special friend. Come, join us on a journey through magic, your seat will be A6. Every detail was meticulously crafted. Nestled amidst the glitz and glamor of Hollywood, the premiere of A Capitol Wife *awaits your presence. Embark with us as we unveil the cinematic marvel that is sure to captivate hearts. 1 night only, be among the first to witness the beauty of our latest creation...*

It spelled out...

'S C E N E 1... W A T C H... B E L T... B U C K L E... I ... W I L L... S I G N A L ... C O - O R D I N A T E S... F O R... B U R I E D...T R E A S U R E!'

'Co-ordinates?' Augusto said, brandishing the sketchbook. 'So the belt buckle taps are co-ordinates.'

'Yes! And what on earth is the *buried treasure?*' Opal shrieked, then resumed in a whisper. '3, 4, then a tap above the buckle. Then 1, 1, 8, and a tap right of the buckle.'

'If it's for buried treasure it must be map co-ordinates. 34 north, 118 west. Her right would be west.'

'Of course.' Opal nodded. 'But how will we find out where that is?'

'My California guidebook could tell us roughly.'

'Fantastic!'

'We'd better keep our voices down,' said Augusto, grabbing her hands. 'You never know who could be following me.'

Opal looked at Augusto's hands, and her eyes flashed.

'That's what Mr Huxley's grubby fingernail was doing,' Opal whispered. 'Writing down the co-ordinates using some pencil lead under his nail. He must have scribbled onto something on his lap – his programme, perhaps. It would look too suspicious to sit there with a pencil or pen. Graphite under the nail – classic spy behaviour. Mr Huxley is a studio spy and Jane was sending him the code.'

'What studio were they spying for?' Augusto said, keeping hold of her hands.

'I'm guessing Cox & Lumière Pictures, if Mr Huxley works for them. But he could be double-crossing Cox & Lumière Pictures for another studio even... who knows. I guess we might find out once we get to this *buried treasure*.'

'Fantastic, we will amass a fortune, dash to Monte Carlo before the taxman catches on and live out our days sketching together.'

Opal went slightly pink and pulled her hands back. 'Buried treasure could be a euphemism for something else. It may not carry much value to us personally. Just to the spies.'

'Whatever this treasure is, we have to go and investigate. It might unlock the evidence that will put me in the clear and avenge Jane.'

'We must act before they ask you in for that meeting. Do you know how to navigate with these kinds of co-ordinates? Daddy used to have special gridded maps...'

'I do. It's in the back of my wagon.'

'You have a wagon?'

'I hired a Ford.'

Opal followed Augusto into the Luncheonette parking lot. His vehicle was looking distinctly the worse for wear with a light film of dust and its once-proud fenders drooped slightly. He pulled up his sleeves, revealing his taut forearms, and dug around in the dark back seat. When he found *The California Guidebook* he had a quick thumb inside.

'It's somewhere in the Mojave Desert. But to find the specific spot we'd have to get a topographic map of the area.'

'Topographic maps, yes, with latitude and longitude markings.' Opal propped her chin in her hands and remembered her father using these. 'But where in blazes does one even begin to look for topographic maps around here? It's only really government agencies that would have those.'

'Perhaps we need a map to find the map?' Augusto smirked.

'Don't be daft. We must think,' Opal said as she tried to stop Napoleon from suffocating inside a bag of potato chips on the floor of the car.

After a brief tootle downtown, where nocturnal characters lurked in pursuits of things that Opal dared not guess, they stumbled upon a little *'mom and pop'* store that was still open. The proprietor, a leathery man with an entrepreneurial gleam, had tucked away a box of maps he'd been trying to flog for years. And among them, the very topographic specimen they needed.

Before their navigation of the Mojave Desert began, Opal had insisted to Augusto that she collect some provisions from her room at Palatial Pines. Binoculars, water flask, Cracker Jacks, Fig Newtons, Spratt's dog cake, the new sun protection fad everyone was on about – *zinc oxide cream* – and a wide-brimmed sunhat for daybreak.

On her way back down the corridor with her bag of bits, she almost jumped out of her skin. Bonfire had yanked open her door a fraction and her hair sprouted out. Tears were streaming down her freckled cheeks!

THIRTY-THREE
MOJAVE NAVIGATION

'Opal is that you?' Bonfire blubbered.

'Good heavens, you nearly made my hair fall out in fear.' Opal clasped her head. 'Yes, it's me. Are you alright?'

'What are you doing?' Bonfire sniffed, glancing down at the bag and large sunhat.

'Oh... I just have to take Napoleon for a walk and burn off his rampant energy. He's being utterly restless and tearing the stuffing out of my pillows. We need to do an extra-long walk into the sunrise so I thought I might need the extra-large hat,' Opal lied. 'But, Bonfire... have you been crying?'

'Yes. I found the money again. I fell asleep early and it wasn't there. When I awoke a few minutes ago, it was. All twelve dollars of it.'

'Do you need to stay in my room again?' Opal asked. 'I won't be back for quite a while so you can spreadeagle.'

'You're such a gal. Thank you, Opal.'

'I promise to help you find out who's been playing these tricks on you. But for now, I really must be off,' Opal said, and dropped her key into Bonfire's grateful palm.

'You took your sweet time,' Augusto smirked, when she joined him outside.

'I got unavoidably detained,' she replied, slinging the provisions into the back of the ride. Napoleon scrambled in after it. 'Toot-toot and tally-ho then!'

With an air of casual bravado, Augusto pointed the old Ford north-eastward, which was as much a leap of faith as it was a direction. They were both navigational novices, but with combined experiences they decided they could make a decent attempt.

There were still enough street lamps to see the map and compass. But they started to become scarcer as they zoomed into the scrubs. Around a bend, perched on a hillside, was a disreputable-looking bungalow. There was a curious hive of activity around it. Trilby hats moved in and out like ants at a picnic, and, very suspiciously, a faint reddish hue flickered through the cracks in the curtains. Red lamps?

'How peculiar,' commented Opal, pointing with one hand and holding her hat on with the other.

'Communists,' Augusto muttered darkly, as if the word were coated in something sticky and unpleasant.

As if on cue, a gust of wind whipped past, carrying with it a flurry of papers. One of them smacked against the windshield and clung there. Opal leaned forward and squinted. The headline read: *WORKERS OF THE WORLD, UNITE!* in red lettering. It then flapped and flew off as Augusto put his foot down and sped away from the revolutionaries and their nocturnal plotting.

'Watch it!' Opal yelped, clutching at the dashboard as the car narrowly missed a huge cactus. 'I nearly tossed the compass clean out of the car! And, just so you know, according to it and the map, the X spot in the desert isn't actually that far away. We could hit it within two hours.'

But even the best of maps couldn't best fatigue. Opal's

eyelids grew heavy, and Augusto, catching her yawn contagion, suggested, 'We'll make no sense of the desert in the dark, Opal. Best we camp out and press on at sunrise.'

'I daresay you're right. I was too keen to get there,' she said, her voice tinged with reluctance, though secretly she felt a giddiness she'd never admit to, reclining in a beat-up car in the company of her handsome pash.

The old Ford soon found itself nestled behind a boulder of a good concealing size, and Augusto gallantly covered Opal in his jacket across the back seat. He stayed in the front and propped his feet up on the dashboard.

'Would you like the rag top overhead?' he enquired, after a moment's silence.

'No, thank you. I've slept under the stars before with Papa. It was by the Sepik River... once you ignored the mosquitos it was just breathtaking, the Milky Way stretched in a ghostly ribbon across the heavens. And then once with the Girl Guides. The Suffolk night sky just looked like a grey old cardigan in comparison, but still peaceful. One rarely gets the opportunity and I rather like it.'

'So do I,' he replied and sighed into the sky.

It became awkwardly silent. Apart from the humming of crickets.

'What a cacophony! Loud little beasts, aren't they?' she muttered. 'You'd never hear such a din in the countryside in England. It's deathly silent in Suffolk.'

'It's like this where I come from,' he replied, and Opal could hear him strike a match and pull on one of his cigarillo's.

'And where exactly is *that*, Mr Augusto Sevilla?' she asked, and she twitched a smirk. She couldn't resist but tease him every now and again about people thinking he was Argentinian.

'Spain. You know this,' he said with a tone of voice that held none of its usual humour.

With this topic of conversation, Opal felt she was edging

close to a threshold she should not cross. It was exceedingly tempting to pull at the thread of his mysterious origins, but what might she find? And would it be the sort of revelation that would strengthen their friendship, or would it create a crack that could never be mended? It could also be a very valuable opportunity for Opal to let him explain on his *own* terms. It would signal to her that he truly wanted to be close. She would wait. She would be patient.

She looked up into the sky and then stifled a giggle. She rather fancied herself in that moment, reclining in a Ford Model A, her mother's aghast visage hovering in her imagination. Lady Laplume, who would have balked at the mere idea of camping, would have fainted on the spot had she known her daughter was traipsing across the Californian sands in a dilapidated motor, in the company of a man with a dubious nationality. She was glad that Napoleon could not tell tales.

She tucked her pup in beside her and her musings drifted off into the galaxy above. It shimmered hazily beneath the veil of Augusto's smoke, and she began counting the stars to sleep.

The next thing she knew, a warm beam of light had prised her eyelids open. The sun was stretching its fingers over the jagged horizon, casting the world in a soft, coral glow. Her watch said six. Her head had crumpled the map in her sleep. *Drats.* She sat up and flapped it out smooth. Napoleon's grumble was staunched by an involuntarily yawn.

Augusto stirred but he'd evidently been up for some time, waiting for her to awaken as he'd gotten through a whole pile of cigarillos. 'Good morning, *señorita*. We must get this show on the road.'

'Quite. We're sure nobody has followed us, aren't we?' Opal said, then inspected the vicinity with a swoop of her binoculars.

'I'm not sure of anything in Tinseltown. Wouldn't surprise me if Napoleon was a spy.'

'Oh, he *is* a spy. My personal one. He spies on you for me sometimes,' Opal said, patting the sleepy pile of fluff and taking a swig from the water flask.

'Oh dear, I'd better stop babysitting then. Don't want him to relay everything I say about how beautiful his mother is,' Augusto said, and stubbed a cigarillo out on the dashboard.

Opal almost spat out the water. He had never said anything of the sort to her before. She felt a flutter of joy prick her cheeks. She swallowed the gulp and rammed her sunhat on to conceal her blush. *Quick, change the subject.*

'Do you think we'll find this treasure?' she asked, manoeuvring herself into the passenger seat next to him and shaking out the map.

Augusto's reply was a grunt, not of discouragement, but of thoughtfulness, his gaze flicking from the map to the rising sun, and then to the endless stretch of sand and rock that sprawled before them.

'The desert has a way of hiding things. But we'll find it, *señorita*. We have the map, the compass, and your sharp eyes,' he said as they set off.

The desert was bathed in a mix of orange and pink hues from the rising sun. The distant hills, jagged and bold, were like sleeping dogs, watching over the barren expanse, while scattered bushes of sagebrush whispered in the breeze. The air was dry and hot, yet there was a crispness to it due to the vast distances between them and the nearest city.

'Now, where's true north? We must orient the map,' Opal said, holding up the compass, which spun uncertainly. 'Seems to have lost it's, er, northern inclination.'

'Here's what we'll do,' Augusto said, rolling up his sleeves to reveal his lovely forearms. 'We'll find north by keeping the sun to our right as it rises, which should be east. Then, we stride forward.'

'Jolly good plan. Though we'll have to go off the beaten track.'

'Of course, we're on an adventure, aren't we?'

'It seems our X on the grid has an L-shaped rock by it. We can keep a look out for this when we get close.'

Napoleon flopped his paws over the side and let his tongue flap in the breeze. He was getting a wonderful, fluffy blow-dry. They ebbed very close to 34N 118W now and a spattering of spiky trees started to appear.

'There it is! It must be the L-shaped rock!' Opal shouted, pointing upfront and bobbing up and down with excitement. The mound was khaki in colour and the morning sunlight exaggerated its shadows, tracing the unmistakable silhouette of an 'L' on the baked ground below. There was also a dark blob next to it, could it be some sort of vehicle?

Augusto reduced his speed and leaned his elbow out of the side of his car, straining to see what the blob was.

'Pass me the binoculars, Opal,' Augusto said in a parental tone.

'What... what is it?' Opal said, handing them over.

He stopped the car in a whirl of dust. He pressed the binoculars to his eyes and Opal waited for him to confirm what it was. But he didn't say anything. She only heard him take a deep gulp.

'*Well?* What are you looking at?!' she demanded.

Augusto didn't answer, got out and lumbered through the sand. Opal jittered her knee up and down nervously, then snatched the binoculars and put them up to her eyes. The field of view encircled a black Chevy. She moved a little further left to capture Augusto, who was standing with his hands in his hair with a look of distress at something below him. She moved the binoculars down a smidgeon. There, bashed into the rock... was a body.

THIRTY-FOUR

DOMINGO

Opal had to take a deep breath to stop her binoculars from shaking. The body was propped up on its knees, the torso and face leaning against the rock. The shirt was stained as if a black-cherry pie had been thrown at it but the red juice had congealed in the sun. The side of the face that was visible was sunburnt raw, but had a distinct dark dot above the brow. *Domingo!*

Opal gasped and the binoculars clattered into the interior of the car. Napoleon barked and leapt out onto the sand. He bounded towards Augusto as if he had detected trouble.

'Stop, boy!' Opal yelled and clambered out after him.

When she got close, Augusto snapped out of his glassy glare and put his hands up as if to implore her to stay back.

'Opal... don't come near! I don't want you to see this!'

'It's alright! It's alright, Augusto,' Opal panted. 'I've seen, I've seen.'

He took out a hanky and mopped his damp brow. He then pulled at his collar like he did when he was in distress in Emmett Zimberg's office. Napoleon inspected the Chevy with his nose but when he came to Domingo's feet he sat back and whimpered, realising what it was. His fur started to quiver.

'I... I guess we've discovered the whereabouts of Domingo finally,' Opal said quietly. 'Come, let's stand under the shade of the tree for a moment.'

Augusto joined her under the shade and put his arm around her shoulders, pulling her close. Another casualty of this beastly town, no doubt, lured here by dreams of becoming some grand editor or photographer, only to be puppet-mastered by a bunch of villains who used him as a stepping stone to scramble up the greasy pole. He was one of the rare artists she'd met who actually wanted to capture reality, and now his talent was all but squandered. *Just you wait, Hollywoodland, justice is coming for poor Jane and Domingo, ruined by your monstrous industry!*

'What do we do now?' Augusto said in a childlike tone, his breath on her temple.

'Well...' she said. 'It would not be silly to deduce that his death, or murder, was something to do with the X on the map. The buried treasure. If we found it, if it's still here that is, then it could help inform us what happened. Let's focus on that for the moment.'

'What about the body?' Augusto whispered, even though nobody else was around.

'Well, we must report it,' Opal whispered back.

'What if they think *we* did it?' Augusto said, pulling at his collar again.

'The evidence does not lead to us, does it. Look,' Opal said, pointing at the ground behind Domingo's feet. 'The track marks. He's clearly been bashed into the rock by a vehicle which has sped away over there.'

She pointed to the killer's track marks that lead far away to a boulder in the distance. She then glanced at the black Chevy parked near the body.

'I'm assuming this is Domingo's Chevy that he used to get here. And the front is untarnished – he wasn't bashed with it. Our car is also unmarked. And our tracks stop where we have left it far back there.'

'Yes, you're right. But I don't feel good about this.'

'And why would we alert the police to something that *we* did? That would surely show our innocence,' Opal said in a soothing tone.

'To avert suspicion?' Augusto said and put his hand onto the tree trunk as if to ground himself.

'Calm down, Augusto. Don't worry so!' Opal said, placing a gentle hand on his arm.

'They're going to pin this on *me*. They're trying to get me, aren't they... Mr Zimberg and that Detective Kensington. How on earth are we going to tell them why we are here?'

'Take a *deep* breath. We will simply have to tell them the truth. Or only the necessary truth. Drink some water and I will have a look around in a moment.'

'We were supposed to just dig up the treasure or whatever it was, as proof that Jane and Mr Huxley were working together as spies, try to spin the narrative on her death. But now there's another body here... I do not want to be involved in that.'

'Water... drink,' Opal said.

Opal didn't really know why she was the calm one. It was as if she had adopted the role because one of them had to. Two flailing wrecks in the wilderness would not be able to survive. This was also the third dead body she'd seen in her life, having been witness to her cousin Clementina's death. This had hardened her somewhat.

'Besides...' she said, splashing some liquid into the cup for her dog and then passing the flask to Augusto. 'We don't need to go to Detective Kensington. He is a *private* detective. We can alert the nearest County Sheriff's office. They don't – or shouldn't – have any ties to Platinum Signet Productions.'

'What's that at Domingo's knees?' said Augusto, pointing.

Opal glanced over and blinked multiple times. '*Oh yes*, there's some papers. Let me go and look.'

THIRTY-FIVE

SEEDS OF SUSPICION

'No,' said Augusto. 'I'll go and get them.'

The man seemed to have pulled his socks up somewhat after the water. He squared his shoulders and marched over to Domingo. After a moment bracing himself, he bent down and retrieved a handful of crumpled documents from under Domingo's knees. Domingo must have been holding them before the vehicle hit him.

'They're scripts,' Augusto said, shuffling through them.

'What scripts?'

'Platinum Signet Productions confidential script proofs. For something they're planning to shoot next year. With a list of investors, it looks like.'

'I wonder what he had those for. He's not a scriptwriter,' said Opal, pinching her chin. 'I'll check his car.'

She leaned over into his vehicle, holding her hat on with one hand. Scattered on the seats were various compasses, a diary and topographic map similar to theirs. Under the seats were metal jerry cans of water and fuel.

'Where's his camera?' asked Opal. 'He always had it around his neck.'

'It's not around his neck now.'

'It's not in his car either... but there is a shovel!' Opal said, lifting it off the back seat. The steel-pointed blade glinted in the sunlight.

'Well, that is convenient! We forgot to bring one.'

'I'm incredulous at how dense I've been,' Opal said with a sigh. 'We risked our necks coming out here to dig up treasure and brought oat biscuits and not a shovel.'

He handed Opal the documents and slung the shovel over his shoulders. He hung his hands over the top of the bar in a roguish, chain-gang kind of style.

'Poor Domingo, he did not deserve to go like this. I wonder how long it would have been before anyone found him?' said Opal, glancing over at the body.

'It is truly horrid. God rest his soul... *que descanse en paz*,' Augusto muttered, then looked up at Opal. 'Do you think Domingo had dug the treasure up already and it was stolen by the killer?'

'Well,' said Opal, wiping some tears so she could inspect the shovel tip. 'The shovel doesn't have any sand on it.'

'It does look clean and unused,' Augusto agreed.

'It's baffling why he had scripts in his hands. He could have been on the same trail as us and *about* to dig up the treasure when he was driven into, to prevent him, perhaps. But *why* confidential scripts?'

'Was he secretly practising lines out here where nobody could hear him?' Augusto said wryly. 'I don't mean to joke. I'm just so terribly nervous.'

Opal did not acknowledge the flat tyre of a joke as she was thinking deeply, blinking at the scripts. 'These confidential scripts and lists of investors are pretty valuable. Any other studio would love to get this kind of competitive, inside information. What if *the scripts* were the treasure?'

'But as you said, the shovel is clean. He hadn't dug yet.' Augusto frowned.

'What if he was *about* to bury the "treasure", i.e. *the scripts*, and got killed before he could?'

'But the invitation said the treasure was *already there*.'

'True. But what if it's a recurrent spy drop? Where confidential documents are often dropped off by Domingo? Jane and Domingo from Platinum Signet Productions worked together to get documents to Mr Huxley at Cox & Lumière Pictures?'

'Well, if we can actually *find* this dig and there's other things in the hole, then I guess you'd be right.' Augusto smiled.

'Indeed. The 38N 118W mark seems to end this side of the rock. A little further up from the body. But could be anywhere in this ten-yard square.'

They both blankly scanned the ground that looked like a giant cracked biscuit, the chocolate chips were pebbles, Joshua tree seeds and little shards of rock. Opal didn't know where to start.

'I can't believe we're here, in the middle of God knows where, after seeing Jane play her belt buckle like it was a xylophone.' Augusto shook his head incredulously. 'What has my life become after meeting the Honourable Opal Laplume?'

'It's a madcap farce, my life,' Opal had to concede. 'But remember the end bit. Jane put her hand under her belt buckle and then tapped her ring.'

'Was that part of the code or just a *fidget*?'

'I don't know... but she had to have given the spies a more specific clue of exactly where to dig,' Opal said as she stared at Napoleon.

The poodle was sniffing where a lizard had disappeared under the rock. His lollipop tail started to twirl in intrigue.

'That's it!' she shrieked. 'Under the rock!'

'What?'

'Jane's final gestures were under the belt and pointing to the rock of her ring. It meant, *under the rock.*'

'*Cielos!* Talk about pulling a white rabbit out of a hat. How do you come up with all this?'

'It's quite simple when you think about it.' Opal flicked a Joshua tree seed off her wrist. 'Now, let's see. The rock juts into 38N 118W point around here.'

'It does look disturbed there,' agreed Augusto. 'Though it may have been an animal.'

'Get digging, I say!' Opal said.

Crunch. Augusto speared the tip into the crumbling yellow surface and started shovelling away like a burly track-layer. Napoleon, not to be outdone, took to the task with his paws in the same spot. His little digits dug rapidly as if he was in a marathon.

'Careful, Napoleon!' shouted Augusto as his paws got in the way of the sharp shovel. 'Opal, why don't you read the scripts under the tree while I dig?'

'I say, what a gent,' Opal replied, with a warm smile.

As she walked to the tree, she noticed that the killer's vehicle track marks led under the tree and away. They seemed to halt, back up a bit then charge forth into Domingo. *Poor chap,* Opal thought, and let out a sad sigh, gazing up into the tree.

The Joshua tree had thick, forked trunks jutting upwards with balls of spiky greenery on the ends. Like a cactus and a walnut tree had been bred together. There was a little thing hopping around inside, round like a robin, except its defining feature was not a red stomach but a yellow cap. His tiny beak, sharp and efficient, was forever pecking at seed pods, and turning his head sharply as though making a mental note of every available morsel in the tree.

I must remember to tell Father about him, Opal thought, as she knew he was intrigued by how desert birds survive. The bird swooped to the ground, pecked a juicy black Joshua seed off the ground, then with a flick of its wings, the bird ascended into the tree and, as though following some well-practised routine, performed its necessary duties. The droppings fell to a spot on the ground.

Opal crouched down and her eyes flickered with recollection. She had seen these kinds of droppings before... grey with black Joshua seed fragments. Was it on the red Lincoln car of George's that Burton had driven her in? Opal dabbed her brow with a glove, her thoughts homing in on George DeLuca and Betty. Their motives for desiring Jane's demise were the same. Both harboured ambitions for Betty to star in *Midnight at St Claire's*. George, the sly old hound, had doused Jane's mantilla shawl in Silver Spur whisky, ensuring Emmett Zimberg would catch a whiff. Meanwhile, Betty had been rehearsing the *Midnight at St Claire's* numbers with suspicious zeal well before Jane's final curtain call. But who, Opal mused, had they enlisted to pull off the delicate business of switching the bullets? And what, pray, was George's sudden urge to mow down Domingo all about? Could Domingo have stumbled upon their dastardly scheme and had to be silenced? Or was it unconnected?

Napoleon barked thrice. It was a bark of self-congratulation. Opal scrambled to her feet, dusted the sand off her knees and dashed over. The dog had uncovered the metal lid of a box.

'Good boy!'

Napoleon sat proudly as if he'd won first prize at the Greater Los Angeles Digging Cup, his tail making a semicircle in the sand as he wagged. Augusto loosened the sand around it with his shovel, and heaved it out.

THIRTY-SIX

THE PAPERCHASE

It had a simple latch and was not locked. Opal clicked it open and held her breath as she lifted the lid. Gleaming, bright white in the sun was a stack of paperwork. A big red CONFIDEN-TIAL stamped across the first page.

'It's more confidential scripts for Platinum Signet Productions!' she said.

Augusto's shoulders slumped downwards, crestfallen.

'Oh, come on... you didn't think it would be actual *treasure,* did you?' mocked Opal.

'Why not? That's what it said in the invitation cipher.'

'Well, *treasure* was clearly a code. Even codes have to be deniable. If someone cracks it and accuses the spy, they can deny the code, saying there was no treasure, because there isn't. That's the whole point. Spy codes have to *imply* and also be *deniable* at the same time.'

'Do we keep all this and take it back with us?' Augusto flapped the documents in the air.

'Well, it would be useful for leverage,' she said, stowing them away in her bag. 'I could possibly exchange them with Mr

Huxley for some information. We will leave the box here. To prove it was a dead drop.'

'Mr Huxley could be dangerous, Opal. He'd also know this location, wouldn't he? If it was for him. Do you think he's the killer?'

'Could well be,' said Opal, but her suspicions had been veering towards George since seeing those bird droppings.

'What are we going to tell the police? *And* Emmett Zimberg, when he comes to hear of it,' Augusto asked.

Opal walked around the tree for a moment and scraped her gloved fingers on the bark as she mused. When she came to a conclusion, she placed her feet together and clasped her hands in front like a Girl Guide. 'We shall send an anonymous tip-off to the police. Say we are a couple of travellers who found the body and Chevy at 38N 118W by the L-shaped rock and that we couldn't stop.'

'What if they can't identify him? He's on the missing-persons list in Hollywood but perhaps not out here?'

'There was a diary with his name on in the car. If they've got a few grey cells working in the old noodle they'll be able to work out who he is.'

'Anything interesting in the diary?' Augusto said and started towards the Chevy.

'Wait, I'd better pick it up as I've got gloves on. That's a point, you better get your prints off that shovel.'

'How do I do that?'

'The handle's metal so would be less porous than wood. Just rub a bit of sand and water on it and wipe with your shirt,' Opal said and plucked the diary off the car seat.

'Nothing particularly interesting. It seems to be his editing hours and a visit to "*Abuela*" in New Mexico.'

'*Abuela* is grandmother.'

'Gosh. The poor granny must be out of her mind since he's

been missing,' she said as she flipped through the pages. 'There's not much in here.' She tossed it back onto the seat.

'Shall we get out of here? I'm starting to feel queasy,' said Augusto.

They walked away from the scene. Opal didn't look back at Domingo, she couldn't bear it.

'Won't the sheriff see our footsteps?' said Augusto.

'Yes, they will, but it doesn't matter, we are the anonymous tippers and we would quite logically have footprints,' she replied. 'Let's inspect what direction the killer's car zoomed off to.'

The culprit's tyre marks lead to a boulder big enough for it to hide behind, and then disappeared south-westward, a similar direction that Augusto's Ford had come from – Hollywood. The Chevy's track marks seemed to blend in the same course. Opal conjectured that Domingo was headed to the spy drop to put the documents in the hole for Mr Huxley to collect later. Someone followed Domingo out here, waited behind the boulder, ran into Domingo when he got out of the car and then sped off.

Opal was so cut up about Domingo she couldn't bear to eat any of the vittles she'd brought. A bag of Cracker Jacks, a box of Fig Newtons, little cakes with a fig filling, and hard candies wrapped in crinkly wax paper didn't manage to tempt her one bit.

She could do with some energy from the sugary lemonade though. From the bottle she slugged back a huge gulp. It gave off the crisp, tart perfume of lemons and summer. It wasn't cold but it was rejuvenating.

She and Augusto pulled the rag top up so that Napoleon could rest in the shade inside. He panted happily, still glowing from his digging triumph, paws twinkling with golden sand.

'So...' Augusto panted, riffling through his California guidebook. 'The nearest County Sheriff's office is Inyo, but there's a sheriff's outpost at Bishop.'

'Great, we shall find a postbox at Bishop, hopefully. I'll drop a note off with my hat covering my face in case one of the small-towners has their eyes peeled and makes a connection.'

Opal made a makeshift envelope from folded sketchbook paper and wrote a note to go inside. She gulped, her throat hot and dry. Her hand steered the pen seemingly with a will of its own. Under normal conditions, she'd have dashed off to report this matter without a second thought. But it wouldn't bring Domingo back. She glanced at Augusto, who, mopping his brow in a distinctly guilty manner, returned her look with equal discomfort. But they had no choice. It only spurred Opal on, a fresh resolve to find out who did this awful thing!

The musical number playing out in front of the cameras made Opal's head spin faster than a well-shaken snow globe. Betty, in a beautician's smock trimmed with rhinestones, stood atop a golden manicure table. Around her loomed giant nail-polish bottles, their tips tilted to send streams of gleaming red silk-like nail-polish waterfalls. Dancers, acting as polish drops, dressed head to toe in crimson, slid gracefully along the flowing streams, landing atop an enormous fingernail prop. There, with one final swoop, they sprawled artfully to 'paint' the nail in synchronised perfection. Betty launched into a spirited refrain of 'You can play it safe with a French manicure, but it's red or dead – I'm passion, for sure!'

At any other time, Opal would have been enthralled watching this lacquered fantasia. But she knew Augusto had had his meeting with Emmett Zimberg and Detective Kensington the evening before and she'd still not heard from him. She wasn't a nail-biter, but she'd removed a glove and was nibbling. She hadn't done that since she was at school worrying that she would be last picked for lacrosse.

'Cut!!!' blared out from George DeLuca's megaphone and

everyone onstage relaxed like jelly. He then started yapping to the choreographer about some of the dancer's knees bending in exact unison.

Opal was distracted by a ruckus happening over by the smoke and fog crew. Three men, collars askew, were huddled around their wheezing contraption at the edge of the set, whispering hoarsely over a crumpled copy of the *Los Angeles Evening Herald-Express*.

'Didn't I tell ya he'd taken a one-way trip to the pearly gates!' said one.

Opal darted over, ignored their lechy comments about her appearance, and politely asked if she could see whatever they were gawking over. On the front page was a portrait of a smiling Domingo, his countenance that of an ambitious and self-assured film editor. And the text below made Opal's blood run cold;

BLOOD ON THE SAND: DOMINGO'S HOLLYWOOD DEMISE

Domingo Lara, 34, film editor, was found dead in the Mojave wilderness on Friday. A suspected hit-and-run. An anonymous drop at Bishop town's post office alerted the Inyo County Sheriff. A local remembers an unfamiliar vehicle swerve by and remembered its registration number. It was when the Inyo Sheriff gave Domingo's employer, Emmett Zimberg, the registration number they connected it to a man who worked in the Platinum Signet Productions precinct. The owner of the car is suspected of trying to avert suspicion by alerting the sheriff anonymously. The name of this man is still unknown to the press.

Augusto! The reg plate! Oh heavens! Opal thought, and burst into tears, burying her face in the paper, making the pages damp.

'I know, I know, we all hoped he was alive out there,' said a sweet female voice, and a warm hand was placed on her shoulder.

Opal peeled her face out of the pages. It was Bonfire, her freckly nose screwed up in anguish, she obviously thought Opal was crying about Domingo. *A good excuse to let rip and wail*, Opal thought. She was also sad about the film editor but she already knew he was dead. To know Augusto was in danger because of her stupid gallant ideas felt horrendous.

'Oh, Bonfire.' Opal sobbed and hugged her friend tight, the ginger frizz a safe cloud to bury herself in. It was a safe place in a land of ladders, not friendships. Everyone had some unshakeable belief about how life is only worth living if one reaches the top, even if that meant using someone as a rung. But Opal did not feel used by Bonfire. A familiar demanding voice spoke behind them. 'Aren't you girls paying attention? One of those cack-handed dancers knocked a rhinestone off my lapel.' It was Betty, of course.

Opal straightened herself up and plucked a needle out of her sewing pinny.

'What's your problem?' Betty said, arms folded, grimacing at Opal's watery face.

'Augu— I mean Domingo!' Opal said and staunched a sob with her fist.

'What? Have they found that celluloid sap?' demanded Betty. Bonfire handed Betty the newspaper and she snatched it. 'Well, well, well. Murder in Mojave.'

'How do you know it was a murder and not an accident?' asked one of the fog-machine handlers, quite innocently, but Betty seemed to take it as an accusation. Opal was wondering the exact same thing.

'Shut your trap, you varmint. This is Hollywood. Everyone's out for blood. Running into a rock off-piste? That's no simple driving error.'

Opal continued to sniff and shakily attempted to sew

Betty's rhinestone back on. She was reluctant to help this woman who could have potentially gotten Augusto wound up in her evil schemes.

'Opal, go and get some water. I'll fix this,' said Bonfire, taking the needle off her.

'Thank you,' Opal spluttered.

She dashed off out of the fire exit, heels echoing in the vast construction. The afternoon sun blinded her and she bent her arms around her head as a barrier as she stumbled to the administration building.

Why, why, why did I convince Augusto we should leave an anonymous letter to the sheriff... how could I have been so stupid!

When Opal alighted at Emmett Zimberg's secretary's desk, she dabbed her face with a hanky and tried to compose herself.

'Pray. Where are Augusto Sevilla and Emmett Zimberg, please?'

'They're not here,' the secretary replied, absorbed in stamping 'Platinum Signet Productions' onto a stack of letters.

'Where are they...?' Opal said, clasping her hands together in a pleading but restrained fashion.

'Never you mind,' the secretary said, pausing with the stamp mid-air.

'Please!' Opal begged, raising her hands into a praying position.

The secretary stamped loudly, sighed and said, 'They've gone in a van to the downtown LA police station. Please don't ask anymore. If you don't go back on set, I'll report you.'

Opal felt awash with sickness. She dashed back outside and headed for Studio Services; she needed to cuddle her dog. Her mind pedalled fast, trying to conjure up a solution. Who can help me? Mr Huxley? Tell him the truth? That I followed his spy instructions? No, I couldn't possibly, it's too dangerous and we don't know what it really all means. Would Peridot help? She had power but who did she really work for? Could Carey assist? No, he could also be a potential killer. Opal sifted through her entire mind's contact book, nobody being a trust-worthy candidate to turn to.

'My dog. The little black poodle, please,' she implored at the Studio Services door.

When Napoleon was finally in her arms she sat up against the wall and sobbed into his fur. He smelt of sweet baby powder. He smelt of home because home was wherever this fleecy angel was. She would come up for a gasp of air and then go back down into it like a dark cloud that made her disappear. She knew she would look like a lunatic but she couldn't help it.

'Opal Laplume?' a young man's voice said. It was Burton, his big ears looking droopy in concern. 'What's the matter?'

'Domingo was found dead and they're trying to blame Augusto,' Opal said bitterly. 'But he's innocent.'

Burton slid his back down the wall into a crouch and put his arm around her.

'Hey, if Augusto's innocent, they will find out. They haven't proven anything, have they?'

'No! But... but they can turn any tale into reality in Holly-wood. It's all make-believe. Oh, Burton, you are such a dear. Thank you for being so kind to me since I arrived. I would have been dreadfully lonely without having you to talk to.'

'You ain't so bad yourself. You've helped my English no end!'

'You aren't... ARRRn't,' Opal corrected him, cheering up for a split second.

'Hey,' said a Studio Services clerk who had poked his head out of the hatch above them. 'Sorry to interrupt. But you know there's an audition for a black poodle at Cox & Lumière Pictures tomorrow... Here, take this flyer...'

Opal pinched the flyer that he hung down over her head.

It was a delightful illustration of a sooty little poodle just like Napoleon, a studio address at Cox & Lumière Pictures and the time, nine a.m. She fluttered her lashes in contemplation at her pet, a moment's distraction from her grief. Napoleon looked up at her naively with his round eyes, and deciding she was happy again, wriggled out of her arms. He then proceeded to chase his own pom-pom tail, and bash his head on a trash can in the process.

Would her mutt be obedient on a film set? Probably not... but it could be her only chance to get inside the Cox & Lumière studios. Then she could try and find out what Mr Huxley's dealings with the spy drop were...

THIRTY-EIGHT
BLACK POODLE AUDITION

Opal, Burton and a freshly clipped Napoleon strutted proudly through the Cox & Lumière studios. Burton had insisted he come along. Opal had previously given him his cash back and he said it was the least he could do after Opal had helped him. She was grateful for the company since receiving the bad news of both her father and Augusto. But Opal suspected Burton had really come for the spectacle and opportunity to step foot in a foreign studio. He swaggered in an adolescently giddy manner, catching his big ears on his flat cap as he tilted it to Cox & Lumière actresses.

'I feel like we're on enemy soil,' he said as they passed under a grand stone arch carved with *Cox & Lumière*.

Opal felt every step she was taking was fuelled by the drive to get Augusto out of the firing line and to get justice for Jane and Domingo. An invisible thread attached to her nose, pulling her and tweaking her head at every possible thing that may lead her to her next conquest... Mr Huxley. He *had* to be able to help her. Napoleon too was keen, but for other reasons...

'Napoleon obviously thinks we're at the Crufts final.' Opal couldn't help but smile a little. Her pup always lifting her spirits. He was almost skipping in pomposity. He seemed to know he had an important appointment.

'What's Crufts?' Burton asked.

'Crufts is a competition where British dogs parade their pedigrees, while their owner's subtly do the same, just with fewer wags and more tweed.'

But upon arriving at their designated audition studio, Opal scuffled to a halt. She felt Napoleon's lead stiffen as he too froze, completely catatonic, staring straight ahead at the endless line of black poodles. He'd never seen so many dogs in his life, let alone *all* poodles and *all* black ones to boot. Forty or more of them, each with a cut, style, or fluff that practically screamed, '*I was born to be famous!*'

Opal, who loved poodles with a passion that bordered on the romantic, was entranced. Napoleon was the absolute epitome of poodle perfection but there were some real contenders here. Her gaze landed on the tiny, teacup-sized poodle perched precariously in the hand of its owner like a fluffy owl. The sight of it gave Opal a sudden, irrational urge to scoop it up and hide it in her handbag. But she resisted, of course.

'Wow,' Burton said. 'I don't know where one poodle starts and another ends.'

'Come on, boy.' Opal tugged the lead gently to encourage her pup. 'Now's your time to shine.'

He didn't budge. He simply looked up at her with bulging eyes as if to say, 'What parallel universe have we crossed over to?'

She picked him up and whispered in his ear, 'Right, boy. We've got to get through this audition. Because if you get the role, we will be invited inside the Cox & Lumière offices to sign a contract, I'm sure. From there I'll be able to sniff out Mr Huxley. We need to do this for Augusto, Jane and Domingo. Okay, boy?'

Opal then carried him into the queue and shifted from foot to foot like an impatient mother at the chemist with her baby bundle.

'I detest auditions,' she whispered to Burton. 'They remind me of the literary pageant try-outs at school. I auditioned for *Sir Gawain and the Green Knight*, and, naturally, I thought I'd make a memorable entrance... chainmail, dramatic cloak and, of course, feathers in my helmet for flair. The girls immediately started jeering the moniker they'd given me 'Carnival Float', because I looked more like a procession than a knight. The moment I spoke, my helmet fell over my eyes, and I ended up reciting the whole speech to a stack of books because I couldn't see the adjudicator.'

'Oh, I hear ya.' Burton shook his head in sympathy. 'I once entered a creative writing contest in school. Poured my heart into a story about a conman who accidently cons himself. Thought it was bestseller material. But they gave first prize to some fella who wrote a heartfelt poem on "the quiet dignity of a seashell". A seashell, Opal! I tell ya!'

'Well, at least it's not us that has to audition. It's Napoleon the great!' she said in a chirpy tone and bounced Napoleon in her arms to try and animate him.

'Come on, Napoleon, why don'tcha try to make pals with the other pooches? You're all the same breed, you should be best friends!' said Burton, bending and almost touching his nose with Napoleon's.

'Yes, Napoleon dear. You know what I always say... meet as many people in this life as you can. It will open up worlds you never knew existed and break presumptions of what personality traits could co-exist in one person. Who knows, you might even meet a girlfriend.'

Napoleon didn't even blink, a frozen ornament.

Opal eyed the competition in front up and down. There was a large, lion-cut poodle with its mane billowing around its head. The owner spoke to it as if it were the next Garbo or Gable of the canine world. She was a very beautiful woman with cupid's bow lips and luscious blonde curls swept above her head. She was sucking on a very long cigarette holder. Seeming to appreciate the sight of young Burton, with a sweep of her blue lids, she pulled her cigarette case out and offered him one.

'No, thanks. I don't smoke,' he said, shaking his head.

She took this as a rebuff. The cigarette case with a black poodle hand-painted on it snapped shut in his face and she turned back around.

Opal, like Napoleon, now froze too. *Burton didn't smoke? Did he not tell her that Jane had chastised him for the behaviour?* Opal eyed Burton up and down, tilted her head and asked, 'Burton... how often do you drive George DeLuca's car?'

'Not often.' He shrugged.

'What about the day Domingo went missing?' Opal asked.

'No, I was at Santa Monica Beach, writing, but I took the train,' he replied. 'I wish I could drive it more, it is a beautiful motor.'

Opal parted her lips to interrogate him further about George's automobile, but an infernal yapping started behind her, a bit like a squeezy sink plunger. She turned and another poodle auditionee had joined the queue. Well... it wasn't a poodle at all. It was a black terrier, who had had the clippers transform him into a Continental Cut Pageant Queen. He didn't have Napoleon's charming pom-pom tail though. It's owner, a lady in pink mules and eyebags that suggested she'd had too many highballs last night, was determined to convince anyone who would listen that her 'poodle' was going to knock the competition out of the Cox & Lumière park.

'My poodle Perdita's been in no less than three major dog food ads,' the lady boasted loudly. 'Once appeared on Broadway, too. Did a stint as a chorus dog in *Ziegler's Dogs!*'

'We asked for a black poodle, not a brunette *yeti*,' muttered a hawkish-looking adjudicator at the doorway, waving one particularly shaggy dog away, before tossing a dismissive glance to the next in line. 'And that one's too *old*.'

Opal winced. If she thought auditions for actresses were brutal, this was something altogether different. Unbelievably cut-throat. Was this how they treated the poor creatures? A dog's age could be so easily mistaken! She wanted to protest, but then remembered it was a competitor.

'No puppies,' the adjudicator snapped at the next, inspecting a small poodle who hadn't grown into its floppy ears yet.

Opal held her breath when it came for Napoleon's turn.

'Fine,' the adjudicator grunted.

Opal thanked her, said farewell to Burton who was heading back to work as she didn't know how long she would be, and waltzed in with Napoleon under her arm like a prize lamb. But then frowned. *Fine?* she thought. Napoleon is far better than *fine!*

Inside was a dance studio that hummed a little bit of doggy but that was to be expected. The dozen or so dogs who'd made it through the entrance stood in a line, their coats in varying arrangements of ruffles, with owners nervously clutching leashes and looking over their shoulders at one another. The atmosphere was thick with a mix of anxiety and expectation, every dog poised as if it might just be one tail wag away from greatness.

The director, a toothy fellow with a polka-dot bow tie and an air of unfounded confidence, handed out a silly bird toy tied to a string to each of the owners.

'Now stand two metres in front of your poodle. On command,' he declared, 'your dog must walk over, look at the toy, and play with it.'

There was a collective murmur of understanding. Opal, took the toy, stood in front of Napoleon and smiled, trying to coax him out of his catatonic stupor. He still looked positively stuffed.

The director turned to face them, gave a theatrical flourish, and shouted, 'And go!'

The dogs leaped into action like well-oiled machines. They batted the dangling toy with paws, nipped at it with sharp teeth, and pranced with delightful enthusiasm. They were picture-perfect, obedient, agile, playful, all except for two; the terrier Perdita, obviously more of an indoors girl, yawned and slumped sideways. And Napoleon, still frozen, his tiny eyes wide and round as if to say, 'Have I multiplied? Or am I looking through a kaleidoscope?'

'Feathers, boy... look! Feathers!' Opal whispered urgently, hoping that the mention of the feathers would somehow snap him out of it. But her heart sank, he wasn't going to budge.

'And you... and you!' The director pointed at Napoleon and the terrier.

Opal sighed and prepared to be booted out.

'You've passed the test!'

'What?' Opal said, utterly flabbergasted. 'But he didn't do as you asked?'

'That's EXACTLY what we were looking for. There will be many birds on set as we will be shooting jungle scenes. We need a poodle that can resist the distraction of them.'

Both Napoleon and Opal tilted their heads in confusion. *How utterly batty.*

'Everyone else, *au revoir*!' the director added dismissively. 'Take your fluffy keisters out of here!'

The final test, to Opal's amusement and dread, was... limbo. According to the director the movie was to be called *Hare-brained in Havana* and there would be a limbo party scene. A couple of assistants set up two low poles. One slightly lower for the tiny Napoleon.

The terrier was coaxed under it with a piece of jerky from the owner's handbag.

'Very impressive!' the director exclaimed.

When it was Napoleon's turn, he became even more stiff; like taxidermy.

'Come on, boy. You can do it... please?' She tried, then turned to the terrier's owner. 'May I please borrow some jerky?'

'No,' was the simple answer from Perdita's owner, who crossed her pink mules and arms stubbornly.

The director, realising that no amount of pleading would move Napoleon, concluded, 'Well that settles it... the role goes to poodle... Perdita!'

Oh, blithering fig! I was so darned close. My only chance of getting inside Cox & Lumière studios taken by a blasted poodle imposter. However am I going to get anywhere with this case and free Augusto?

THIRTY-NINE

A CHOCOLATE ECLAIR AND A PRAYER

An assistant cleared her throat, tapped the director on the shoulder, and said in a barely audible voice, 'I regret to inform you, sir, but Perdita the poodle is actually a black *terrier* with a... haircut.'

The director raised an eyebrow, gave the terrier a second glance. 'Yes, yes, I suppose that is a valid point. Okay well... the preferred candidate for the role of the *poodle* goes to... NAPOLEON... *THE POODLE!*'

The director and the assistants clapped merrily towards Napoleon. Napoleon was about as animated as a teddy. But Opal bounced on her heels like an athlete ready to race into the studios, find Mr Huxley and get every morsel of information on Domingo and their dealings together she possibly could. It could be dangerous but not as dangerous as leaving Augusto in the jaws of prison.

'But it's like a stuffed toy, it doesn't *move!*' Perdita's furious owner said.

'Because you weren't generous with the jerky,' the director scolded her. 'When we don't play fair, it bites us in the keister.'

Perdita's owner huffed and spun on her heel, and tugged her terrier out of the audition.

'Well, I say. I did not foresee this result. But we are thrilled. And, yes, indeed, Napoleon will move for food, don't you worry,' reassured Opal.

'He's got the right look and that's all that matters here in Hollywood when it comes down to it. Now over to the executive office and we'll sort out a contract.'

Opal, with pet in arms, was whisked down a shiny hallway. Sunlight streamed through rectangular-paned windows, painting the linoleum floor in cheerful stripes. The energy of the place had a distinctly more relaxed culture to Platinum Signet Productions. People were whistling and smiling and walking at a normal pace. At Platinum Signet Productions Opal was used to everyone walking as if on hot coals, always hours behind where they should be with their projects.

Opal kept her eyes peeled for which department she might find Mr Huxley's office. The 'Production' corridor looked promising. But she was jettisoned off in the other direction to 'Animal Handling'.

Napoleon was balanced on a set of weighing scales and photographed from all angles, measured and dentally inspected. He started to slowly be himself again now that he wasn't surrounded by clones of superior size.

'Gosh... quite the little Betty Caruso, isn't he?'

'She wishes,' Opal found herself saying, the sheer anger towards that woman for getting Augusto in trouble was just overwhelming. 'Do you mind if I leave you to it for a moment?'

Opal could sense that Napoleon would be alright and that the trainer was gentle and wanting to get to know him. Napoleon would probably not even realise she'd gone since his eyes were riveted on the treats that were being handed to him from every direction.

'Sure, we'll probably need him till about four. Just need to play a few games with him to see how he moves in front of the camera.'

'Alright,' said Opal. 'I won't be long.'

She ambled down the 'Production' corridor, getting friendly nods from young male producers chewing pens. Sure enough, Mr Huxley's office was near the end.

She knocked.

'If I get one more knock, I'm going to take that pen and write varmint over your forehead,' a ruffled-sounding Mr Huxley said from beyond the door.

'It's the Honourable Opal Laplume.'

'Oh... Miss Laplume. I'm sorry I thought it was one of those bothersome young men.'

The door was opened by the man that Opal recognised as Mr Huxley's driver.

Mr Huxley smiled at her, his feet up on his desk, a napkin round his neck and an oval platter of pastries beside him. 'Do forgive me, grab a pastry. I don't have long to chat, mind.'

Opal sat down and leaned forward to inspect the golden goodies. Her nostrils couldn't help but flare as they caught scent of the butter, vanilla and icing sugar humming around the silver platter. There were flaky croissants, eclairs gleaming under a rich chocolate glaze and cream puffs dusted with powdered sugar like pillows.

She popped the end of an eclair in her mouth and bit down with her front teeth, careful not to ruin her lipstick. Its crisp exterior gave way to a smooth vanilla custard that was cooling to the tongue, followed by a velvety embrace of chocolate sauce.

'To what do I owe the pleasure?' asked Mr Huxley, licking icing sugar off his thumb.

Opal put the eclair down, swallowed hard, looked Mr Huxley in the eyes and said, '34 north, 118 west.'

Mr Huxley's smile fell like a juggler's plate. He pulled his napkin off and flung it on the desk. His eyes seemed to brew with a dark-navy colour and Opal's shoulders jumped as the door was closed behind her.

'Quince...' Mr Huxley said in a drawn-out and dark tone.

The driver's hand pressed gently but threateningly onto Opal's shoulder. Opal shuddered and immediately regretted coming in here. *Lord help me.* Mr Huxley sat up with a jerk and steepled his fingers like a bank manager who was about to deny an overdraft.

'Let's watch... *The Last Laugh,*' he said, with his head on one side and a grin that could have been read as exceedingly kind or exceedingly evil.

The second hand of the driver gripped Opal's other shoulder, slightly harder this time, holding her in place.

'What? Who's last laugh?' Opal stammered. 'Let me go!'

'Please don't be alarmed. Come with us.'

Opal shut her eyes and inwardly said a little prayer...

FORTY

LET'S WATCH THE LAST LAUGH

Huxley, with a cryptic nod, directed them to the office window, which he yanked open. The three of them stepped out. There was nothing much else Opal could do but obey. They were in a tight wedge, almost touching the next building. Further along loomed a crumbling, concrete staircase leading into the bowels of Cox & Lumière Pictures. Down they descended into a dank cavern, past rusting pipes and the faint smell of coal dust. At the bottom, they passed the neglected archives of films from the last decades, boxes of brittle reels stacked haphazardly, their labels faded and curling with age. Opal felt benumbed with fear. She was clinging to the security of knowing she had a pair of scissors in her handbag she could resort to if needed.

Huxley yanked a light switch hanging on a chain and amber bulbs crackled into a glow. There was a coal shaft, an ancient relic of the studio's more industrious days, that was cleverly disguised, its wooden doors resembling nothing so much as a utility closet. With a quick glance to ensure no one was watching, Huxley gave a discreet tug on an iron bolt, and the shaft creaked open. Behind the shadowy pile of coal, a hidden latch clicked, and the wall slid aside with a low, protesting groan, revealing a narrow, dimly lit passage that led to a room.

'Here we are, my private reel room,' announced Mr Huxley, with a wave of his arm.

It was chilly and small, more of a crypt than a cinema, with barely five mismatched chairs arranged in front of an ancient projector that hummed like a cat with a grudge. There was a pile of reels on a bookshelf, wrapped in old, crinkled paper and bound with twine. The labels on the cannisters were hand-written.

'A little mausoleum for my favourite German silent films,' Mr Huxley said proudly and plucked one off the shelf that said, '*The Last Laugh.*'

'I... I'm confused,' Opal said. 'Are we actually going to watch that? *The Last Laugh?*'

'I'll pop it on... it's a must-see.'

Opal stammered nervously, 'Oh! I'm relieved. I thought I might be here for some... nefarious reason,' and let out a high-pitched giggle.

Mr Huxley chuckled back. Quince, the chauffeur, blocking the doorway, kept a very serious expression indeed and simply blinked once.

Mr Huxley carefully unspooled the reel onto the projector and with a dramatic twist of the hand, the projector began to hum. He turned a crank and a faint smoky glow began to bleed through on the screen, the images appearing as though they were emerging from a fog. The room was bathed in a spectral illumination, casting elongated shadows across the walls.

Mr Huxley gestured for her to sit and then he sat facing her. He was silhouetted by the projector and she couldn't really see his expression, apart from the whites of his eyes.

'Now, tell me exactly how you know about those... co-ordinates,' he said, his voice very low.

'Well, I intercepted you,' Opal said, she felt honesty was the best policy in this situation as she didn't want to risk upsetting him even more. 'I saw your strange invitation and knew Jane used the acrostic method to learn lines and that she'd used the same method writing a code in your invitation. I saw the scene that Domingo left in the edit of *A Capitol Wife*. I navigated out to the Mojave Desert and found Domingo dead... and the documents.'

'What a clever girl,' he said in a kind of awestruck tone, not angry at all. But then his voice became stern. 'Do you have the documents?'

'Yes,' Opal replied, nervously pulling at the fingers of her gloves.

Mr Huxley breathed what could have been a sigh of relief, then said, 'Okay, Miss Laplume. And why did you come to my office?'

'Because I think George DeLuca may have killed Jane and Domingo and I want your help to prove it.'

He took a moment to answer and then said, 'Who are you working for?'

'Nobody. Well Jane, I suppose. To find out who had her killed. And Domingo. And to help get Augusto out of the firing line.'

'Augusto?'

'He's a security guard. Emmett Zimberg wants to pin Jane's murder on him just to feel satisfied he's got someone to blame. And that Detective Kensington just wants an easy pay cheque.'

'What makes you think George DeLuca had Jane Margeaux and Domingo killed?'

'George and Betty had been plotting to take Jane down so that Betty could take her roles and George believed it would help his career. They tried to make her look like a drunk on set. Betty had been practising Jane's songs before she'd even died and there were bird droppings on George's car that match the ones at the tree near Domingo's body.'

'George DeLuca eh? It's certainly plausible that he'd do such a thing. We're going to need better proof than that though.'

'So, you'll help me?'

'I too have been trying to find out what happened to them both. I was paying them both to help me spy on Platinum Signet Productions. Jane wanted to come over to our studio but she's been tied up in an awful contract with them. Domingo did it for the money. They would bury the confidential Platinum Signet Productions documents in the desert for me or Quince here to collect bimonthly. We'd change the dead-drop location from time to time. I should have gone out there to check when Domingo went missing, but I didn't expect him to have died out there. Quince went to check the site after Domingo's body was announced in the papers and the documents were gone. I guess you took them, Miss Laplume.'

'Yes,' Opal said.

'And the accused man in the *Evening Herald* yesterday I guess was Augusto.'

'Yes. My conjecture is that Domingo knew somehow that George and Betty had killed Jane, and George followed Domingo into the desert. He didn't know anything about the dead drop but rammed him into the rock when Domingo got out. That's why the documents were still there.'

'This is possible.' Mr Huxley nodded.

'Domingo may have had some tangible proof. Or he may have only been an eyewitness to something. But if he did have tangible proof... where would he have been likely to have hidden it?'

'I can't think right now.' Mr Huxley rubbed his chin. 'I may come up with something. But I'll need those documents first, young lady.'

'When I give you the documents, do you promise to help me and to free Augusto?' Opal said, folding her arms.

'I do. Jane and Domingo were good friends of mine, I want

justice for them.' Mr Huxley also folded his arms. 'But there is another thing. Once it's revealed who the killer is... whoever it is... are you not going to tell Emmett Zimberg about our spy ring?'

'No,' Opal said simply.

'Why not?' Mr Huxley said, tilting his head on the side.

'There's no point. They may investigate, but you can deny it. Aren't spy operations designed to be deniable?' said Opal.

'Indeed. It's all fully deniable.' Mr Huxley nodded again.

'Mr Huxley, sir,' Quince said in a very deep voice, pressing his hands against the door frame as a blockade. 'If you don't mind me saying. I don't trust this girl.'

'Well, I do. And we're going to help her avenge our friends. Whether George DeLuca and Betty were behind it or not.'

Opal looked at the projection of German gentlemen in overcoats walking through a set of swing doors and remembered the swing doors that whisked her away from Augusto in Paris.

'Why is this film on? I'm utterly bamboozled,' Opal said.

'Jane, Domingo and I used to come here to discuss matters. Whenever we needed to meet, we'd say "Let's watch *The Last Laugh*." I put it on from time to time as it creates a nice ambiance.'

Opal thought it more eerie than ambient. She tapped her foot, then asked, 'How did you use the confidential Platinum Signet Productions documents?'

'They helped us understand what films Platinum Signet Productions are set to make so that we can compete with similar titles before they can produce them. The list of investors lets us know who we can make offers to and undercut Platinum Signet Productions where we can. A very wicked business is show business.'

'You're telling me,' said Opal. 'Can I get out of here, please. It's dreadfully stuffy?'

'Not quite yet,' Mr Huxley resumed in a low voice. 'Where did you hide the documents?'

'The deal is that I will hand them over to you once you've thought of, or found out, where Domingo could have hidden some evidence? His camera, perhaps? That wasn't around his neck and he always had that.'

'I'll need a few days,' said Mr Huxley, leaning back in his chair.

'Alright, but we have to think fast because I don't know what they're going to do to Augusto. I thought perhaps I should try and go to the police station where they're holding him?'

'The LA police won't listen to a young girl like you. Don't you worry, he'll still have to stand trial and that will take a while.'

'In the meantime, I can grill Peridot Ellington, Adrian and Bonfire, who all think that George or Betty did it. I hope they have something.'

'Peridot Ellington is a deep encyclopaedia of everyone's secrets, that's for sure,' scoffed Mr Huxley.

'Please, Mr Huxley, may I go now? I have to get back to my dog... he's won the role of the black poodle in *Hare-brained in Havana*,' said Opal, looking over at the boulder of a man, Quince.

'Really? That's one of my movies!' Mr Huxley said with a wink. 'Make sure you ask for at least five hundred dollars a week for that dog. Don't let them fob you off with a hundred. Tell them to speak to me if they do!'

Opal found Napoleon in the exact opposite state he was in earlier. Much as he was in the Salon des Artistes in Paris. Exhilarated by all the attention. He had been brushed and pampered into an even fluffier candyfloss than usual. His coat glossy, eyes black diamonds, and tongue hanging out as if lapping up the love.

'Yes, you're a movie star now,' said Opal and scooped him up.

'Can you sign the Animal Actor Contract, please, Miss Laplume. It's one hundred dollars per week.'

'I don't mean to be vulgar,' Opal said and lowered her voice to a whisper. 'But Mr Huxley informed me I should be asking for five hundred.'

'I shall get this amended,' the agent said with a sigh.

Napoleon emitted a sharp volley of barks in the corridor. The sort of barks he reserved for those select individuals who he both recognised and held in the highest esteem.

'*Ah quel beau caniche! Il a l'élégance parfaite!*' The words were spoken in the velvet voice of Chanel.

Opal popped her head out. 'Oh, Madame Chanel!' she said rather coyly, she still hadn't got over the fact the fashionista had caught her buffeting from the bin.

'Opal, Opal,' she said and beckoned her. 'I was just speaking to Peridot Ellington. She wants to do an article called *Style Setters of Sunset Boulevard* and feature you and me and some other fashionable Tinseltown ladies for *Photoplay* magazine.'

'I say. That sounds simply ripping,' Opal said, and the smallest glimmer of joy briefly pulsed in her heart for the first time since Augusto had been taken away. The article would be wonderful publicity for Laplume Millinery, but it would also be a prime opportunity for her to pin down the elusive Peridot Ellington and see if she could shed a deeper light on why she was suspicious of that blister George and piranha Betty!

'Yes, you'll be wearing my newest collection – and, perhaps, some of your hats.'

FORTY-ONE
JUST MODELLING

'Why, that's a pretty hat, young lady,' a photographer said through teeth that were clamping a cigar stub. It was so well chewed it might have been part of his diet. He removed his battered fedora with a touch of ceremony, but almost knocked over his enormous box camera with his elbow.

'Thank you, sir,' Opal said in a jittery manner. She could even feel the items inside her hatbox quivering in her grip. 'I'm being photographed. Where do I go?'

'Oh, a model!' He beamed. 'I'm mighty glad to be the one snapping *your* picture.'

'I'm not a model... I'm just modelling,' said Opal coyly.

'Same difference to me, sister,' he said with a wave of his cigar, leaving a trail of ash floating to the ground. 'They'll doll you up right fine behind those screens over there.' He jabbed a thumb in the general direction of some draped partitions.

The photoshoot's glorious setting was the courtyard of the Egyptian Theatre on Sunset Boulevard. Oversized concrete blocks, echoing the splendour of Egypt's desert architecture, stood boldly ahead of her. The walls were adorned with murals of sphinxes, pyramids, and hieroglyphics, their vibrant hues almost sizzling in the August sunlight. Four twenty-foot-tall columns flanked the entrance, which could be reached by a vast courtyard, lined with oversized pilasters crowned with lotus capitals.

Opal's four-legged shadow trotted excitedly ahead towards the dressing area, quite sure, now that he was an actor, it would be *him* that was to be made up. Opal followed at a more subdued pace. The prospect of telling Mother her Laplume hats were featured in a Hollywood rag was enticing, but her real interest lay in extracting information from Peridot Ellington about the cryptic couple, George and Betty.

Behind the folding screens was a bustling melee of fashion-photoshoot activity. A railed dressing area was crammed with dresses, shawls, and 'unmentionables', while a hair and makeup station brimmed with combs, brushes, and pots of makeup.

Opal was parched in the heat, so was exceedingly grateful that someone had set up a refreshments table, its white cloth billowing faintly in the warm breeze. Glistening under the benevolent sun were jugs of cut glass, their contents dappled by refracted light, filled with citrus nectars so vibrant one could practically hear the fruits burst. Opal poured a glass of orange juice and brought it to her nose. It exuded a scent so fresh it could have been bottled straight from an orchard at dawn.

On plates lounged sliced fruits cut in triangles and arranged in spirals. The grapes, plump and bursting with juice, lay in clusters, daring passersby to pluck them. Opal eyed up the strawberries, still carrying the scent of dew, waiting patiently to be crushed by teeth. Opal munched on one and the taste was so intoxicating that she felt a tad scandalised.

Standing apart from the beautifying crew were faces that Opal recognised. Loud Peridot Ellington stood presiding over the scene like a general directing troops, her large toque hat flapping dramatically with every gesture. Nearby, Chanel was perched on a small stone sphinx, observing everyone silently through vines of smoke.

And then there was... *Lotus Hartley!* Opal's tummy turned a somersault as she spotted the woman pawing through the rows of dresses with the enthusiasm of a cat in a canary shop. This was her chance, she would have to interrogate Lotus about the gunfight she witnessed, but was terrified of what she might say about her father.

'Opal,' Lotus cried, overemphasising the 'O' and the 'P'. 'We're modelling together today! Isn't that *fantastic!*'

'Good morning, Miss Hartley. I say, what a simply ripping surprise! I could swoon!' Opal replied, immediately regretting her overplay.

'Darling Opal. I'm over the moon we finally get to do this shoot and interview.' Peridot zigzagged through the crew. '*Style Setters of Sunset Boulevard* would not be an article without you.'

'I'm utterly flattered to be included,' Opal replied, the corners of her mouth a polite crescent. 'Peridot, I need to speak to you at some point today...'

But Peridot had already buzzed off into the backstage chaos. 'Did you bring the Laplume hats?' Chanel materialised beside them, her dark eyes appraising Opal's hatbox.

'Madame Chanel. Yes, yes, I did indeed. I hope they are fitting with what I'll be putting on.'

'There are two looks for you today,' she said and riffled through Opal's box. 'This Baku-straw cartwheel hat for look one, and this cloche will work excellently with look two. A little too burgundy, but it doesn't matter as the photography will be black and white.'

Before Opal could politely reply, she was whisked onto a chair and two pairs of nimble hands started to work on her with a comb and powder brush. Napoleon sat gazing up in evident dismay at the sight of his mistress being brushed and fussed over when it was clearly *his* role.

Opal, now draped in Chanel, radiated such chic that even the palm trees seemed to lean in for a better look. It was a mint-green, drop-waist dress, its pleats a marvel of construction, the sleeves like a jellyfish caught in silk. Lotus, in Chanel's 'garçonne' style, sported a crisply tailored ensemble in a champagne hue, the jacket nipped in. Lotus perched on a short column in front of the mural and Opal posed behind her, delicately holding the corners of her wide cartwheel hat.

'Are my earrings glinting in the sunlight?' Lotus asked boastfully. 'They ain't paste, you know, they're real.'

Oh, how dreadfully déclassé to say such a thing, Opal thought, feeling a wave of second-hand embarrassment. 'Glorious. Where did you find such treasures?'

'A small gift from a certain... English lord.' Lotus twisted her finger around the emerald droplet, as if she was joyfully toying with Opal's mind.

Opal didn't have much time to reply as the shoot had commenced. Opal felt quite the amateur. She'd only been snapped by the papers in Paris after being mistaken for someone else and had done the odd bit of flouncing in the school literary pageant. But the way the photographer guided her with his cigar stub as a pointing stick was very helpful indeed. She'd spent so many hours studying and drawing fashion figures she had a good idea of what shapes models made with their bodies. With every snap and wind of the camera she edged closer to confidence.

'Smile, Opal, show us those pearly whites!' encouraged Peridot.

Opal's lips hesitated as they stretched, lifting the apples of her cheeks to the sun. It felt very queer as you were never supposed to smile in portraits in England. But when in Rome...

The blonde and brunette were then instructed to pose back

to back while the photographer's assistants scurried to adjust reflectors, corralling sunlight to make the most of the golden morning. It was proving to take time.

'I'm not sure how long I'm going to last in this heat,' panted Opal, 'It's very much reminding me of Indonesia.'

'Oh yes, I know exactly what you mean from touring the islands with my band,' Lotus replied.

'This is what I've been meaning to ask you about... Your story of the gunfight over the diamond. Who... who exactly were the lords in question?' Opal asked, turning to Lotus, but could only see the back of her head.

'Lord Sterling Peregrine and Lord Edmund Laplume,' Lotus said and turned back to look at Opal with a serpentine side-eye.

Opal had to stop herself from swaying and falling over. Lord Sterling Peregrine? She never thought she'd hear his name all the way out here in Hollywood. The man who had kidnapped her in Paris. Her father's enemy. The implications of what Lotus was inferring was simply too nightmarish to bear, that her father was a murderer!

'Oh!' Lotus's eyes flashed in mock-innocence. 'Your surname is Laplume, isn't it... Gosh how does it feel to know *your father* is the murderer of young Reggie Peregrine?'

The very air around Opal became charged, as if a tropical storm were brewing. She was livid.

'He is *not* a murderer,' she hissed, keeping her voice low so as not to alert the crew to the fight.

'Oh yes he is,' Lotus said in a sing-song tone, clearly enjoying it. 'I saw it all happen.'

'Please convey exactly what you saw and include all the details you remember,' Opal whispered. 'And keep your voice down.'

It wasn't that Opal in any way believed Lotus. But something inside her needed that extra inch of reassurance. Something in Lotus's tale must have inconsistencies or something she could prove wrong.

'Your father, Lord Laplume, stood by a canopy tree, clenching the diamond in a cloth bag. Master Reggie Peregrine and his poacher friends were simply asking if they could see the stone. Lord Laplume aimed his gun at Reggie. The poacher to his right shouted, "Stay Back!", and fired a warning shot into the canopy, which swiftly brought down a branch. The next sound was Lord Laplume's muffled shot as it hit Reggie's body,' Lotus said, her words like stinging bullets of air.

Opal shuddered, then ground her teeth. 'Papa is *not* a murderer. He refuses to even kill birds and only studies specimens who have died naturally. Why would he shoot a teenage boy?'

'Alright, alright. Don't shoot the messenger. I am relaying what I saw. I'm sorry it's rattled you,' Lotus said, her voice dripping in false-lament.

'I just think you must be mistaken,' said Opal, much louder than she meant to. She was clenching her fists so hard it was a wonder her nails didn't burst though the fingers of her gloves.

Napoleon, currently in the wardrobe mistress's arms, growled and struggled as if he'd noticed Opal's distress and wanted to chase Lotus off. *The Honourable Opal Laplume needs me!* he seemed to squeak.

'Stop whispering, girls, this is highly unprofessional. The reflectors are now in the right place,' Peridot Ellington scolded. 'We need to get in position.'

Opal tossed her head and stood once more, back to back with the spiteful Jezebel. She tried to focus on the sky as she pasted a false grin across her face, when inside she felt like kicking the camera lens. Once the photographer grunted, 'Alright we've got it in the can,' Opal tried to dash back behind the dressing screens before she burst into tears.

'Hold up, Opal. Come here, Lotus,' said Peridot, beckoning

them together with her bony fingers. 'Now, girls, I have to speak to you. That was a real smash. That shot will be on one side of the spread. The other side will feature ONE of you girls. There's no space for you both. See it as a little contest as to who gets the best shot.'

'Jolly marvellous,' Opal said, looking at Lotus with sharp-as-a-hatpin eyes. How dare Lotus accuse her father of killing the Peregrine boy!

Peridot jutted her chin, taken aback by Opal's sudden hostility towards Lotus. Lotus put her hands on her hips and smirked as if to say 'game on'.

Opal lifted Napoleon up and gave him a huge cuddle behind the screens. She almost blubbered into his fur but managed to staunch it. The absolute audacity of that vicious minx! Opal was starting to wonder if Lotus was lying on purpose and not innocently mistaken. Was she in Hollywood for a more sinister reason than trying to get her face on the silver screen?

At least Opal had gained some extra information about Master Reggie Peregrine's shooting. If it wasn't poppycock, then the echoing and muffled sounds and the fallen branch could be good clues to prove Lotus wrong. One thing was certain, Lord Sterling Peregrine had not given up on trying to destroy Opal's life.

Once dressed in 'look two', Opal went to fetch her headgear to top it off. After angling it over her eye in a precise fashion, she then dove into her handbag for her favourite hatpin. But she blinked when her eye caught sight of something black. Tiny legs emerged from the bag, crawling at a leisurely pace, then with alarming speed, scurried up her hand and onto her forearm. It had the red kiss mark on its back, her old friend, the black widow.

'Oh, good morrow little black widow!' said Opal, quite forgetting it was deadly. 'Let's find a bush for you, eh.'

'Did someone say black widow?' the hairstylist said, spinning around in panic and bumping into Opal.

There was a collective gasp as everyone's eyes bulged with fear at Opal's new pet.

'Ouch... I think I've been bitted!' cried Opal, her heart thumping in panic. 'Help me!'

FORTY-TWO

THE GLASS JAR

'I'll call a doctor immediately!' the set dresser yelled. 'My uncle died from a black widow bite! It's deadly serious.'

'Don't worry, Opal, I'll save you,' yelled the photographer and swung a *Photoplay* magazine from above his head at the little critter.

Opal, her morals still set on protecting God's creatures even though it had bitten her, dodged aside. The magazine caught the side of Peridot's jaw on its trajectory.

'Jumpin' Jehoshaphat!' Peridot cried, stumbling backward into one of the dressers.

The dresser, startled, flung an elbow that knocked a makeup brush from an assistant's hand. The brush soared through the air, landing in a tin of powder, which exploded in a dramatic puff directly into the lighting assistant's face... and Lotus's. Lotus, stoically brushed the powder from her face, not a hint of concern over Opal. Blinded and coughing, the assistant staggered into a clothes rack with the grace of a marionette with half its strings cut. The rack groaned and collapsed in a clatter of hangers.

Opal thought she might faint. She flopped onto a stool and

fanned herself with her hand. Someone ran for a telephone. The rest of the crew fussed around her with water and checking her pulse... until Opal noticed the hairdresser had hatpins sticking out of her blouse pocket. Opal inspected her bite. It was only one hole. A spider fang bite would be two punctures.

'Wait!' Opal said, revitalised by the knowledge that there wasn't poison coursing through her veins. 'I'm terribly sorry, everyone. The hairdresser must have pricked me when she bumped into me. It's not a spider bite.'

Chanel surveyed the wreckage with the air of a queen watching peasants' squabble over breadcrumbs. Exhaling a perfect ribbon of smoke, she arched a single brow and drawled,

'Well... The spider's caused less damage than half the directors in this town.'

'You'd better be darn sure, Miss Opal Laplume!' said the photographer.

'Look! The spider's in your hat!' yelped Peridot.

Everyone stepped back. The photographer went for the magazine again but Opal dashed off. She'd get the little eight-legged lady to safety. Dodging the honking cars, she headed for the flora across the street and found a group of date palms vibrating in the breeze. She took her hat off and realised that the spider had nestled inside the feathers. she tried to get it off with a stick but it wouldn't budge! And now she'd destroyed the feathers. *Blithering fig!* She removed the feather bundle, with the spider still clinging inside and gently placed it in the grass.

'Goodbye, you lipstick-smacked little troublemaker,' she said and watched its red-marked bottom wriggle away.

She'd now have to attach something else to the hat! She foraged for a few of the dried palms on the ground. She dashed back and with her scissors she snipped then into attractive spear shapes with some fronds cascading out. To punctuate her little hat brooch, she added a red bougainvillea flower and with quick fingers stitched it to the side of the headgear where the feathers had been.

'*Très bon!*' Chanel said with a swirl of her cigarette. 'That looks even better. We're not going for black widow, we're going for blue debutante.'

Lotus, who was in the middle of shooting now, pursed her lips, looking utterly disappointed at Opal's triumph. The sheer bitterness on her face was most definitely ruining her takes.

On the dresser lay Lotus's handbag and the sunlight glinted off a glass jar inside. Opal stepped closer. Inside, another two black widows sat on a leaf.

No, No, No! Lotus Hartley! You've been trying to kill me! You snide viper, Opal cursed under her breath. *I know now you also slipped one in my bag at Mr Huxley's abode. Perhaps while we were in the powder room together. Lord Sterling Peregrine is behind all of this, I swear. She must be his accomplice. I just can't believe after the whole ordeal in Paris that he is STILL after me? Whatever am I going to do?*

Opal retrieved the jar and slipped it into her own bag. Planning to free the little arachnids later... Disarming Lotus was the only pertinent thing to do. She would keep quiet, and think how best to deal with Lotus later. And Lord Sterling Peregrine, for that matter. He was clearly after the entire Laplume family and was not going to stop unless she did something!

At that moment Peridot came around the screens, still looking a little dazed from her magazine wallop earlier. Opal realised this might be her best chance to pick Peridot's brains about Domingo.

'Peridot,' Opal said. 'If you have a moment, I'd like to speak to you in the shade over there, please.'

'As long as it's print-worthy,' smirked Peridot.

'This goes beyond print-worthy, I'm afraid, Peridot. For the time being, at least,' Opal whispered by a shady pilaster. 'On

Santa Monica Beach you said you suspected Betty of having orchestrated Jane's death.'

'I have an inkling, yes.' Peridot's ink-drop pupils dilated at the topic of murder.

'Well, I *am* jumping ahead of myself, but I believe Domingo may have known who was behind Jane's death, and was killed for it.'

'Witnessing things is not a wise pastime.' Peridot shook her head gravely.

'I too have a strong suspicion that Betty and George as a *duo* destroyed Jane and then Domingo for knowing about it. Do you know where Domingo may have kept any evidence about Jane's murder? Say, if he kept an incriminating photograph, for instance? Where would he likely store it? His camera is missing, you see.'

Peridot inhaled through her nostrils as if giving herself a moment to decide how to reply, then seemed to relent. 'Well, he did used to follow the odd person and take photographs for me. He'd do anything for cash, Domingo would. I wouldn't be at all surprised if he'd blackmailed Jane's killers with some evidence. And he was constantly documenting things with his camera, you're right.'

'Do you know if he stashed his photo negatives somewhere?' whispered Opal.

Peridot glanced over her shoulder to double-check nobody was in earshot. 'He did. I know exactly where. Hidden in plain sight. It's where he and I used to do our... *dealings*.'

'Where?' breathed Opal, trying not to jump up and down.

'I'm not telling you.' Peridot smiled, enjoying the game. 'But I will *show* you. I'll drive you there myself. Tomorrow night. I can't be left out of the action... I'll pick you up outside Platinum Signet Productions at eight. And in return, you'll tell me all *you* know!'

FORTY-THREE

THE PHANTOM BENEFACTOR

Opal rolled over in her bed with all the grace of a poorly executed omelette. It was morning and her eyes felt puffy from crying over Augusto's plight and Lotus's wickedness. Her dreams had been a grotesque patchwork: Augusto slumped in a dank cell, his beard like a neglected shrub; and her father shooting at the Peregrine boy in the forest, a look of murder in his eye like he'd been possessed by some alien being. Napoleon, ever the well-meaning fool, attempted to lift her spirits with a vigorous slathering of dog kisses.

She was so exhausted she didn't even try to calm him down. Just opened her eyes slowly, trying not to let the light in too fast. Then, a rat-a-tat-tat came at her door. It was Bonfire, brandishing a handful of banknotes in her fist. They were quivering and her face was filled with fear.

'This has gone far enough,' Opal said. 'We must find out *why* this is happening to you. Follow me.'

She swirled a shawl over her nightclothes, slipped on her shoes, grabbed Bonfire's hand and pulled her down to the front desk.

'Please listen. This is frightfully unsettling,' Opal

demanded of the maid. 'Bonfire has been waking up to piles of money on her nightstand. It just appears as if put there by a ghost in the night. A dozen or so dollars at a time. You are the only ones who have a spare key. Have you any idea what's been going on?'

'No, mam.' The maid shook her bonnet. 'Why would anyone give someone money for nothing?'

'Precisely. And how the devil did they get it into her room?' pressed Opal.

'With all due respect, mam...' The maid looked Bonfire up and down. 'You haven't been out bending the elbow at night, have ya?'

'What?' Bonfire frowned.

'Hittin' the juice... and forgot that you put it there?'

'No, no I wasn't *"hittin' the juice"*,' Bonfire reproached.

'Want me to hold onto it until we figure out who it really belongs to?' asked the maid, offering her palm.

'I don't think so,' Bonfire said. 'But thank you.'

'Let's inspect your room, Bonfire, come on,' said Opal. 'We're getting nowhere here.'

They had just begun climbing the stairs when Bonfire froze, a terrified look springing onto her face and electrifying her hair. 'What if the maid thinks I'm some fancy woman who got drunk and forgot she'd seen a gentleman caller? I'll be out on my ear!'

Opal felt her cheeks flush pink. She clutched her shawl as if it might shield her from disgrace and hurried up the steps. 'Don't worry, Bonfire, we will catch the phantom benefactor. Just think... what's the significance of the amount of money? What would a dozen or so dollars buy?'

'I don't know. A goat?' Bonfire shrugged.

'Serious answers, please.' Opal sighed.

'Half a month's rent? A man's pair of trousers? A second-hand typewriter? It's a bit of a waste of time guessing,' Bonfire said exasperated.

'I see your point. I was just wondering if it would jig something in the old conk,' Opal mused, then whispered, 'Were you keeping a secret for anyone?'

Bonfire shut and screwed her eyes up as she thought hard. 'Let me think...'

Once they got to Bonfire's room Opal inspected the window, which was dusty around the frame, and then glanced down at the nightstand. She asked Bonfire to place the cash on the table how she had found them. She splayed them out in the messy way they had been put there. It was not a neatly stacked pile. It was like someone had thrown the money down.

Opal gathered up the notes and studied them close to her nose. She blinked several times to improve her focus on the paper edges. 'How queer,' she said after a moment. 'There's sawdust on the edge. And on all the other notes too. They obviously hadn't been in anyone's pocket or the dust would've rubbed off.'

Bonfire wrinkled her freckled nose as she inspected them.

'Perhaps they've been stored in a wooden, dusty place,' Opal pondered. 'A wooden box? Wooden wallets don't seem to be the fashion in Hollywood. Not yet anyway.'

She flapped the notes in frustration. *What was someone trying to tell Bonfire?* Napoleon got excited as if the bundle of flapping money were little bird's wings and started trying to snap at them, dribbling in case it was indeed edible.

'Oh no, boy, you're not going to eat money again. We can't have that fiasco we once had at Barclays on Fleet Street with that poor old blighter's pension.'

Napoleon, once wound up, could not unwind without expelling the energy somehow. He jumped up onto the bedside table and yapped again at the notes. The table wobbled somewhat, shaking the room and a little fleck of sawdust fell from the ceiling above. If it had not been caught by the morning sunrays through the window, Opal would have missed it.

'Look!' Opal pointed up to where the sprinkle of dust was coming from.

The ceiling was wooden boarding with had a joist cavity separating it from the floor above. An air-sandwich of boards. Opal removed her pet from the nightstand and stood up onto it herself.

'Careful, Miss Laplume,' Bonfire said, and held the nightstand steady.

Opal squinted her eyes at the slim gaps above. She could just make out a little slither of green... *Was it... Money?*

'Good grief!' Opal exclaimed. 'I think someone has been stashing money up there that has been falling through the gaps!'

'Really?' Bonfire said. 'Boy oh boy, am I relieved! Nobody was breaking in at night then.'

'So now we must do the decent thing and go up and return it all,' Opal said, hopping down and brushing her hands together in satisfaction.

'All of it?' Bonfire's freckles seemed to quiver in agitation.

'Oh... have you blown it on trifles and fripperies?' Opal asked.

'Well, no, I still have it but...'

'Bonfire, they're going to figure out it's been falling into your room when they count it and realise some of it slid through the gaps.'

'I know, I know. I just thought after all this grief I could at least go to the Max Factor salon for a haircut.'

Opal sighed and put her hands on her hips. 'Bonfire, if we manage to wrap this film alive... I'll take you to Max Factor. And you don't need a haircut, your hair is simply *ripping* as it is.'

'Thank you,' said Bonfire, scrunching some curls with her hand. 'I wish I was rich and could go to Max Factor every day.'

'That would soon get boring. Remember, having a sizeable bank account can expand your horizons but quality family and friends... like you... heighten your zenith!' Opal smiled at her. 'And that is far more fulfilling.'

'You're a really swell gal, Opal Laplume,' Bonfire said. 'When I first met you, I got the impression you were a little bit of a nosy parker, always staring and blinking at everyone. Earwigging too. I also didn't always understand your accent and what blithering fig meant.'

'I thought you said I was swell.' Opal laughed nervously and patted perspiration on her brow.

'Oh, that was only my first impression. But then you're so thoughtful and shrewd and real smart. I try to keep friendship outside the studios but I really do think we'd make swell pals. You've probably got lots though.'

'That is so kind of you to say, Bonfire.' Opal smiled, though she hoped she didn't always come across as conceited on first impressions. 'I actually don't have many friends, well any long-term friends.'

Napoleon pawed at her leg and whimpered. 'Well, yes, of course, Napoleon. I have you, that goes without saying. We are both mammals and we understand each other when it comes to a lot of things... like food, cuddles and danger. But human friends... I have a lack of.'

'Why's that?' asked Bonfire. 'I can't seem to shake my old school posse, and I have more siblings than a family of mice.'

'I'm the exact opposite. I was too déclassé for the society lot and too plummy for the ordinary set to relate to. I'm in the London millinery shop alone all the time or I'm travelling. I lead a terribly lonely existence, even though I always seem to be surrounded by characters.'

'Really? That's not what I expected.'

'There's something about this town...' said Opal, looking out of the window, 'that's quite bleak. And I feel like I can hear tumbleweed all the time.'

'That's Hollywood. It's the loneliest place on earth,' said

Bonfire. 'People are usually only nice if they think they can get something off you. But I'm the bottom of the pile. The underling of the underlings and you're still kind to me.'

'Well, why wouldn't I be? You're positively smashing. Now, I'll throw some proper clothes on and we'll go up to the gentlemen's quarters.'

Now Opal was attired appropriately, they found themselves up on the opposite sex's floor, and stopped at the room which they assumed must be above Bonfire's, due to the position of the adjacent tree outside. Rat-a-tat-tat. Bonfire knocked sheepishly, her fist clenched with the banknotes.

'That room's been empty ever since Mr Lara vanished,' said the maid behind them, making them both jump. 'And you shouldn't be up here.'

'This was Mr Domingo Lara's room?' Opal asked.

'Yes, mam.'

'We think the money he'd been stashing under his floorboards has been falling down into Bonfire's room. That's where it's been coming from! Can we please go in and check, you have the key, don't you?'

The maid frowned. 'Yes, I do. Are you saying there is a stash of money in there? Who gets to keep it?'

'Um...' Opal said, and she and Bonfire looked at each other. They knew what the maid wanted. 'Well, the police really. But we will give it to you to pass on...'

This was apparently the correct answer and the maid smiled and unlocked the door.

The room was set out identically to the girls' rooms. It had evidently been cleared of Domingo's possessions. It was sweltering and Bonfire switched the fan on.

'So terribly sad about poor Domingo.' Opal sighed. 'Did his family come to take his things?'

'Yes, mam, a very sweet old lady. I'm assuming it was his grandmother; she only wanted his camera though. She had no use for the clothes and books so we gave them to the Hollywood Presbyterian Church.'

'Oh, his camera?' asked Opal, walking over to the area where the money must be hidden. 'I guess she wanted the film for memories.'

'No, there was no film in it. She was disappointed about that but she was happy to keep his beloved camera.'

No point in seeking Grandma out if there was no film in his camera, Opal thought.

The floorboards to the left of the window were indeed loose. Domingo must have got lazy and just slotted them down the gaps and not laid them within the joist cavity. Opal looped her finger under a corner of the board and lifted.

She gasped.

What she saw in the hole made her eyelids shoot back and her mouth drop open.

FORTY-FOUR

THE STASH

Stashed inside the joist cavity was *not* money. The room with the money must be next door and they had mistaken which one was actually above Bonfire's room. No, this secret cache was something far more sinister. There was a long silence as Opal stared down at the contents. All that could be heard was the ceiling fan, swooshing around scenarios in her mind. Nausea crept up to her throat.

Crammed into a tight ball was midnight-blue fabric, tangled with the soldier's mask, its frozen smile grotesque. Resting on top of the mask, shiny and gold, was a single bullet. A blank, but no less menacing.

Opal felt a sensation like a black widow creeping up her spine... *Did Domingo kill Jane?* 'Well? How much is in there?' demanded the maid. 'Some lunkhead left the sink looking like a grease-pit down the hall and I've got to scour it, I don't have all day.'

'I'm terribly sorry. We've got the wrong room. It must be next door,' Opal said, but her voice cracked nervously. She closed the lid and stood up.

'Next door to the left, or right?' asked the maid.

'I guess it's to the left as the tree trunk adjacent to Bonfire's leans more in that direction,' Opal said.

'The boy's room? If he's been stashing money then we can't take it,' said the maid disappointed.

'What boy?'

'I think he might be a script clerk, he's always got scripts. Big ears. He drives me nuts the amount of Butterfinger wrappers he leaves on the floor.'

'Burton,' Opal and Bonfire looked at each other and said in unison.

'I wonder if he is in?' said Bonfire, marching round to his room and knocking.

They all waited at his door for him to answer.

'He must be at the studio already,' concluded Bonfire. 'I guess we can ask him later?'

'No...' Opal said. 'I think it would be best to find out now. Can you unlock it, please?' *If he's hiding money*, Opal thought, *what else might he be hiding in there?*

'Why?' asked the maid, hands on hips. 'The only reason I let you into Domingo's old room is because it's not invading any living person's privacy.'

Opal thought fast. 'Well, we need to count how much money he *has* in there. Just in case Burton tries to say that Bonfire has kept more of the money than she's owned up to.'

'Good thinking,' said Bonfire. 'I mean, Burton is very sweet, I can't imagine he would try and pull something like that, but you never know. Folks are desperate around here.'

'You're telling me,' said the maid and sighed. 'But I might need a little more persuading.'

'Listen,' Opal said. 'We can't give you any of Burton's money. But we can... I don't know... launder some of the bedsheets at Platinum Signet Productions to take some of your workload off?'

The maid looked Opal up and down and folded her arms.

'Laundry day's Friday. Be ready for a sack.' She then unlocked Burton's door.

'Thank you kindly,' said Opal, a little apprehensive of what size of sack she'd be lumbered with and how she'd pull it off.

Burton's room was indeed littered with Butterfinger wrappers. A dated typewriter with mismatched, replaced keys was balanced on the bedside table: his makeshift desk. Opal could see that the floorboard below it was indeed disturbed and loose.

She popped up the corner with a finger and slid the board aside. Yes. Yes, indeed there was a scatter of banknotes. He must have gotten lazy and slotted them down without lifting the board up to place them safely, and they'd been slipping through into Bonfire's room.

'How much is there?' Bonfire asked, crouching down next to Opal.

The girls reached inside the joist cavity and took handfuls of notes out to count.

Bonfire counted the money and Opal grabbed an unopened Butterfinger bar off the floor. It was a thick slab, coated by a thin shell of chocolate. Opal bit a piece and contemplated it. It was the sort of chocolate that, while serviceable, suggested an American enthusiasm for sugariness over the European devotion to artistry. Certainly nothing like Cadbury's. But it was the interior that truly intrigued her. The thing disintegrated into peanut crumbles, then melted into a sort of nutty, buttery delirium. It stuck to her teeth.

'Okay he has seventy-five dollars. And I have forty-five dollars in total.' Bonfire sighed. 'I guess I'll have to give it back.'

'Yes. Let's put this back inside the hole and you can go and tell him. It is jolly decent of you and I'm sure he'll be grateful.'

While walking Napoleon to Platinum Signet Productions. Opal had a dilemma on her mind. Should she go to the police about the stash in Domingo's room? She most certainly was not going to go to Detective Kensington, as all he cared about was a quick payday and Augusto in chains. The police would be safer... But... what if Mr Zimberg had paid the police to go along with Detective Kensington? She needed more proof. Tangible, hard proof. She would keep shtum until she found out more. Burton could certainly be in the soup.

FORTY-FIVE

THE CHARIOT OF GOSSIP'S DARK OVERLORD

Peridot's knuckles gripped her steering wheel with the tenacity of a woman whose occupation was wringing scandal from the tight-lipped. Her mouth parted with a moist little smack, and she said with the breezy malevolence of a Hollywood Lucifer, 'Get in.'

Opal, pulling her fedora over her eye for composure, slid onto the cool leather seat. Napoleon paused, one paw raised in hesitation, as though weighing the ethical consequences of climbing into the chariot of gossip's dark overlord. Opal lifted him onto her lap and heaved the door to. She had no choice but to go with the woman, she'd gotten to the end of her sleuthing rope.

'Where *are* we going, Miss Ellington?' Opal asked, a quaver of apprehension in her tone.

Peridot's ink-drop pupils remained fixed on the road ahead. 'You'll see, you'll see,' she said. 'Not far... you've been there before.'

And with that, the green Packard Deluxe Phaeton departed. The street lamp reflections swept across the bonnet and glinted cheekily off the car's enormous headlights as they glided out onto Washington Boulevard. The air was sweet with the scent of orange blossoms, spiked by a whiff of gasoline. Peridot's silk scarf fluttered frenziedly behind her. The great movie houses flashed 'Grand Premiere Tonight!' and a gaggle of hopeful starlets, dressed to the nines, congregated on a street corner, clutching portfolios of headshots.

Further out, the Packard purred its way up the winding trail, the beautiful, bombastic HOLLYWOODLAND sign loomed. Towering above the hills in letters, some forty-five feet tall. It's four thousand bulbs twinkled like stars.

As they passed the W letter, Opal noticed a little scene under the central arch of the W. It was none other than Mr Huxley, dressed in a white tuxedo, on his knees! At his side was a blonde lady. Was it? It was indeed that awful Lotus Hartley. Mr Huxley was slipping what appeared to be a small meteorite onto her ring finger and as the lady accepted, a small congregation of witnesses applauded.

'Well, I never. He's proposing to the Australian warbler! He's got photographers and an audience of studio underlings,' said Peridot.

'Goodness, I can see the ring sparkle from here!'

'She has a face on her but when she sings, I get an overwhelming admiration for the man who invented earplugs,' Peridot said loudly over the engine. 'She's clearly a fortune hunter, the same as that Carey Margeaux.'

'I'd taken Carey out of the box of being a fortune hunter, since he made that ostentatious cheque out to the orphanage,' Opal said, glancing sideways at Peridot; she knew this comment would get an energetic response.

'Did you notice that slimy display of sainthood didn't make so much as a footnote in the papers? Thinking he could outmanoeuvre Peridot Ellington was foolish.'

'I got the impression you weren't so pleased with his stunt at Cocoanut Grove. Getting you onstage like that,' Opal added.

'He thinks I made up my orphan past for public appeal, but I didn't. I suffer from childhood amnesia and that is all I am saying about *that*.' She then put her foot down and they lurched forth. 'Let's change the subject to your future, my dear. Who will the Honourable Opal Laplume be wed to?'

'I don't know. Mother wants me to marry Viscount Turkey – Cecil Turks-Leyton – but he's such a damp squib. I'm coming to the age where I must make a choice, I suppose,' said Opal, sighing up into the starry sky.

'Choose when you are ready. There is a lot of pride in getting older. It comes with the perk of feeling the veil of hogwash lift, all the societal pressures that you're supposed to believe in and adhere to becomes piffle. You wish your younger self had the same level of clarity and confidence. Don't choose someone when you're young and dense,' Peridot said.

Opal blinked at her in surprise, it was the most level-headed and warm thing she'd ever heard her say. Perhaps it was why Peridot herself was not married?

They arrived shortly after. And indeed, Opal had been before. It was Colonel Thwack's Miniature Golf course. Napoleon strained on the lead, desperate to get some ball action again. But it was deadly quiet inside the course and he squeaked in confusion.

'No more games tonight, ladies, we're closed. I leave in a moment,' said a steward with a bunch of clubs under his arm.

'Oh no, we're just here for the lockers,' Peridot said and marched straight passed him.

The lockers had tall, slim metal doors that had been painted a gay green. Peridot stopped in front of one with the number 48 on it, fiddled with the numbers on the padlock, furrowed her brow and gave a withering look.

'Domingo used to give me the code for this infernal thing,' she said, tapping her foot in a manner that suggested she'd like to kick it. 'Darn it, though, he was always changing them. Well, that stops us dead in our tracks, doesn't it?'

Opal pinched her chin and blinked in thought. 'When was his birthday?'

'God knows,' replied Peridot with a theatrical wave of her hand.

'Well, what else do we know? His room number? His motor registration?'

'All I really knew about that man...' – Peridot folded her arms and shook her head – 'was that he was a shameless opportunist. He'd steal the sugar out of his grandmother's tea if he thought no one was watching.'

Opal blinked rapidly, as though she'd just been startled by a passing train. 'Grandmother... Yes, yes! He had an entry in his diary for her seventieth birthday. It was on... February 17th. Now, what's seventy years ago?'

'Don't look at me for sums, girl. I've always been more of a words' woman. Arithmetic gives me hives.'

Opal's fingers began dancing in the air, counting invisible numbers. '1861! February 17th, 1861. That's it. 17.02.61!'

'That's your English way with dates. We Americans have 02.17.61.'

She twisted the number wheels and there was a soft click. With a flourish, she swung the locker open and peered inside.

'It's empty!' Opal groaned, throwing up her hands in despair. 'Drats!'

'Empty? Not a chance,' said Peridot, and extended a pointed nail to the top corner of the back panel. She gave it a press and with a faint pop, the panel shifted forward.

'A false back!' Opal said triumphantly.

Peridot tugged it free.

What lay behind made Opal let out a strangled squawk.

'No... no, no, no!' Opal said, clutching the sides of her face and digging her nails in. She could not believe what she was seeing. Her mind spun backwards like a reel in a broken movie projector, the grim frames clicking into view with dreadful clarity. She wished she could stop it. After holding her breath for a moment, she let it out in a relieved sigh. At least... she would now be able to prove Augusto's innocence!

The setting of the photograph was clearly the editing suite where Opal had found Domingo the fateful day Jane was shot. A lone bulb lit a figure in a toy soldier costume, hastily wrestling with a brass button. The mask and helmet were off, beneath them, tousled hair, sticky-out ears, and the unmistakably anxious face of... Burton Ford.

'Now,' Peridot said in a low pitch, placing a hand on Opal's shoulder. 'Before I let you take this photograph away, you're going to tell me everything you know.'

FORTY-SIX

AS RED AS A CARDINAL'S SASH

'Can anyone hear us?' Opal said, looking up and down the locker area and peeking through the hedges behind. Napoleon trotted up to a janitor's cupboard which was ajar and inspected it. No one.

'I don't think so. The steward has left,' said Peridot, her ink-drop pupils dilated. 'Now *tell* me...'

Opal spoke in a low tone. 'That photo will free Augusto from police custody. It proves that Burton killed both Jane *and* Domingo.'

'Dammit,' said Peridot, folding her arms. 'I was hoping it was Carey. Burton Ford? Such a young boy. What happened?'

'I know, I'm flabbergasted because Burton was my first friend since moving here,' Opal said, looking down at her feet sadly. 'But his moral compass seems to have spun off in a very dark direction indeed. We owe it to Jane and Domingo, whose murders are very much connected, to get justice.'

'Get to the goods... I'm waiting,' said Peridot, tapping her toe.

'The plot involves spying for Cox & Lumière Pictures,' Opal whispered, enjoying keeping Peridot waiting for answers.

'Burton Ford was a *studio spy*?' said Peridot, a little louder than she should have.

'No, not Burton. It was Jane and Domingo. They were both collecting a pay cheque under the table from Cox & Lumière Pictures for... spying on Platinum Signet Productions.'

Peridot gasped and covered her mouth with her hand. Opal could detect a smirk of enjoyment under that hand. 'Emmett Zimberg is going to explode like the sky on the Fourth of July. Do go on...' she said from behind her hand.

'Despite the spying, that was not the reason Jane and Domingo were "bumped off", as you Americans like to say. This may have put George and the Platinum Signet Productions bigwigs in the suspect line as the spying would directly affect him. No, Jane's murder was an act of impulse. An act of fear and paranoia.'

'What scared Burton, the little lamb?' Peridot asked.

'I'm not particularly knowledgeable on politics but I've gotten wind that the CPUSA, the Communist Party USA, is not something you'd want your Hollywood bosses to know you're a member of.'

'He's red?' Peridot raised her eyebrows. 'The young ones are always so impressionable.'

'As red as a cardinal's sash.' Opal nodded. 'He tried to write films for Jane that promoted his beliefs but these were constantly rejected.'

'One wouldn't have thought Jane Margeaux would touch those scripts with a ten-foot pole and gloves on,' Peridot said.

'The sudden act of violence towards Jane came after she uncovered his membership to the CPUSA. It happened in less than a few seconds. Witnessed by Betty, Burton handed Jane a handkerchief when she was sneezing. Out from that pocket, a red pamphlet fell. He had originally claimed it was a red Marlboro cigarette box for which Jane reprimanded him. But he slipped up later when he revealed he didn't actually smoke.

Jane saw the communist pamphlet and uttered the words that sealed her fate. "You won't last long around here", or something to that effect.'

'So Burton cracked like a cheap deckchair...'

'Yes. Burton, taking Jane's words as an imminent threat,' Opal continued, 'decided he'd have to kill her before she could tell on him. He had to be fast. The shooting stunt was coming up. What if he swapped a real bullet with the blank? He mucked in with the hordes of extras in the adjacent studio space. Once dressed in one of their toy soldier costumes, completely concealing him head to toe, he snuck back to the sound stage and knocked over the water barrel. He waited for our security guard, Augusto, to leave his post to right the upturned barrel. Then he went to Augusto's table, picked up the unattended gun and removed a live bullet. Later, when nobody was looking, he swapped it for the blank in the gun kept in the weapons case. He chambered the round.'

'That smooth little operator.'

'The next activity was Burton's – and consequently – Domingo's undoing. Burton got changed back into his normal clothes in the film storage closet inside the editing room. He did not realise Domingo was in there. We all know Domingo and his photography obsession. Taking pictures of everything he found interesting, and he took a photo of Burton in the costume with the mask off.'

'And that's what this is. He doesn't look too bad as a toy soldier,' Peridot said, taking the photograph out of the locker and inspecting it. 'Then he cut the lights?'

'No, he didn't. He would have been jolly well flummoxed when the lights went out. This happened by accident. The water from the fallen barrel caused a short circuit in the main electrics. Nobody actually switched them off.'

'That must have been damn terrifying,' Peridot said, shaking her head.

'When it was decided that everyone should come here to Colonel Thwack's to give Jane a send-off by participating in her favourite activity, Domingo insisted Burton pair up with him. On the last hole, Domingo hid the incriminating photo for Burton to find when he sank his putt. I witnessed their body language. Domingo put the photo back in his pocket, obviously threatening the boy. Domingo, ever the hustler, would have gained more monetarily if he blackmailed Burton than dobbed him in to the police.'

'That sounds like Domingo alright. Trying to pry money from a boy's hand,' said Peridot. 'But he should have thrown Burton in the can when he could!'

'Indeed. Burton had killed once. Domingo should have known he was next. Burton had been watching Domingo's moves very closely, working out the best time to strike. Domingo was doing his routine drop-off of documents to the Mojave Desert in his Chevy. Burton, in George DeLuca's car that he often drove, decided to follow Domingo. Domingo parked up near the dead drop. Burton hid his car behind a large boulder. Once Domingo started to walk towards the L-shaped rock, Burton charged and crashed Domingo into the rock. Leaving him for dead.'

'What connects Burton Ford to that scene exactly?' Peridot asked.

'Unfortunately, the droppings from a cheeky bird that perched above the car were seen on the vehicle. Those droppings with Joshua tree seeds only come from that particular area.'

'The grimy little varmint used George DeLuca's motor for his dirty dealings!' Peridot laughed.

'Then I found that mysterious money was landing on the bedside table below Burton's room. I realised it was coming from gaps in the ceiling boards. When we first went to investigate, we got the wrong room. It was Domingo's old room.

Burton had been trying to frame Domingo for Jane's death by hiding the toy soldier outfit and blank bullet in his joist cavity. He must have put it there after he killed Domingo and stole his room key off his body. Just in case Burton was ever caught, he could point the finger at Domingo.'

'Now we have the incriminating last piece of the puzzle,' said Peridot, spinning the photo in her hands. Opal felt slightly nervous, like she might dash off with it.

'Not so fast...' said a male, adolescent-sounding voice.

FORTY-SEVEN
BUCKINGHAM PALACE

Opal whipped her head around, her fedora almost falling off. Immerging from a bush was... Burton Ford, brandishing a club above his head. It glinted under the moon.

'Hand over the photograph and nobody is going to get hurt,' Burton said very slowly so that his words could not be mistaken. His expression was one of thunderous fury, his ears quivering like outraged satellite dishes scanning for Opal and Peridot's next move. He had a golf-club bag over his shoulder and the chunkiest, heaviest club braced in both hands ready to swing.

From the back of Napoleon's throat came a rumbling warning sound. He lowered the front of his body, ready to pounce. Then, like a furry cannonball, he went for Burton's shins. Burton swung the club and Napoleon leapt over it like a skipping rope.

Opal darted forth to protect her beloved pet. 'You swing that thing at my dog again and I'll—'

'You'll what?' he spat and hurled the club at Opal. It somersaulted in the air and narrowly missed Opal's cheek, clattering to the floor. Opal and Peridot jumped out of the way, slamming their shoulders into the lockers.

'Run!' shouted Peridot, and threw her arms above her head so dramatically you could see why her acting never took off. The photograph was clamped firmly in one hand.

They clamoured in the direction of the miniature golf course, Napoleon at their heels.

'Split up!' Opal shouted and dashed down towards the Eiffel Tower sculpture. She instantly regretted it as she realised Peridot was the only one with a car. But then again, Peridot was the one in possession of the precious evidence so would be targeted.

Burton bounded after Peridot, who was hopping over the elephant feature and then scrambling under the footbridge. All Opal could hear was Burton's club whipping the air as he swung it and the thuds of sculptures being vandalised. Opal decided to crawl along a hedgerow to see if she could help Peridot in any way. The panting journalist was currently cowering behind a purple windmill, the photo clutched at her breast.

Burton was searching high and low, whirling his club like it was an axe and he was the Prince in *Sleeping Beauty*, slicing through the thicket. He was positively rabid. Chopping the arms off cacti and smashing the mini Tower of Pisa even further lopsided.

'Come out now! I have my own tales I can tell the police. That photograph means nothing,' he wailed like a coyote.

Oh yes? thought Opal. *Why are you losing your marbles over it then?*

Opal spotted the large Buckingham Palace golf puzzle. It was directly in between herself and Peridot. Opal waved her arms to try and grab the woman's attention. She spotted Opal and mouthed, 'HELP ME'. Burton decapitated the head of the Statue of Liberty and it went splashing into the river.

Napoleon struggled in Opal's arms to dive in and fetch it but Opal held him fast. She pointed at the Buckingham Palace sculpture which was hollow at the back apart from a few pipes for the ball to slide down. Peridot clocked on and they both crawled towards it. Peridot kept the photo in her teeth.

Opal had to twist her limbs in order to fit and Peridot had to stick a foot up. They looked like a couple of mime artists posing static in a wild, kicking Charleston. Napoleon couldn't quite fit between their tangled limbs.

'Napoleon, go behind one of the King's Guards,' whispered Opal and tilted her head towards the little plaster soldiers. Napoleon's black bouffant became a perfect woolly extension above the bearskin hat. His black marbles for eyes gave the only clue that the hat may be alive.

Burton became worryingly silent. *He must be creeping close*, thought Opal. She peeked through the palace balcony windows and twitched the tiny curtain. Burton was ten or so yards away. He'd noticed the bearskin hat with eyeballs and tilted his head in bafflement. Napoleon did the same back.

'Ah ha!' Burton yelled, brandishing his golf club like a truncheon. 'I can seeeeeee you!' he said creepily as if it was a playground game. 'All you need to do is give me the photograph.'

Opal swallowed. There was nowhere to run. Peridot's automobile was all the other way at the end of the park. *Unless...* She'd seen a possible getaway vessel. The chimneys of the miniature *Titanic* came sailing around the bend of the park's river feature. It was the bonus game for people to try and score balls in its chimney funnels. It sailed on a fast current all the way around the park and most importantly... past the car park.

'After three,' whispered Opal, 'we're going to leap on the *Titanic*.'

'I can't swim!' said Peridot.

'Neither could many of the original set aboard, but don't worry, it's within leaping distance.'

Like a bunch of drunken monkeys, they leapt onto the mini-

Titanic, holding its chimneys like tree trunks. Napoleon was a professional doggy paddler so cannoned in, getting Peridot's skirt wet. He happily swam behind.

They were too out of reach for Burton now. The current was swiftly washing them to safety. The mini-*Titanic* golf replica was evidently designed far better than the real thing. They hopped off when the stream curved by the parking lot and clambered into Peridot's green Packard.

Burton, like a villainous meerkat, bobbed up above the hedgerow and saw what they were up to. He dashed to George DeLuca's red Lincoln.

'Quick, Peridot!' Opal said, yanking the chrome door handle with an unhealthy cracking sound. 'Get the motor started.'

'Where... where are we headed?' Peridot yelled over the engine's vibrato.

'The police station, of course!' Opal replied. 'Put your foot on it.'

They lurched away. Napoleon's paws were flopped over the back seat. Yapping at and taunting Burton behind.

'Isn't the police station the other way?' yelled Opal, holding onto the dashboard with all her grip. 'And you're crumpling the photo!' She took it out of Peridot's hands that were pressing it against the wheel and pinned it safely inside the cigarette clip on the dashboard.

'I know a short cut,' said Peridot and carried on south.

Burton veered dangerously close, almost bumper to bumper.

'Christ, he's trying to knock us off the cliff!' Opal exclaimed.

FORTY-EIGHT

O-DEAR

'We were better off just clinging to the *Titanic!*' Peridot said, her scarf flapping frantically.

Only their headlights beamed out like a ghost chase along the winding hills.

The twinkling HOLLYWOODLAND was coming up ahead. Opal noticed the gaggle of people below the W. Mr Huxley, glowing in his white suit, was still there with his brand-new fiancée and the audience of friends and flash cameras.

'Mr Huxley!' Opal screamed from the top of her lungs. 'Help! Burton is trying to kill us!'

Mr Huxley looked up, his hand shading his brow. 'Opal! Opal! What? Who is trying to kill youuuu??' he yelled back.

Opal was about to shout Burton again, but noticing the cluster of avid shutterbugs, sparked a cunning idea.

'Jean Harlow!' she bellowed.

'Jean Harlow?' Mr Huxley shouted back, a look of utter perplexity almost making his eyes cross.

The click-happy minions jolted into action and fiddled with their bulbs. *'Jean Harlow has gotten road rage! This will be a great shot!'* they said to one another and huddled into the bushes by the side of the road. Mr Huxley and Lotus simply hugged in a scared and befuddled manner.

Peridot's wagon hurtled past them. Burton approached with a ferocious trundling of his wheels. Just as Opal had wanted, the shutterbugs leaped out of the undergrowth and their flash-bulbs exploded like wartime artillery, hitting his vehicle with lightning. It became a freakish, overexposed daytime for a split second and the look on Burton's face was like he'd been pelted with white flour.

Blinded and panicked, Burton yanked at the wheel and his automobile bounded off the road, scattering earth. Up through sagebrush he lurched, up and up until with an almighty clonk, he introduced himself to the bottom of the 'O' in HOLLY-WOODLAND. The sound was reminiscent of a grand piano being dropped from the sky, followed by the mighty letter swinging back and forth, bulbs bursting in crackling pops of outrage.

Everyone held their breath. Peridot pulled on the brakes to watch. Napoleon barked up into the hillside, almost jeering the 'O' on to fall. Burton attempted a hasty reverse, his wheels kicking up dust. The great iron ring detached from its poles with a theatrical creak and collapsed forward, swallowing his car like an alphabetical lasso.

'O-dear,' Opal said with a giggle. 'I'm truly O-vercome.'

A blubbering sound came from Lotus. 'Jean Harlow was so wonderful in the *Hell's Angels* movie, and now she's gone!' She sobbed into the pocket square she'd pinched from Mr Huxley's suit.

There was a loud grunt from inside the car wreck, that echoed about the hills.

'Hey, that ain't Jean Harlow!' one of the photographers yelled. 'Unless she's grown huge ears and stubble.'

'It's not Jean Harlow,' said Opal, stepping out of Peridot's car with Napoleon under her arm. 'It's Burton Ford and he tried to kill us. We have to keep him inside that O until the police arrive.'

'What? *Burton Ford* was trying to mow you down?' Mr Huxley asked, pulling his fiancée close.

'I daresay it's true. Peridot and I...' Opal began to explain but was interrupted by the unholy screeching of tyres.

Opal whipped around. Peridot had straightened her vehicle and was speeding off, pedal to the metal... towards... Platinum Signet Productions. Opal slapped a hand on her forehead. Of course! Peridot had the photograph. Why on earth did she trust the Royal Highness of Hearsay with the evidence? Peridot was almost certainly barrelling towards Emmett Zimberg's office, prepared to dangle the photo under his nose. He would no doubt be expected to part with an eye-watering sum to keep his 'heart attack' cover-up intact.

'Quick, Mr Huxley, can you drive after Peridot? She's got the evidence that will get justice for Jane and Domingo and free Augusto!' Opal yelled, spotting Huxley's Rolls-Royce behind a rock.

Mr Huxley nodded at once. 'Anything to take Peridot Ellington down and avenge Jane is fine with me.' And he bundled Lotus, Opal and her dog into his elegant motor.

Peridot, realising she was being followed, resorted to flinging things out of her car to hinder pursuit. An entire flurry of typewriter paper went swirling into their windshield. Napoleon, snapped up a good many in his jaws, his tail wagging at the novelty of the game.

They came to a fork in the road. Peridot's turning was blocked by a sea of protesters. Bright red CPUSA banners and torches bobbed aggressively in rows. With no choice but to divert, Peridot careened towards the Santa Monica coast, finally pulling on the brakes at the Pacific Electric railway station.

The Empress of Earwigging tumbled out, her hat askew, her eyes fixed on the locomotive approaching in the distance. It would be her getaway with the photo. Mr Huxley pulled up close.

'Stay back!' Peridot shrieked, one foot out of the car, her hand hovering near the photo on the dashboard. 'Or I'll ruin you all!'

Opal spoke with the dulcet tones of one addressing a madwoman on a ledge. 'Peridot, please. I need that piece of evidence. That photo will clear Augusto's name.'

Napoleon, meanwhile, had noticed something far more imminently important... potential snacks. He sprang out of the car and trotted to a bin filled with discarded seafood. He snuffled about in it on his hind legs. In the process, he unearthed a portfolio of headshots, one of which was splashed in prawn cocktail sauce. Deciding the smell was good enough to merit further investigation, he pulled it onto the ground and proceeded to lick it.

A seagull, one of those extra-large, greedy ones, swooped down and plucked the photo, quite rudely, from where Napoleon was tasting it. The scavenger soared into the air with triumph and flew over Peridot's car towards the beach.

Opal's eyes fluttered with sudden inspiration. She pointed skyward with a dramatic finger. 'Oh blast! The seagull's got the photo!' she yelled.

Peridot let out a scream of unfiltered panic. 'Stop! Someone stop that seagull!' And with that, she was off, arms flailing, chasing the bird as if it had a cheque for a million dollars in its beak.

Opal wasted no time. She reached out and salvaged the actual photograph from Peridot's dashboard. She turned to Mr Huxley with a satisfied sigh. 'Next stop, the police station, please, Mr Huxley.'

'Right! Darling fiancée, do come on...' Mr Huxley crooned at Lotus.

She'd not wasted a second to declare her engagement to a

group of strangers strolling the promenade. They were oooing and ahhing over the cluster of carats on her left hand. She had it stretched out and was saying she'd never been so devotedly in love in her life.

'Just a moment, Mr Huxley,' said Lotus, she was enjoying the gushing strangers too much and had proceeded to show off her emerald peacock-design earrings.

'You must call me Herb now, angel,' he said. Then added, a little jealously, 'And I guess you wouldn't have worn the earrings from your old beau Lord Sterling Peregrine if you knew I was going to be proposing to you tonight.'

Opal's mouth dropped open. Lotus stopped coooing and looked at Opal sideways.

'Lord Peregrine? He *was* or *is* your lover? That makes complete sense! You gold-digging tramp. That's why you were trying to kill me! He set it all up. You put black widow spiders in my bag twice! And he was probably paying you in jewels to do it!'

Mr Huxley stood in front of Lotus protectively. 'Now, now, Opal, calm down. I don't know what this is about. but my angel wouldn't hurt a fly. You've no business causing a scene like this.'

Napoleon stood in front of Opal, her protection officer, his tail upright and affixed. He bared his teeth, not forgetting his sacred duty as sole defender of her honour, ankles, and afternoon tea.

'I'm not the only one she's tried to kill. She's tried to kill *your* reputation, Mr Huxley!'

The crowd gasped and even the seagulls seemed to shut up.

'What are you talking about?' Lotus said in an innocent voice when Mr Huxley looked at her, but when he looked back at Opal her eyes turned into spears.

'Miss Cuthbert,' Opal said with a lisp and hands on her hips, then sympathetically to the man who she quite liked. 'I'm sorry, Mr Huxley.'

The crowd frowned in perplexity and looked at the gent who had turned red as a beef tomato. He turned to face Lotus square on.

'You've betrayed my trust, Miss Hartley. I cannot marry you and I cannot help you with your career.'

Lotus let out a scream of anguish and frustration, stomping her heels, 'I'll still make it without you, Mr Huxley! Just you wait!'

'My dear, a career only works if there is desire, opportunity *and talent*. If one of those is missing, it doesn't work,' Mr Huxley retorted as he plucked the ring from her finger with the nonchalance of a man plucking lint from his lapel, then walked away.

Lotus made incredulous scoffing noises and dug her fingers into her hair in utter disbelief. She watched her Hollywood future drive away in a Rolls-Royce Phantom into the distant seascape.

'You've got nothing left now. So why not tell me the truth?' Opal asked, hands on her hips. '*Why* are you after me?'

'Perhaps you're right. I am a gold-digging tramp. Lord Sterling Peregrine endowed my jewellery box with rocks that could make a sultan's eyes water. I just had to help him out a little with one of his sinister stratagems.'

'How could you get involved with such a wicked man?' Opal seethed, restraining the boiling-over Napoleon.

'Yes, wicked as they come, my Sterly-pie, but well, he had a certain charm, and next thing I knew, I was his "special friend" for six months or so. I stayed with him while touring in Papua. But I'd got it in my head he was stepping out with some other woman. So I did what any sensible girl would, I followed him one day when he was headed to the outskirts of the village. And that's when I witnessed your murderous father shoot Reggie.'

'You failed at killing me with poisonous creatures and your fibbing skills seem to have taken the day off. I've found holes in your little tale – the echoing shots in the trees you heard actually exonerate my father. Sorry about that.'

Lotus swelled up with indignation like a bullfrog and drew back her handbag as if she meant to launch it at Opal. Napoleon puffed up and growled like a small but ferocious bear. Lotus shakily lowered the bag again.

Opal thought it best to leave the vile girl to stew and inevitably get the next boat to Australia. She crooked a finger at Napoleon, and together they swept aboard the Pacific Electric railway train. Clutching the invaluable photograph to her breast, Opal set her sights towards town. Time to free Augusto from the clutches of the LAPD.

FORTY-NINE

THE HOLLYWOOD LAPD

Opal got to the police station in time to see Burton Ford in handcuffs being led up the steps. He had a squashed metal bar still around his body that had broken off the HOLLYWOODLAND 'O'. Opal wondered if he'd also be picking up the tab for repairs to the sign.

Moments later she was sitting at the slightly grimy police interview table, filling them in on all the evidence she had discovered. The air was stuffy, smelling of stale coffee. Emmett Zimberg, Detective Kensington and the LAPD homicide detective sat at the other three sides of the table, their cigars smouldering like miniature volcanoes. The three men were all peering down at the photograph.

There he was, Burton Ford, present in two dimensions but guilty in all three. The toy soldier costume proving the damning fact that he was, inescapably, the murderer of Jane Margeaux.

Opal waited for them to swallow their pride and to admit she'd done a darn sight better job than they had. On the table there was also a heavy glass bowl, smudged with fingerprints, filled with chalky white peppermint lozenges. Opal popped one in her mouth and sucked on it with involuntary smugness. They were good. Crisp, breath-freshening, aggressively medicinal and dissolved into a sharp, coolness that lingered on her tongue.

Emmett Zimberg looked tired and exasperated. Like a man who had sat in too many boardrooms and negotiated too many shady deals. 'A seventeen-year-old boy did all this.' The Platinum Signet Productions boss shook his head. 'It's tragic.'

Detective Kensington, to Opal's surprise, said nothing. His face was a picture of muted humiliation, he clearly felt the sting of having been outwitted by a young woman who adjusted hat ribbons for a living.

'So, you must free Augusto?' Opal demanded. 'Where is he now?'

'He's being detained not far from here at Lincoln Heights jail,' said the homicide detective. 'I'll request the suspect's release order from the watch commander.'

'So, you can't let him out tonight?'

'The paperwork might take a while as the case was tied up with... bureaucracy. But he will be released.'

'Who at Cox & Lumière Pictures were Jane and Domingo working for?' asked Detective Kensington accusatorially. He wasn't about to give up his private eye duties yet.

'I'm not at liberty to say,' Opal said, lacing her hands and tilting her chin up to Detective Kensington smugly. 'But you're the detective, so I'm sure you can work it out.'

Detective Kensington sneered and looked to Mr Zimberg for a reaction.

Mr Zimberg ignored his inept gumshoe and addressed Opal, his glasses shining like gold coins. 'Now, what's happened to those confidential Platinum Signet Productions documents you found?' His voice was kind and fatherly.

'Oh... I have them, sir,' said Opal, thinking about the coat lining she'd sewn them into. 'I can get them back to you.'

The conversation was interrupted by a ruckus out in the corridor. The sound of feet shuffling and a lady's heel stamping.

Then came a discombobulated moan, the kind you'd make if you'd slipped off a merry-go-round. Opal couldn't help but go to the window hatch and twitch the blinds up with a surreptitious finger.

There were two LAPD officers propping up a woman under her arms, whilst she tried to twist and shrug them off. It was Peridot Ellington, whose skirts were soaking wet, a piece of seaweed dangling from her hat, in quite a tasteful arrangement Opal thought.

'I don't need the asylum. I wasn't talking to seagulls. I was simply frustrated because the wretched bird had a very important—' Peridot stopped when she came past the window hatch Opal was peering out from. With a gaping mouth like a codfish, she glanced at Emmett Zimberg and the prized photograph on the table.

'Never mind,' she said, and her limbs flopped, letting them whisk her away.

'I always thought it'd be a matter of time before that dame cracked,' Emmett Zimberg said.

Opal finally pushed open her door at Palatial Pines, exhausted as a dachshund after a steep uphill trot. She removed her long hatpin and took off her cloche, shaking her cropped curls with her eyes shut and emitted a long sigh. When she opened them again, she noticed something of delight. Lying expectantly at her feet was letter from her beloved papa. Never had a piece of paper brought such happiness.

Beloved Opal,

I pray this letter finds you unharmed. My darling, clever bins, making hats for the stars and what not!

I am so sorry to have kept you in the dark while you were in

Paris, but I did not want you to be frightened, and I'd hoped everything would clear up. I am thoroughly cut up about your poor cousin Clementina's death.

As you will know now, I discovered the Apolline Diamond just as I was having a spot of luncheon at the Taritatu River. But my downfall was that I wasn't very quiet about the treasure I'd found. I told a local missionary and a farm hand, and as I was boasting about having it weighed and documented, my voice must have carried amongst the trees. I believe Master Reggie Peregrine overheard me in the underbrush somewhere.

They tailed me all the way to the bank and ambushed me with rifles pointed. Panicked, I fired a warning shot into the canopy above. One of the poachers fired also, but at that moment Reggie Peregrine lunged at me, taking the poacher's bullet to his temple. Lord Sterling Peregrine is convinced I fired the fatal shot, even though I have been cleared of all charges. It must be why he was out for revenge, and tried to even the score in Paris by kidnapping you.

Dear Bins, I am so sorry for everything that's happened. Everything is alright now, and I hope you can forgive me. Will you come to Papua before we travel to Britain together? The jungle and its feathery creatures have missed you, and so have your darling papa and mama.

Ever your loving father,

Lord Laplume

FIFTY

HARE-BRAINED IN HAVANA

A clapperboard was held aloft. It was chalked with 'Hare-brained in Havana. Scene 55. Take 17.' *Snap!*... as sharp as a guillotine cued the jungle-themed nightclub into action.

Crouched behind a papier mâché banana tree, Opal flicked a jerky-laden fishing rod onto the dance floor. Across from her, Napoleon stood poised at the limbo pole. His ears pricked, paws twitching, every whisker aflutter. Cameras whirred, lights sizzled, and a Latin band on a treetop podium burst into a rollicking tune, heavy on maracas, marimbas, and rum-barrel bongos.

Eyes locked on the jerky, Napoleon lifted his paws, waggled his hindquarters, and shuffled forward as if in his former life he'd been tutored in the cha-cha-cha. Under the pole he wriggled... front paws. Yes! Head and ears folded back. Yes! The crew held their breath. The director's fist hovered, primed for triumph or to unleash verbal carnage.

'Yes, yes, go on, boy,' Opal hissed, fingers white-knuckling the rod. 'Seventeenth time lucky!'

Napoleon would have done it, if it wasn't for his Achilles

heel: his pom-pom tail. Almost through, it clipped the pole... *clink!*... knocking it to the floor.

A collective groan came from the crew. The band whimpered into a musical collapse, trailing off with an awkward cymbal bash.

The director inhaled, ready to erupt in colourful idioms that would have made the parrots learn some very bad language. But before he could, Opal stepped out from behind the tree.

'Excuse me, sir,' Opal piped up, jerky still dangling. 'Why don't we just glue the pole in place?'

Silence. The director blinked at her as if she'd just found his lost wallet in his own pocket.

'Well, I'll be damned.' He beamed. 'That's the best idea I've heard all year! Props! You heard the lady... get on it! Move, you sedated sheep!'

As studio minions scrambled, Opal stifled a giggle.

'Take five while they fix the pole!' the director bellowed through his megaphone.

Opal scooped up her little starlet and joined the gaggle of audience who'd come to watch Napoleon's starring moment. Adrian was slow-clapping and Bonfire was bobbing up and down with excitement.

'You came to watch?' Opal asked, delighted. 'Though I'm not sure what you're clapping for, this one has not mastered his trick yet!'

'Well, we need a bit of poodle limbo in our lives after all we've been through,' Adrian said, giving Napoleon a head pat.

'I heard you made the two dancers' turbans? At last, Opal! Your designs will be on screen!' said Bonfire.

'Yes. Adrian was sweet enough to get me the gig and I whipped them up in a few days.' Opal beamed, glancing back on set at her magnificent creations.

'Well... open the magazine!' insisted Adrian impatiently,

flapping the thing in front of her nose. She had no idea that the thing was out on the stands!

Opal flipped slowly through *Photoplay* to find her feature. And bang in the middle, there she was. The first picture was with that vicious jezebel Lotus but it was *she*, not Lotus, who had won the solo spot on the adjacent page. '*Style Setters of Sunset Boulevard.*' Opal giggled with pride. *What is Mamma going to say? She will be positively jigging with joy.*

With the affixed limbo pole, Napoleon was able to master it in one go. The scene unfolded and Napoleon was awarded a golden cigar case with the '*holy grail of all cigars*' inside with a special gold band. The script said nothing about Napoleon snapping the cigar in his jaws and running off with it. But that's what he did, resulting in the frazzled director calling for '*Lunch!*'

Opal scurried after her dog, hoping they had more than one holy grail cigar prop. His pom-pom tail disappeared out the stage door. A moment later, a puff of smoke billowed back from where the dog had exited. *Napoleon with all his talents was now a smoker*, Opal made herself cackle. When she went to investigate, the person smoking the holy grail cigar was the one and only, cleft-chinned, dark-eyed, Augusto Sevilla.

'Thanks for the Cuban, Napoleon,' he said, removing his trilby. Napoleon ran in circles around his favourite marshal, yapping in high-pitched joy.

'Augusto!' Opal breathed. 'You're back.'

A flurry of all the sweetest emotions washed over her, relief, happiness, excitement.

'Thanks to the wits and brains of my little English detective, I am, yes. The District Attorney's office authorised my release!' he shouted, opening his arms wide.

'I'm so relieved. I just couldn't bear for you to be in trouble.' She stepped into his arms for an embrace and then looked up at his face. 'Were the police beastly to you?'

'Let's just move on to happier times,' he said, and put his hands on his hips. 'What's this you've got?'

'Oh. It's my magazine feature. I'm wearing Chanel, it's all frightfully surreal.'

'I wish I could kiss that girl,' he said, peering at the pages then looking into her eyes.

Opal scrunched up her toes and felt her face heat up. *Say something, say something. His face is getting exceedingly close. I so want to kiss him but I just couldn't possibly.* Opal quickly lifted up the magazine in between them and pressed the page onto Augusto's mouth. 'There you go, you can kiss her!'

He pushed the magazine down without any of the humour that Opal was expecting. He placed a strong hand on the small of her back. Like a magnetic force he pulled her close and planted a kiss onto her mouth. It was soft, sweet and lightly intoxicating, like brandy butter.

She pulled away and opened her eyes. He looked at her and didn't say anything.

Opal wrinkled her toes. 'You'd better let go of me, Mr Sevilla. You're crumpling my *Photoplay* magazine.'

'We can buy more, they're on all the newsstands.'

He tried to kiss her again but Opal felt she might faint. It was ecstasy. She managed to pull back.

'I'm going to miss you when I go away again.' Opal ran her fingers over the magazine spine, her voice tinged with wistful sorrow.

'You're leaving?' he asked, and his brows ascended his forehead in distress.

'I have to go and see my parents in Papua. I leave in a week,' Opal said, looking down at Napoleon. His eyes and nose were three shiny blackcurrants quivering with emotion.

'I'll follow you,' Augusto insisted, lifting her chin to look at him. He then produced two glass bottles of root beer and a brown paper bag of jelly doughnuts from the depths of his jacket. 'This is to celebrate my prison release.'

Opal clinked cheers and gratefully swigged the sweet beverage. 'Honestly though, Augusto, you can't follow me. Don't be a plonker. You have lots of opportunities here in Hollywoodland.'

'What is *plonkers*? I've never heard that word before,' he said, wiping his mouth with a sleeve.

'Well, I don't know how quite to describe it... it's a blithering nitwit.'

Augusto contorted his mouth in perplexity and put his hands on his hips.

'A halfwit with delusions of grandeur?' Opal tried again, giggling into her bottle top.

Augusto bit into the doughnut and chewed with his tough jaws as he looked Opal over.

'I may be deluded, but I have no opportunities in Hollywoodland if the Honourable Opal Laplume isn't in Hollywoodland.'

Napoleon barked up at the doughnut as if it was made of pure gold. Opal ruffled his curly hairdo, grateful for the interruption to the intense way Augusto was looking at her.

'But... what do I tell my parents?' she asked. 'They'll be awfully suspicious of me bringing along a handsome man in tow. Mama would say it's dreadfully inappropriate.'

'Why?'

Opal wanted to say it was because her mother was hell-bent on marrying her off to Viscount Cecil Turks-Leyton. Moniker: 'Turkey'. But didn't want to insult Augusto.

'Because in my world, the only men a single young woman is supposed to be around is a chaperone, a butler, a papa, a brother or an uncle and you, Augusto, are *none* of those.'

'What about if I was your butler?' said Augusto, taking a big bite of doughnut and smiling like a court jester.

Opal burst out laughing. 'It takes decades to master the art and we haven't had one of those since Copperfields Hall.' But her lashes fluttered in the unmistakable manner of a mind hatching a plan.

'Perhaps... perhaps a *protection officer*,' she said and took a chuffed gulp of root beer. 'It's your true profession, after all, and it's not the first time they've had to hire one for me. It seems Lord Peregrine isn't finished terrorising my family.'

'That's perfect, *señorita*. I'm going to hand in my notice here,' said Augusto, dusting the sugar off his fingers by brushing them together.

'Hold on. I'd better ask them in person, then you can join us later. I can't just show up with you. Besides, Father will have to pay for your voyage.'

'Where is the holy grail cigar?' yelled an extremely furious props manager from inside the studio.

'We'd better vamoose like a shot! Or you'll have *"banned from Platinum Signet Productions & Cox & Lumière Pictures"* on your résumé!' Opal whispered.

Augusto grabbed her hand and they dashed off, giggling with abandon, Napoleon galloping alongside in his limbo suit.

A LETTER FROM MILLICENT

Thank you so much for taking the time to read my second book – *Murder in Hollywood*. It was thrilling to write! I do hope you enjoyed it and that you felt part of the adventure with Opal and Napoleon. If want to stay updated on my latest releases, please do sign up using the link below. Your email address will never be shared and you can unsubscribe anytime.

www.bookouture.com/millicent-binks

I have always loved this particular setting – 1930s Hollywoodland. I first saw Busby Berkeley's *Gold Diggers of 1933* when doing an art foundation course when I was about nineteen. I was absolutely blown away by the scale and imagination behind the epic productions. The synchronisation and whimsy. You could tell the dancers were taught as strictly as an army regiment. I think it was my first exposure to the very zenith of glamour.

I was impressed with how they managed the mechanics of it all with very little help of technology. It was charming when I wondered how the pianos were spinning on their own in exact unison and squinted and saw people's legs in black tights underneath, supposed to be invisible, carrying the pianos on their backs. The directors really went to great efforts to soften what was going on economically.

Then I learned dark tales about Hollywoodland. Rumours that Judy Garland's maid, who she'd thought was a close friend, had been spying on her for the studio bosses. And about how some actresses' contracts dictated every aspect of their lives including their wombs and whether they'd be allowed to bear children. Human beings were clearly less important than the movies themselves, and some were even sacrificed in the making of them. For example, *Hell's Angels* 1930 by Howard Hughes had such dangerous stunt sequences several pilots and an assistant died. Hollywoodland at the turn of the thirties is the perfect setting for infinite murder mysteries since everyone's motives have such high stakes. There is also that wonderful dramatic irony that they created utopia on-screen using a machine greased with corruption.

I adored writing this and had many giggles to myself as well as devious cackles when inserting the red herrings. My cat Queenie, who sits above my writing desk, would twist back her ears in alarm. I do hope you follow us on our next escapade... Napoleon's pom-pom tail will be shaking the snow off and rolling in the castle grounds of yuletide Scotland!

I would LOVE to hear from my readers – for any reason, ideas on new book themes or adventures that Opal could go on or even just to chat – you can find me if you search Millicent Binks on Facebook, Instagram, Tiktok and X. You can also contact me on my website.

Millicent Binks x

www.millicentbinks.co.uk

instagram.com/millicentbinks

PUBLISHING TEAM

Turning a manuscript into a book requires the efforts of many people. The publishing team at Bookouture would like to acknowledge everyone who contributed to this publication.

Audio
Alba Proko
Melissa Tran
Sinead O'Connor

Commercial
Lauren Morrissette
Hannah Richmond
Imogen Allport

Contracts
Peta Nightingale

Cover design
Tash Webber

Data and analysis
Mark Alder
Mohamed Bussuri

www.ingramcontent.com/pod-product-compliance
Ingram Content Group UK Ltd.
Pitfield, Milton Keynes, MK11 3LW, UK
UKHW042329180725

460946UK00002B/3

9 781836 189169